Gold Mountain

Gold Mountain

A Klondike Mystery

Vicki Delany

DUNDURN
TORONTO

Editor: Matt Baker
Design: Jesse Hooper
Printer: Webcom

Library and Archives Canada Cataloguing in Publication

Delany, Vicki, 1951-
    Gold mountain : a Klondike mystery / Vicki Delany.

Issued also in electronic formats.
ISBN 978-1-4597-0189-2

    1. Klondike River Valley (Yukon)--Gold discoveries--Fiction. I. Title.

PS8557.E4239G65 2012   C813'.6   C2011-906001-9

1   2   3   4   5   16   15   14   13   12

  Canadä

We acknowledge the support of the **Canada Council for the Arts** and the **Ontario Arts Council** for our publishing program. We also acknowledge the financial support of the **Government of Canada** through the **Canada Book Fund** and **Livres Canada Books**, and the **Government of Ontario** through the **Ontario Book Publishing Tax Credit** and the **Ontario Media Development Corporation**.

Care has been taken to trace the ownership of copyright material used in this book. The author and the publisher welcome any information enabling them to rectify any references or credits in subsequent editions.

J. Kirk Howard, President

Printed and bound in Canada.
www.dundurn.com

Dundurn
3 Church Street, Suite 500
Toronto, Ontario, Canada
M5E 1M2

Gazelle Book Services Limited
White Cross Mills
High Town, Lancaster, England
LA1 4XS

Dundurn
2250 Military Road
Tonawanda, NY
U.S.A. 14150

For Caroline, Julia, and Alex

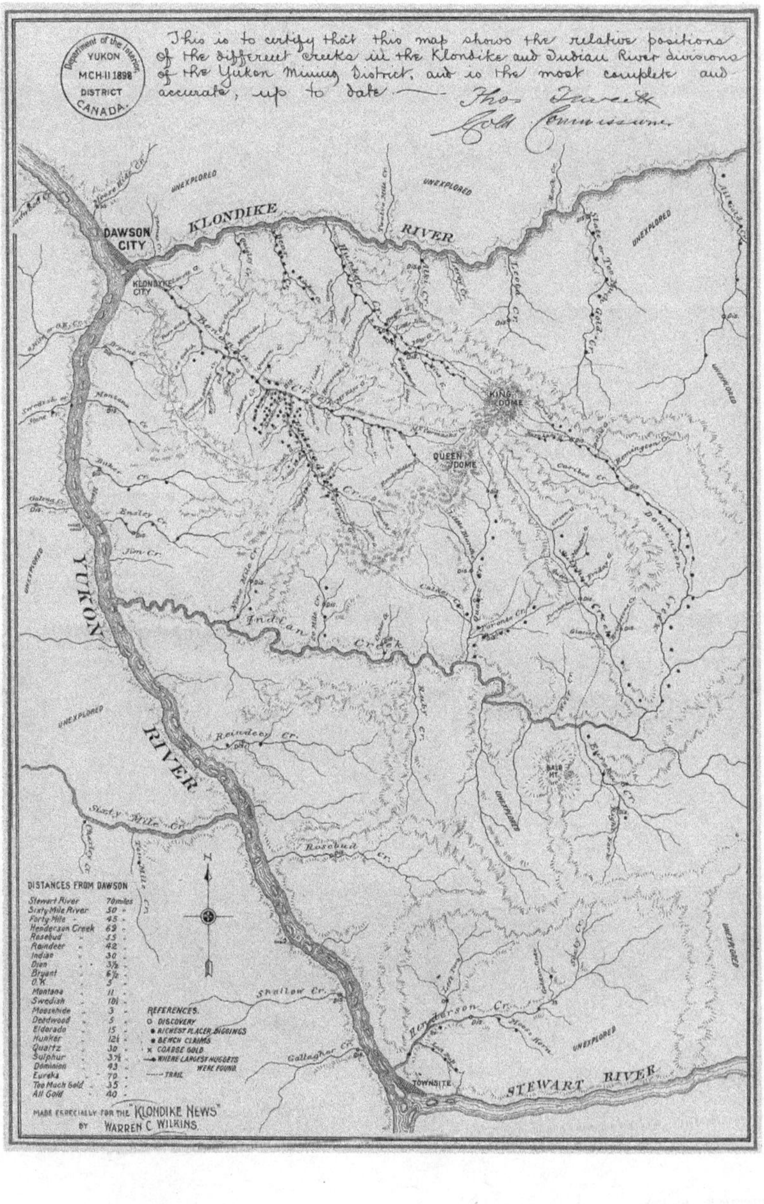

Image courtesy of the Dawson City Museum

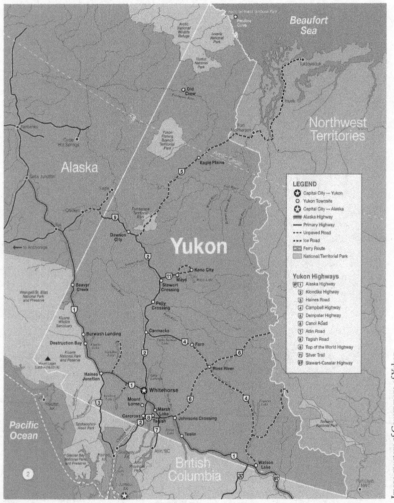

Prologue

Blood is so difficult to wash out of good clothing.

Two men came tumbling out of the gambling room in a flying mass of fists and feet, unwashed clothes, manure-encrusted boots, mining dust, Front Street mud, and months of pent-up disappointment. I had barely enough time to dance backward, avoiding a spatter of blood destined for the bosom of my red satin gown. I fell backward into someone, tall and hard-muscled, and I felt his strong arms wrapping themselves around me and rough hands taking advantage of the opportunity to caress my shoulders.

Without looking to see who was holding me, I felt the roaming hands now moving away from my shoulders and inching toward my breasts. I drove my elbow backward into his midsection, then raked the heel of my boot down his leg and planted it firmly into his instep. The arms released me and the man grunted softly.

"I'll have you for that, you lying son-of-a-bitch," the larger of the fighters shouted, spitting out a tooth along with a mouthful of blood and saliva as he struggled to be the first one back on his feet. A flock of gamblers, eager to follow the action, spilled out of the back rooms. They still clutched chips or cards in their scarred hands with cracked nails, stained black with dust and mud. But, of course, not everyone deserted the game — the croupier's voice could still be heard, calmly saying, "place your bets, gentlemen."

The larger man, whose tooth was now lying in a slimy puddle in the middle of the floor, lunged toward the other, swinging a wild fist. The punch landed, and the smaller man staggered backward, falling into the crowd of drinkers crowded around the bar. Old Barney's stool swayed dangerously, but he merely clenched his glass tighter and took another swallow. Maxie screamed in mock terror and pretended to faint dead away, in a flutter of cheap fabric and many-times-mended stockings. Unfortunately for her, no one reacted, and she hit the floor with a distinct thud followed by an indignant shriek. Her skirt flew up high above her ankles, and at the sight of all that exposed leg, men rushed to offer her assistance.

Irene stood safely back from the melee, watching it all with a smile of mild amusement. A young fellow, dressed as if he were going shooting for grouse in Scotland, extended his arm. She sized him up in an instant, accepted the offer with a gracious nod, and allowed him to escort her to safety.

"One hundred dollars on the big guy," came a shout from the back of the room. A chorus of voices took him up on it. The smaller man shook his head and threw himself back into the fight. He landed a powerful right hook that belied his scrawny frame. The larger man flew backwards, crashing into a circle of drinkers watching the fight. A glass shattered on the floor. "Why you …" the glass's owner shouted, raising his fist to send the other man back the way he'd come.

"Stay out of it, Williams," one of his group yelled, grabbing at him. His blood up, Williams drove his meaty fist straight into his friend's stomach. The friend — former friend? — blanched and vomited.

"Hey, that was a dirty trick," a third man said, striking Williams solidly in the jaw.

The violin player, who had been halfway across the room when the fight broke out, clung to the walls, clutching his delicate instrument to his chest as if it were a newborn.

"Ray," I bellowed, wading into the altercation, calling for my business partner, "where are you?"

Murray, one of the bartenders, dashed out of the gambling room and reached the secondary fight, which was now threatening to spawn a tertiary engagement. "Take it outside, boys." Murray pushed the antagonists apart.

At last I could see Ray. He had pulled a well-used baton out from beneath the long counter of the bar and was advancing on the men who'd started the whole thing.

"That won't be necessary, Walker," a voice cut in. It belonged to one of the two Mounties, radiating authority in their scarlet tunics, broad-brimmed hats, and polished black boots. "We'll take care of it."

The patrons moved aside politely to allow the law passage. A forest of arms lifted Maxie to her feet. Betsy stopped scream-ing and fluttered her eyelashes at the younger policeman, but he ignored her. The man who was taking bets on the outcome of the fight moaned in disappointment. Each Mountie grabbed a fighter by the back of his collar and propelled him toward the door. "It's a blue card for you two," the older officer said, "and make no mistake."

The moment the doors shut behind them, the room returned to normal. The gamblers went back to their games, the drinkers surged toward the bar for another round, and the dancers and the musicians — including a pouting Maxie and a weeping violinist — departed to get ready for the night's show. Barney, not much caring if anyone was listening or not, droned on about the old days. Murray politely asked the man with vomit all down his shirt to go home and change before having another drink, and Ray replaced the baton behind the bar with scarcely a blink. Helen poked her nose out of the back room and groaned at sight of the mess she'd have to clean up. I touched my hair, making sure every strand was tucked neatly in place, checked that my best-quality fake pearls were still draped around my neck, and straightened the skirt of my red satin gown. I waved to Ray and indicated that I would take a breath of air for a few moments.

I watched the crowds flowing up and down and across Front Street. *What had I gotten myself into*, was my first thought. *A great deal of money*, was my second.

Owning a dance hall in Dawson, Yukon Territory, in the summer of 1898 certainly beat dangling from a rope tossed out of the second-story bedroom of a Belgravia townhouse on a rainy February night, dressed in men's clothes — all in black — with a pocket full of rings and necklaces and a sack of the family's good silver tossed across my back, trying not to breathe too loudly while a constable, tardy on his rounds for one cursed night, stood below, sneaking a quick smoke.

I laughed deeply, winked at a shiny faced cheechako passing by, and returned to the lights of the Savoy with a flick of my skirt.

Chapter One

The next night, we seemed to be busier than ever, if that was even possible. It was July of 1898 and the entire world was caught in the grip of Klondike gold fever. Thousands upon thousands of people had arrived in Dawson over the previous weeks, and still they came by every sort of watercraft available. Keep this up and it might require building an extension onto the Savoy Saloon and Dance Hall. The question was, where would it go? The buildings along Front Street, tossed up virtually overnight with little thought to aesthetics, safety, or permanency, stood cheek-to-jowl. Out the back, beyond the alley, was another row of stores, including a mortuary and a dry goods shop.

Neither of which lacked for custom either.

The days were hot, the nights long and warm, and people had come through so much hardship simply to get here, they seemed almost desperate to spend what money they had as fast as possible. The lucky few who'd found gold, such as my favourite barfly Barney, didn't know the meaning of the word restraint.

All the better, because I myself know perfectly well the value of a dollar — and what it's like not to have one.

It was shortly after midnight when I saw him.

Paul Sheridan. So tall, so thin. So unwelcome in my bar and in my town.

The first round of dancing had just begun. He was with Lady Irénée, the most popular dance hall girl in Dawson. She acted Lady Macbeth or Hamlet in the plays, sang a few songs, and closed the stage show with a languid, sensuous dance performed in yards and yards of multi-coloured chiffon. Not a Lady, nor even christened with the fancy French name of Irénée, she was plain old Irene Davidson of somewhere in the Midwest. As a headliner, she wasn't required to remain after her performance to dance with the men, but Irene knew her enormous popularity depended in large measure on her approachability. Besides, she loved attention, soaked up every bit of it, basked in it. She also basked in the money they threw her way. Last week as she took a long languid bow in the one remaining length of chiffon wrapped around her once-white shift, an old sourdough threw a gold nugget the size of my fist onto the stage at her feet. She scooped it up fast enough and gave the man a wave and a cheeky wink.

I wondered if that's where the rumour got started: they say that Klondike gold lay at one's feet, waiting to be scooped up. The only people I ever saw collecting nuggets like windfall apples were dancers.

Irene wasn't pretty, at least not in the way that actresses in the big cities of the east might be. She looked like what she was, a tough farm girl who'd taken a chance and climbed the Chilkoot Trail. The Yukon was not a place for delicate women.

Irene had recently, much to my displeasure, taken up with Ray Walker, my business partner and half-owner of the Savoy. I knew things about Irene she wouldn't want to be made public, and thus I knew why she was suddenly enamoured of Ray, whom she had consistently discouraged until last week.

It's not my job to guard the morals of my employees nor to save my business partner from having his heart broken.

But it was my job to keep the Savoy the most popular dance

hall in the Yukon, and I feared dissent amongst the employees as much as I feared running out of liquor.

I was on the balcony floor above the dance hall. Tables and chairs were set up so the better-heeled customers in the boxes could observe the dancing below. Men were quaffing champagne — at forty dollars a quart — straight from the bottle, dancers balanced on their knees. Betsy, dressed in a rather ugly shade of mustard, was throwing back her head and laughing heartily at something her companion had said. He lifted the bottle of champagne to his mouth and took a long drink. He belched heartily and wiped his mouth with the back of his right hand. His left hand was under Betsy's dress.

My employees are not prostitutes.

Some of the other dance halls don't try too hard to disguise the fact that their girls are available for additional forms of entertainment after the show, but mine know if I find out they're whoring on the side, they'll be out of a job. Being unobtainable helps to keep my dancers popular.

I gave Betsy a warning look, but she avoided my eyes. Betsy had been stepping out with Ray (and I had no doubt there was more staying in than stepping out involved), but he'd thrown her over the minute Irene batted her stubby eyelashes in his direction. If she didn't keep her resentment to herself, she'd be out on the street fast enough.

I glanced over the railing to the crowded room below. Irene was dancing, laughing and smiling at Paul Sheridan, who towered above everyone in the room. He was extremely tall and thin, looking much like a lodgepole pine with a filthy mop of hair and scraggly beard glued to the top of it.

My stomach clenched.

I made my way down the stairs in record time, not even bothering to smile at men as I shoved them out of the way.

I ran through the gambling room, scarcely noticing the piles of chips and bills and gold dust in front of the poker players.

Ray worked behind the bar, his scarred and chapped hands moving as he poured drinks, his eyes moving as he watched for trouble.

I pushed my way through the crowd. The men were always happy to see me, but for once I ignored them. "Ray," I shouted. "Come here."

"I'm busy, Fee," he replied. Ray hailed from the back alleys and shipyards of Glasgow. His accent could be almost undecipherable to the uninitiated. A Scotswoman myself, even I had trouble understanding him sometimes.

"Get over here," I said. "I have to show you something."

I rarely spoke to Ray in such a tone. He managed the bar and the male employees; I supervised the women and kept the accounts. We were a good team.

He must have read something in my face and my voice. He put down the bottle of whisky, told one of the other bartenders, the fellow I call Not-Murray, to take over and came out from behind the long mahogany counter.

"Problem, Fee?" he said.

"Might be. I think I recognize someone."

I led the way to the dance hall at the back. It was after midnight, but this far north in early July it was still daylight outside. The windows were small and dirty, so kerosene lamps were lit throughout the building.

"You can't miss him," I said. "The one dancing with Irene. Please tell me it's not who I think it is."

Irene was by far the best-dressed of the dancers. Almost as well-dressed as I. Which didn't particularly please me. We had shared a dressmaker for a short while, until that business most abruptly shut down. With my blue evening gown unfinished, I might add.

Tonight, Irene was in jet-black silk with flashes of scarlet in the skirt panel and folds of the sleeves. The percentage girls, employed only to dance with the men after the stage show, wore their street clothes to work, and most of them were a muddy brown or homespun. Irene stood out like a peacock. She wasn't the most popular dance hall girl in the north for nothing. Like all great pretenders, she believed she was what she wanted to be, ergo she was.

For once, Ray didn't have eyes for Irene. He sucked in his breath at the sight of the man holding her in his arms. He was about six-foot-five and might have weighed 150 pounds if his pockets were stuffed with gold dust. He was dressed in a tweed suit — nothing out of the ordinary. His waistcoat was threadbare around the edges, his bow tie had seen better days, and his hat and jacket could use the attention of a laundry maid.

The music stopped in mid-note and the dancers skidded to a stop. They pushed past us as the girls led their partners to the bar. Many of the men tipped their hats to me, some slowed as if to stop and talk, but their partners dragged them away. At a dollar a minute, time was definitely money.

The tall man's hand was pressed against the small of Irene's back. She said something to him, he nodded, and they began to move toward the bar.

The floor between us was momentarily empty, and the man caught sight of Ray and me watching.

His face split into a huge grin. He was missing most of his teeth and what remained were cracked and discoloured.

"It's him all right," Ray said. "Paul Sheridan. Goddamnit, Fee. Do ye ken he's here on his boss's business?"

I let out a long breath. "Why else?"

"Mrs. MacGillivray. Fiona, my darling." Sheridan extended his arms, as if about to wrap me in a hug. I put my own arm out to stop him. "You're looking even more beautiful than I remember. Walker, how ya doin'? You're as ugly as I remember." He laughed heartily. Irene looked baffled as neither Ray nor I returned the man's greetings.

"Ye're not welcome here, Sheridan," Ray said. "Get out." He signalled to one of his men to join us.

"Is that a way to greet an old friend? Fiona, are you going to let him talk to me like that?"

"Get out, Paul," I said. "Irene, find someone else to dance with."

"He hasn't paid ..."

"I'll cover it."

Irene walked away.

"Not only out of my establishment, but I suggest you get out of town as well. Do the Mounties know you're here?"

"No need. I've left my former life behind. I'm going straight, Fiona. And that's why I'm so glad to see you."

Ray and his bouncer each took one of Sheridan's arms. They began walking him in the direction of the door. He didn't resist, but continued talking to me over his shoulder. "See how agreeable I'm being, Fiona. No trouble. I have an offer to make you. Supper tomorrow?"

I didn't bother to answer. They reached the door, and Ray shoved Sheridan into the street.

The man stumbled a few feet, then turned and touched the brim of his hat. "Shall we say seven o'clock? You can suggest the restaurant." He kissed the tips of his fingers, extended them to me, and then turned and walked. A spring was in his step.

"I'll have a word with Corporal Sterling tomorrow," I said.

"Aye. The Mounties'll want to know Soapy Smith's arrived in Dawson."

Chapter Two

Angus MacGillivray hated every minute he spent working in Mr. Mann's shop.

At twelve years old, he should have been devoting his time to preparing for his future. At the moment, he was undecided if he were going to become a writer, like his friend Martha Witherspoon, or a Mountie, like Corporal Richard Sterling. Perhaps he could be both. He could work as a policeman and write about his adventures, under a different name.

He wondered what name he could use. His mother was very proud of being Scottish, as was he, so he should take a Scottish name as his *nom-de-plume*. He didn't know what his mother's maiden name was, had never thought to ask. She had no family left, and he hadn't grown up knowing any grandparents or cousins or aunts and uncles. His father had died before he was born, and for all of his life it had just been the two of them. Angus and his mother.

Mrs. Mann fussed over Angus as much as if she were his grandmother. She was their landlady, and that made her sort of a servant, but it wasn't like any of the servants they'd had in Toronto or London.

More like family.

"I said how much do ya want for this here pot?"

A large woman, her bosom like the prow of a ship, waved

a stockpot with a broken handle at him. "Are you deaf or just stupid?" she added.

"Sorry ma'am. I didn't hear you. It's a quarter."

"A quarter! It ain't even got two handles. Look, this one's broke."

"I see that."

"If you think I'm paying a quarter for a broken pot, young man, you can think again." She slammed the item down on the counter and stalked off.

Angus guessed the woman had just arrived in town. She'd find out soon enough that prices in Dawson bore absolutely no similarity to prices in the Outside.

And Mr. Mann's shop bore absolutely no similarity to stores in the Outside. It consisted of a couple of lengths of canvas strung up between logs so unfinished they still sprouted crumbling leaves, and a roughly-planed plank served as the counter. A tent next door was the warehouse.

Stores no fancier than this one were packed along the waterfront. They not only sold, but also bought. And there was a lot to buy. The trip to the Yukon had been so spirit- and back-breaking, the town travellers had given their all to reach so disappointing, that many simply sold everything they had the moment they arrived and turned around and headed back south.

Mr. Mann was negotiating the price of a rifle. Its owner had been up and down the line of tents, increasingly incredulous at the low price he was being offered. In Dawson the weapon had no value at all — the Mounties outlawed carrying firearms in town.

With a burst of curses that would have had him arrested if a Mountie were in earshot, the man shoved his rifle at Mr. Mann, took his money, and left. Expressionless, Mr. Mann made room on the counter for the new item by moving aside a pair of long johns that had seen better days.

He glanced over to see Angus watching him. He shook his head. "Foolish, such men," he said.

Angus sighed. Miss Witherspoon had told him that every experience was fodder for the writer's pen. He reminded himself that he would write about the Klondike some day, and all of this would then seem worthwhile.

"Angus, my boy. Wouldn't have expected to see you here."

Angus stared at the newcomer, open mouthed. The man thrust a hand across the counter and instinctively Angus accepted the handshake.

"Surely, your ma hasn't fallen on such hard times that you're forced to take work as a shop clerk. Why, I saw her last night, as lovely as ever." His eyes opened wide, "Don't tell me that rat-faced weasel Walker cheated her out of her money, and you're forced to labour here. Why I told her ..."

"No, Mr. Sheridan. Mr. Walker hasn't cheated anyone. The Savoy's the most popular dance hall in all of Dawson." Angus slid a glance at Mr. Mann, now helping a lady sort though a box of sewing supplies. "I'm ... I'm ... I'm uh, learning a business. So I can help Ma with her own business affairs someday. It's a great honour."

Sheridan looked dubious at that. As well he might.

"What are you doing here, anyway?" Angus said. "Last time I saw you, you said only fools and easterners went chasing gold."

"So I did, my boy." Sheridan tapped the side of his nose. "I have my reasons. I'm having supper with your mother tonight and I'll tell her my plans then."

Angus laughed. "You're having supper with my mother? Not if she has anything to say about it."

Sheridan took no offence. As Angus remembered, the man could be totally blind to anything that contradicted his view of the world.

Sheridan studied the line of goods for sale. His eyes came to rest on the Winchester. He picked it up, balanced it in his hands, lifted it, and peered down the length.

"One dollar, fifty cents," Mr. Mann said.

"A buck fifty?" Sheridan said. "What, doesn't it work?"

"You can't use it," Angus said. "Mounties'll confiscate it if you have it in town."

"Not planning to stay in town."

"Can't take it to the Creeks either."

"Not planning to go to the Creeks. Didn't I tell you, Angus, man's a fool who goes where every other man goes. Gotta strike out on your own. I'll take it. And a box of cartridges."

Mr. Mann looked to Angus for an explanation.

"Cartridges, bullets." Angus mimed loading the weapon.

Mr. Mann shook his head. "You wants gun? Is one dollar, fifty cents."

"What the hell? Rifle ain't much use without cartridges. Damn strange town you have here. Does anyone else sell ammunition?"

Angus shrugged. "You can ask."

"I'll do that." Sheridan handed a tattered American dollar bill and a couple of coins to Mr. Mann, who tucked them away in the small apron he wore around his waist for just that purpose. "Your ma will probably tell you about our plans later tonight. I think you'll be pleased."

Sheridan gave Angus a wink and walked away, head and shoulders bobbing above the crowd, Winchester balanced on his hip.

"I have to go to the police," Angus said.

Mr. Mann's eyes quickly travelled across over the jumble of items on the counter, searching for something missing. He knew the location and value of everything on display, as well as all the boxes, bags, and loose items stacked under the counter, against the length of canvas that was the back wall, and piled in the tent warehouse.

Finding nothing missing, he said, "Why?"

"That man. Nothing but trouble."

"Wees wants no trouble here. Yous go to seh police."

Angus came out from behind the counter and took off at a run, heading into town.

Chapter Three

Corporal Richard Sterling of the North-West Mounted Police put his feet up on his desk and leaned back with a contented sigh. He puffed at his pipe — a rare indulgence in the middle of a working shift. At about 30,000 people, almost all of whom had arrived in the last two months, the town of Dawson was growing fast. The powers-that-be had decided that, in addition to Fort Herchmer, they needed an office in town, and they set it up in a small building on Queen Street at the corner of Second Avenue. Nice and close to the cribs in Paradise Alley and the bars and dance halls along Front Street.

Richard Sterling had a staff of four constables, and one special constable to cook, clean, and generally run errands. Life was looking up. He had been a sergeant, once, but was busted down to constable, lucky to still have a job, after punching out an officer. He'd been one of the first Mounties in the Yukon, sent to Forty Mile with Superintendent Constantine in the summer of '95 when the government in Ottawa, in its wisdom, extended the forces of law and order to the untamed, largely unpopulated territory. It was a tough place to live and work, but he loved it. It beat working on the farm in the Carrot River Valley in Saskatchewan, where he'd grown up.

The office walls were thin, the wood full of cracks. He heard the front door open and a boy's high voice greet the constable out front. Sterling dropped his feet to the floor and grabbed a piece of paper off the desk. He was reading an official report when he heard a knock on his door. He hesitated for a moment, before calling, "Come in."

As expected, it was young Angus MacGillivray. Angus had hopes of being a Mountie some day and hung around the station — and Richard Sterling — to a point just short of annoying. But he was a good lad, smart and principled.

It didn't hurt that the boy's mother was Fiona MacGillivray, who ... Sterling coughed and sat up a bit straighter in his chair.

"What brings you here, Angus? Quiet down at the store today?"

"No, sir. We're really busy. I'm here on police business. You need to know ..."

They heard the street door open again. Fabric rustled and sharp heels sounded on the wooden floor. The scent of good soap and light perfume drifted in. Sterling jumped to his feet as a woman's soft voice asked the constable for Mr. Sterling.

"Mother," Angus said, "what are you doing here?"

"Angus," Fiona said, her head popping around the corner, "what are you doing here?"

They both spoke at once. "Someone you should know about ..." Angus said. "Man in town ..." Fiona said.

Sterling held up one hand. "Mrs. MacGillivray, please have a seat."

She smiled at him and sat, arranging her skirts around her. She wore a two-piece white day dress that almost took his breath away. White was a highly impractical colour in Dawson, where mills worked night and day producing lumber for the fast-growing town, and the sawdust covered everything. What's more, even the smallest rain shower turned the streets into rivers of mud. Yet somehow Fiona had managed to keep the hem of her dress immaculately clean. Unlike a lot of women, Fiona MacGillivray wasn't adverse to pulling up her skirts and tucking them into her belt to wade across the street. Sterling shoved aside an image of shapely ankles encased in high-heeled, buttoned boots.

She straightened her already perfectly straight hat. "A most unsavoury person of my acquaintance came into the Savoy last night," she began.

"Paul Sheridan," Angus interrupted.

"You've seen him?"

"He was down at Bowery Street this morning. Stopped at the store and said hello."

"Plenty of unsavoury persons in town," Sterling said. "What makes this fellow of interest?"

"Soapy Smith," Angus and Fiona chorused.

"What?"

"Sheridan is ..."

"Soapy must have ..."

"Hold on. Only one of you talk at once. Mrs. MacGillivray, what does this Sheridan fellow have to do with Smith?"

Fiona took a deep breath. Underneath the white fabric, her bosom moved. Sterling tried not to think about that and instead to concentrate on the matter at hand.

"On our way to the Yukon, Angus and I passed through Skagway. Our passage was most speedy, I might add, once I understood the situation in town. Mr. Paul Sheridan is, to put it simply, one of Soapy Smith's gang."

"More than just one of the gang, he's like a lieutenant or something."

"Angus, I believe Corporal Sterling has requested I tell this story."

"Sorry, Ma. I mean, Mother."

"As Angus so rudely said, Mr. Sheridan is one of Mr. Smith's top-level assistants. Highly trusted, I believe, in the sense that Mr. Smith and characters of his ilk trust anyone."

"Why's he in Dawson?"

Angus and Fiona exchanged glances.

"I have no idea," she said.

"He told me he has a plan," Angus said. "He said he's having dinner with you tonight, Mother. Is that right?"

If Fiona hadn't been a well brought up English gentle-woman, Sterling thought she might have spit on the floor. Instead, she sniffed. "Hardly. Whatever delusions Mr. Sheridan continues to maintain about me are neither here nor there." She rose in one long, liquid motion.

Sterling leapt to his feet, knocking his right knee against the underside of the desk. He stifled a groan. "Thank you for coming, Mrs. MacGillivray."

"It is no more than my duty," she replied. He wasn't quite sure, but he might have seen a spark of mischief in the black depths of her eyes.

"Before you go, can you give me a description of this person?"

"Angus will see to that. The boy's powers of observation are quite astute."

Angus preened.

"He didn't say anything to you about why he's in Dawson?"

She smiled. "No. Ray Walker and Mr. Sheridan did not part on the best of terms. Ray escorted him to the door quite unceremoniously. Good day, Corporal. Angus."

They watched her leave and close the door to Sterling's office silently behind her. Then they heard the street door opening with a clatter that might have had it falling from its ill-fastened hinges, such was the young constable's haste to assist her.

Sterling took his hat down from the shelf. "You say this man's high up in Smith's organization?"

"Not that Soapy has an organization as such," Angus said. "I mean with ranks and all. Just a bunch of men who do what he tells them. But yeah, Mr. Sheridan is pretty close to Soapy."

"The last thing we want is Soapy Smith and his gang trying to cross into Canada." The NWMP kept a Maxim machine gun at the border crossing at the top of the Chilkoot Trail, expressly for the purpose of keeping out Jefferson Randolph Smith, aka Soapy, the gangster who controlled Skagway, Alaska. "I'm going to the Fort to report this. Tell me about it on the way. First, how do you know so much about Smith and his doings?"

"Soapy wanted my ma to be his business partner," Angus said.

Sterling stopped dead. "Your mother ... and Soapy Smith." He shook his head. "Your mother really is the most interesting woman. This Sheridan, do you think Smith sent him to talk to her about doing business in Dawson?"

"No. He just wants to marry her."

Chapter Four

I was rather pleased with my performance. If Angus hadn't been there, I would have told Corporal Sterling all I knew about Paul Sheridan. But Angus could do the job just as well. Of late, I had been beginning to suspect that Richard Sterling was becoming ... fond of me.

How I felt about him, I was not entirely certain.

Nevertheless, it is always a good idea to leave them wanting more.

Regardless of any feelings toward the handsome corporal that I might or might not entertain, I most definitely was not in Dawson to find a man. This gold rush wasn't going to last forever: some who were in a position to know privately said there wasn't really all that much gold. I intended to make my money and get Angus and me out in a year or two. I did not need complications.

Men are always complicated.

So far I was enjoying living in Dawson. Most of the time. Last winter had been highly unpleasant, as the town slowly began to starve and some unfortunate souls succumbed to frost bite and scurvy. But now that the authorities were insisting that anyone coming into the territory from the Outside have enough food to last them a year, the winter ahead should be easier.

Unfortunately, the police could do nothing about the mud that coated everything, the perfectly dreadful food, and the shortage of accommodations that had Angus and me crowded into three rooms in Mr. and Mrs. Mann's boarding house. I didn't even have a lady's maid, such a creature being rare in the Yukon.

"Yoo hoo." I looked up to see a woman on the other side of the street, waving at me.

I gave her a genuine smile and waved back. It had rained last night and the street was thick with muck. She ploughed across, dragging her skirts behind her.

"Martha," I said, "lovely to see you. How nice you look."

And she did. She was large and plain and formidable of feature, but her cheeks were pink with pleasure and her eyes glowed with new love.

It might almost be enough to make a romantic out of me.

Martha Witherspoon and Reginald O'Brien, whom everyone called Mouse, had fallen head over heels in love almost from the moment of meeting. Martha had come to the Yukon intending to write a factual account of the gold rush. She still clutched her ever-present notebook, but rather than interviewing miners and dance-hall girls, she now intended to produce a volume of tips and hints to assist family women heading north. Considering that her writing talent was practically non-existent, a shopping list of necessary items was more suited to her skills than breathless prose.

I slipped my arm through hers and we continued walking. She chattered happily on about all the things she planned to buy for her new home when she and Mouse set up housekeeping.

We parted outside the Savoy. At this time of morning, the place was somewhat less hair-raisingly frantic than in the evening. Our doors opened at 10 a.m., and a crush of drinkers, gamblers, and general layabouts could then be guaranteed to pass through the hallowed portals.

It was my custom to go home at 6 a.m., when we closed, get a few hours sleep, and come in to do the accounts in the quiet of the late morning, take our loot ... uh money ... to the bank and then head home for a bit more sleep.

Helen Saunderson, maid of all work, was on her knees in the corner by the water barrel, scrubbing at the floor. She looked up as I entered and I made a gesture of lifting a cup to my mouth. Murray was behind the bar, managing not to look too dreadfully bored at some old sourdough's ravings of a valley, sacred to the Indians, warmed by hot springs, full of riches beyond imagining. Never to be found by the white man.

Better, I thought, than having to listen to the thousandth telling of the tale of the discovery of gold on Bonanza Creek. I climbed the rickety stairs to the second floor and unlocked the door to my office, unpinned my hat and placed it on a table, settled myself behind my desk, opened the drawer, and pulled out my accounts ledger. I checked the bottom-most number.

Highly satisfactory.

Footsteps coming up the stairs, moving down the hall. My friend Graham Donohue popped his head in.

"What's this I hear about Soapy Smith's gang being in town?" He failed to offer me greetings.

"Not exactly the 'gang,'" I said. "But one gang member. It's true."

Graham dropped into the visitor's chair in front of my desk. "You know this person, Fiona?"

"Regretfully, yes. Odious man."

"Do you think more gang members are following? The Mounties won't put up with that."

"To be honest, Graham, I don't know. A year ago, I would have been positive Soapy wouldn't be such a fool as to come directly up against the forces of her Majesty, but who knows what the intervening time has done to him. Rumour has it he's losing control in Skagway. Perhaps he's desperate enough to think he has no choice but to move into the Yukon."

Graham peered at me. "Are you telling me, Fiona, you know Soapy Smith? Personally?"

"Regretfully, yes."

Graham pulled out his notebook and pencil.

"Put that away," I said. "I am not granting you an interview."

"An informal interview. Authoritative yet unnamed sources and all that."

Graham Donohue was a newspaperman. A reporter with a big American paper, here in the Klondike to report on the hottest story in North America, if not the world. He was no taller than I, lean and wiry, and he sported a ferocious moustache that clashed with his schoolboy complexion, sparkling brown eyes, thick black eyelashes and perfect bone structure. Any one of my dance-hall girls would be more than happy to give him the time of day, but Donohue never seemed interested in them. I patted my hair. Graham, well I knew, had eyes elsewhere. He was always attempting to lure me onto the badly sprung couch in my office.

"Angus and I were in Skagway in August of last year," I said. "Sensing that the environment for an independent person of business was not, shall we say, welcoming, I decided it would be best to decamp for Dawson."

Graham's pencil stub hung over the paper. "And?"

I smiled at him. "And, it is time for me to get my accounts done. I am running behind this morning, having made a stop at the police detachment office to report the arrival of one of Soapy's henchmen."

Another round of footsteps coming up the stairs and down the hall. Helen came in, bearing a tray with a single cup plopped in the centre. Most unrefined, to be serving tea already prepared, but I'd given up trying to insist that Helen bring the milk and sugar in separate bowls. "Oh," she said, "didn't know you was here Mr. Donohue. Shall I fetch another tea?"

"Yes, please," Graham said.

"No," I said. "Mr. Donohue is leaving momentarily."

She put the tray down and hurried away.

"Come on, Fiona. What was he like? Smith wasn't in Skagway when I went through."

"Graham, go away." I took a sip of tea. Barely satisfactory. Helen had added too much sugar. I prefer lemon, but needless to say, citrus is non-existent in the Yukon.

Grumbling, Graham stood up and returned his notebook to his pocket.

"You may take me to tea this afternoon," I said. "Four o'clock at the Richmond. Provided you promise my name will not appear in any way in your epistle."

He touched his hat and left.

I picked up my own pen and bent my head over the ledger. I found it difficult to concentrate. Like every other building in town, the Savoy had been constructed with great haste out of green wood and inadequate materials. The noise from below came right up through the floorboards. I pushed away from my desk and went to stand at the window. I could see across Front Street, over the mudflats to the river and the hills beyond. The shore was packed with watercraft of every conceivable type, from steamboats to barges to a mismatched collection of logs slashed together to form a raft. Boats were tied to boats tied to other boats far out into the river. Tents and shacks lined the waterfront, and men and horses struggled through the river of mud that was Front Street.

Ray and some of the men had strung a banner Angus had created across the street: The FINEST, MOST MODERN ESTABLISHMENT

IN LONDON, ENGLAND, TRANSPORTED TO DAWSON. Our sign seemed to be achieving its aim. As I watched, five men came down the street, their hats and jackets thick with grime, their faces dark under unkempt beards and dust. One of them stopped and looked at the sign. He spoke to his companions, gestured to it, perhaps reading it to them, and then pointed to the door of the Savoy. As one, they nodded and trooped up the step and disappeared from my sight.

I studied the faces on the street below. Almost all were male, with a scattering of women and even fewer children. I recognized a few of the men — those who came to the Savoy, whom I'd seen on the streets, who worked in restaurants, banks or shops which I frequented. No one from Skagway.

It had been a year since I was there. Hundreds of men might have joined the gang since and come over the Pass with Paul Sheridan.

He had been alone last night in the Savoy. Enjoying himself, dancing with Irene. No one in Soapy's gang would have stood by and watched one of their fellows being evicted physically from the premises.

It was unlikely Paul had come alone, but not impossible. Perhaps he'd had a falling out with Soapy — easy to do — and decided to strike out on his own.

He might be on his own, but if he were here to dig for gold, I'd join a nunnery.

I felt a prickling of unease as I remembered running into Angus at the NWMP office. Paul had approached my son. That I did not care for one bit.

Chapter Five

It had been only a year ago when Angus and I departed Toronto with an unseemly degree of haste. We took the first train pulling out of Union Station, paying no heed to where it was heading.

We ended up in Vancouver in July of 1897.

Every person we encountered was talking about nothing but gold. Yukon gold. On July 14, the steam ship *Excelsior* had arrived in San Francisco carrying half a million dollars worth of gold, and then on the 17th, the *Portland* pulled into Seattle with a million dollars worth. Newspaper headlines screamed the weight of the precious metal; store fronts were instantly covered in advertisements for the equipment one supposedly needed to go prospecting; waiters and butlers and shop clerks and police-men discarded their uniforms and walked out the door, heading for the Klondike.

Although a great many didn't exactly know where that was.

Or what they would find there.

I stood on the street corner outside our hotel while the bellboy unloaded our trunks and Angus peppered him with questions. He told Angus that his three older brothers were preparing to leave, that he wanted to go with them but his widowed mother was beg-ging him not to abandon her.

I watched a cart go by, laden with pickaxes, burlap bags of flour, wooden boxes stamped canned corn, and three men, the youngest of whom was seventy if a day. "Ho! The Klondike! Ho!" they cried to cheering onlookers. A group of small boys and a scrawny dog ran after them. The boys waved and shouted. The dog barked.

The bellboy took our things into the hotel, and we followed. It wasn't a particularly good hotel. Definitely second rate, not the sort of establishment I was accustomed to frequenting.

Which was, of course, the point.

I was likely being sought by one Mr. Jonathan McNally, whose wife's jewellery was resting comfortably in the valise that never left my hand.

* * *

Jonathan McNally was a fat, red-faced man in his late forties who dabbled at being a banker but in truth was dependent on his mother's family fortune. She was a daughter of one of the old-money Protestant families who controlled the financial life of Eastern Canada. Jonathan's wife — as plump and plain as he — and their six children spent the entirety of the summer at the family vacation home on Stoney Lake. At the weekend Jonathan would travel up on the train to join his progeny. During the week, he would entertain me.

Shortly after he had made my acquaintance over an excellent dinner at the Royal York Hotel, I told my paramour that my house had been discovered to be infested with vermin. I shuddered prettily and said that, as I was in temporary accommodation, I couldn't possibly invite a gentleman around for an after-supper drink, now could I?

He looked slightly unsure — they always did. Then he gave in — they always did — and said he'd be delighted to show me his home.

One of Jonathan McNally's virtues, for me, was that an excess of drink put him straight to sleep. I suggested brandies before retiring, and sure enough he was asleep as soon as his head hit the pillow. I left him snoring lustily and examined the house. Most specifically, his wife's dressing room. She hadn't taken the best of her jewels to Stoney Lake. The drawers to the desk in the library were locked but looked easy to pick.

The weekend arrived and Jonathan, as was his custom, departed to join his family. Saturday night, I used the copy of the key I'd made from the one in Jonathan's jacket pocket and entered the house.

Unfortunately, the butler was up in the night. Also unfortunately, a delicate pie-crust table had been placed behind a door where it hadn't been previously, and I knocked it over. What the butler thought he was doing upstairs in the family bedrooms when no one was in residence, I cannot imagine. Hearing the table fall, he armed himself with a candlestick and came face to face with me, dressed in trousers and a multi-pocketed working man's jacket, all in black, exiting Mrs. McNally's boudoir.

The butler was not accustomed to ladies who'd been taught to fight as if in a bare-knuckle ring.

I screamed, only half-pretending shock, dropped my sack, mumbled something about having left my late mother's necklace behind, burst into tears, and reached out as though to weep on his chest. Instead, I grabbed him by the shoulders of his night attire, pulled him toward me, and drove my knee deep into his jewels. He screamed, I let go and stepped back. He bent over, protecting his vitals, overcome with pain. I brought my knee in again, this time driving it into his face. His nose burst in a spray of hot, sticky blood.

I ran, having the presence of mind to first pick up my bag.

I estimated I had sufficient time to collect my things and my son and get out of town. Fearful of the possibility of scandal, or the rage of the elder Mrs. McNally, the butler wouldn't call the police without his employer's authorization. And even then, McNally might not be too welcoming of the sort of questions the authorities would ask. Such as how I'd obtained a key and knew the layout of his house.

He'd told me they didn't have a telephone at the lake. Something about Mother objecting to the vile instrument. Knowing who was the boss — Mother — Mr. McNally might want to instruct his butler to break a window and leave large muddy boot tracks across the carpet before contacting the authorities.

No, I wasn't afraid of the police.

His mother's money or no, McNally was a wealthy man, and wealthy men had their resources. Rich or poor, no man was fond of being made a fool of.

Particularly by a woman.

I hurried home and dismissed the cabbie. I roused the footman and told him to find me a cab, quickly. Letting the rest of the servants sleep, I stuffed the best of my possessions into only two trunks. The scented cedar box containing jewellery, as well as the pieces for possession of which I was forced to flee, went into a valise. I stuffed cash into envelopes for my staff. More than enough to make up for lack of notice, but also to ensure some degree of loyalty, hoping they wouldn't sell me out to the first person who came calling.

I ordered the cab to Angus's school, where I roused the headmaster in the middle of the night. Angus was sent for and told he had ten minutes to pack his truck. The headmaster and his bony, nightgown-clad wife protested earnestly, something about the importance of strict regimen and rigorous attention to routine in the development of a young man's character. I told them I'd leave a donation to the school, which went a long way to mollifying them, slapped another cash-stuffed envelope on the table, and went outside to wait impatiently by the cab.

Angus was back in seven minutes, trailed by a porter wheeling his trunk in a barrow; his possessions were loaded onto the top of the cab, and we were off again.

On our arrival at Union Station, while Angus patted the horses' noses and thanked them for bringing us, and the cabbie went in search of a porter, I slipped into the building alone, telling Angus to deal with the porter and meet me inside. The cavernous station was dark and quiet. The sound of my footsteps disappeared into the great vaulted stone ceiling.

I changed into a plain dress of brown cotton, wrapped my long black hair into an exceedingly tight bun and topped it with a most unattractive hat, propped a pair of spectacles containing plain glass onto my nose, and slipped a cheap wedding band onto my finger. I rubbed a bit of dirt, scooped up while waiting for Angus, onto the hem of the dress. To his credit, Angus barely batted an eyelid when I emerged in my new costume. I purchased our tickets in a flat Canadian accent, blinked myopically at the man behind the counter, and fumbled through my reticule for a few coins to tip the porter.

"What have you done this time?" was all Angus said as we boarded the train.

During the long journey across the continent, I'd decided to head for the United States. San Francisco, perhaps. It was supposed to be a rough-edged town. I had sufficient funds to find a place for Angus in a good boys' school, rent a house in a respectable part of town, and hire an adequate household. Whereupon I would make my living as I had since I'd been eleven years old.

Stealing.

*   *   *

Standing in the hotel lobby in Vancouver I changed my plans.

Enough of climbing up drainpipes and escaping by the skin of my teeth. Enough listening to fat old men snore in the night.

And enough of missing my son. Angus was eleven years old. I hadn't wanted to put him in boarding school, but once he reached the age of awareness I could hardly have him living with me when I entertained the gentlemen who, usually unwittingly, provided my income.

We'd left London four years ago with as much haste as our recent departure from Toronto. It was time to provide my son with a bit of stability.

"Angus," I said, as we stood in the lobby of the second-rate Vancouver hotel. "How would you like to go to the Klondike?"

"That'd be grand, Mother."

"Where," I asked the hotel clerk, "is the shipping office located?"

I hadn't intended to actually go to the Klondike. It sounded like a most difficult trip. I certainly had no intention of prospecting for gold. Unlike what had been suggested by the talk I heard in Vancouver, then Victoria, and then on the *Bristol*, heading for Alaska, I suspected that gold nuggets were not lying about on the ground waiting to be picked up by men who'd last week been bank clerks or cooks or farmers.

But where there were men, lots of men, away from their homes, full of dreams, there was always money to be made.

And legally, too.

I'd find a profession in Alaska that would allow me to have my son living with me, and not necessitate bracing myself every time I saw an officer of the law heading my way.

This place called Skagway seemed like a good destination. I'd open a theatre and employ women to dance and perform stage plays. I exchanged Mrs. McNally's jewellery for cash and bought supplies and two boat tickets to Skagway.

Skagway turned out to be more than even I had bargained for, and eventually Angus and I joined the long line of fortune-seekers climbing the Chilkoot trail.

Chapter Six

Corporal Richard Sterling had told his constables to be on the lookout for the tall thin man and to let him know if they spotted him.

Settled down to dinner in the back room of the detachment office, which served as the dining hall, Sterling decided to confront Mr. Paul Sheridan personally. He told himself it wasn't because Sheridan had offended Fiona MacGillivray — definitely not, he would never let his personal feelings interfere with the performance of his duties. But if Sheridan was a scout for Soapy Smith, this needed the attentions of someone more experienced than a raw constable fresh from the Outside, still shaking the dust of the Chilkoot off his scarlet tunic.

Dinner consisted of the ubiquitous beans, this time served with a slab of overcooked meat of indeterminate origin. At least the bread was hot and fresh, and it came with a scraping of butter.

"Sir," Constable McAllen came in. He didn't look quite old enough to shave yet. "Sorry, don't want to disturb your supper."

Sterling pushed the plate away. "Not worth worrying about. What is it?"

"I think I spotted the guy you're after. Tall, very thin. He's in the Monte Carlo. Playing roulette. Losing big."

"Thanks. Let's look into it."

*   *   *

It was six o'clock in the evening and the Monte Carlo was busy. Men eyed the police officers as they came through the front doors. Sterling nodded to the man behind the bar and kept walking. The gambling room was about half full. Still early for some of the bigger players.

Gambling, like prostitution, was illegal in Canada. But when the men in charge of this tiny police force, in the town fast becoming one of the biggest — certainly the busiest — in Western North America, realized what they were about to be faced with, they decided it was better to control vice than to outlaw it. The authorities in Ottawa were a very long way away, and the officers and men of the North-West Mounted Police were on their own. So they allowed gambling and prostitution but kept a strict eye out to ensure business was as properly conducted as possible. Places could be and were shut down if they stepped too far over the line.

A crowd had gathered around the roulette table. As Sterling and McAllen entered, a man placed a pile of chips onto the table. "Seventeen," he said.

"You been playin' seventeen all night," a grizzled sourdough said. "It ain't come up yet. When you gonna try somethin' new?"

"That's my plan, old fellow. At some point seventeen will come up. And then I'll be a winner."

The old man's face said what he thought of that plan.

The croupier spun the wheel. He passed his hand over the table and said, "No more bets."

Everyone, Sterling and McAllen included, watched the ball.

"Sixteen," the croupier announced in a flat tone. He scooped up most of the chips, then counted a couple out and placed them beside the ones on red.

The old sourdough, the owner of that bet, chuckled and collected his winnings. He put them in front of the man who'd bet on seventeen. "Luck ain't with you tonight, my boy. Why don't you quit while you can?" With that, the sourdough stood up from the table and took his leave, passing the two police officers standing in the doorway. "Corporal," he said in greeting.

Sterling knew the man — one of the very few who'd actually found gold. Lots of it. He'd prospected up and down Alaska and the Yukon for more than twenty years and was lucky enough to be close to the Creeks when word spread of the great discovery. He had staked his claim within days and pulled a great deal of the gold metal out of the ground since. He came into town once a month, stayed for two days, showered his favourite dance hall performers with gold nuggets, visited the cribs on Paradise Alley, gambled at the Monte Carlo and the Savoy, usually losing all the gold he'd dug up since he'd last been in town, and then disappeared back to his claim with a month's worth of supplies, empty pockets, and a smile on his face.

Sterling approached the roulette table as Sheridan was placing the chips the old miner had given him onto number seventeen. The croupier lifted one eyebrow when he saw the police.

"Mr. Paul Sheridan," Sterling said.

The man didn't look up. "Yes."

"I'm Corporal Sterling and I'd like to have a word with you."

"Can't right now, Officer. My luck's about to turn."

"A night in jail and your luck will definitely be turning."

"I haven't done anything."

"Glad to hear it. Then we can just talk. Randy, give the man back his chips." The croupier pushed them over.

"Keep them," Sheridan said. "And save my place. I'll be back."

"Free with your money, aren't you?" Sterling asked, as he led the man though the bar and out to the street.

"I'll be getting plenty more soon."

Sterling didn't bother to ask where. Half the men who arrived in the Klondike seemed to expect gold nuggets to be lying on the ground or hanging from the scruffy pine trees like fruit ripe for the picking. But some people were starting to leave, giving up the dream, heading back to the south. Telling others they passed on the trail there was no point in carrying on. No more gold was to be found, no jobs except hard work on another man's claim.

Still they came. Optimistic to the end.

"Where'd you come from?" Sterling asked. They stood on the wooden sidewalk, a few feet down from the Monte Carlo's doors. McAllen watched the street.

"Told you about me did she?" Sheridan shook his head. "Naughty minx. Or was it her boy?" His eyes darkened. "You wouldn't have a *personal* interest in this would you?"

"I've no idea what you're talking about. Where was your last place of residence?"

"As you know, Skagway. And yes, I was in the employ of Soapy Smith. Although I never did anything illegal, you see. I worked in one of his establishments. All above board, of course."

"Of course. Did Smith send you here?"

"Nope. These days, Soapy isn't sending anyone anywhere. He's losing control, Soapy is. I could see the writing on the wall. Time to get out of town."

Sterling believed the man. Rumour drifting over the passes said Soapy was running into trouble. On one hand criminals, new arrivals, weren't about to take orders from anyone, and on the other hand Skagway townsfolk were muttering about taking the law into their own hands.

"Planning to stay in town for long?"

"Nope. I'm getting married and then my lady and I will be heading north."

"North? There's nothing north of here."

Sheridan tapped the side of his nose. "Not telling. These men," he nodded to a group of grime-incrusted, long-bearded, probably lice-infested miners, heading out of town carrying equipment and supplies, "they're wasting their time. Bonanza Creek. Eldorado. Child's play. There's a mountain of gold out there. And I'm the only one knows where it is."

"If you say so. Be sure you keep your nose clean while you're here, will you."

Sheridan tipped his hat and sauntered away, whistling, hands in pockets. He didn't go back to the Monte Carlo.

McAllen lifted his hand to his head and drew circles in the air.

Sterling laughed.

Chapter Seven

The word *chaos* had been invented to describe Skagway in the late summer of 1897.

Angus and I had arrived in Alaska aboard the good ship *Bristol* out of Victoria. The town didn't even boast a dock; ships had to anchor at sea and ferry passengers and cargo to shore with boats. Horses — scrawny, terrified beasts, every one — were shoved overboard to sink or swim. We humans, along with all our possessions, were unceremoniously dumped on a muddy patch of rocks and seaweed. Fortunately, I was possessed of sufficient charm, plus the proceeds of the sale of Mrs. NcNally's jewellery, to hire a man to ferry our trunks to the best hotel in town. I tried to barter down from the outrageous $50 an hour the foul-breathed man wanted to charge, but he shrugged and said, "You want to wait a couple hours, lady, rate'll go down to twenty. 'Course by then tide'll be high."

I paid.

All I felt on my arrival in Alaska was sheer horror. Angus, on the other hand, stared at everything with wide-eyed wonder and boyish enthusiasm. Viewed from the boat, the town was nothing but a disappointing cluster of white canvas tents, immediately beyond which a dark line of trees loomed. Snow-capped mountains filled the sky. At low tide, the air stank of rotting fish and vegetation and mud. To one side of the scattering of tents lay wilderness, on the other the ocean, and I wondered uneasily what I had gotten myself into.

My unease only grew when we set foot on land.

The town boasted no more than a couple of actual buildings. Everything else, commerce as well as housing, was in tents. The main street, grandly called Broadway, was nothing but a line of tents. Why, tree stumps stuck up from the middle of the muddy roadway!

Nevertheless, I was here, and I immediately set about establishing my business venture. I'd made the acquaintance of a large number of people — first among those waiting for ships in Vancouver and Victoria and then aboard the *Bristol* — whom I might be able to employ. Women, for the most part, who called themselves actresses or dancers. Those I suspected were heading for the Klondike for another line of work, I avoided. On board the ship, I auditioned a group of male musicians and a vaudeville entertainer and offered them employment. They were all enthusiastic, and I felt confident about the venture.

I had plans of renting a building to use as my theatre, but now that I saw the town, I was beginning to have doubts I could locate anything suitable.

There was hope, however. Buildings were rising from the forest, virtually before our eyes, the air full of sounds of sawing and hammering.

"Isn't this absolutely grand, Mother," Angus said happily while we ploughed our way through the mud after our porters, there being no room on the cart for passengers.

I had taken two steps on so-called dry land and already the muck dragged at my skirts. Propriety be damned, I yanked my skirts up, folded the excess fabric into my belt, and stalked after my son and our worldly belongings.

Immediately upon checking into our hotel, I stripped the bed, bundled the sheets into a ball, threw them (and all their occupants) into the hall, and remade the bed with sheets I'd brought. With a considerable degree of foresight, I'd packed expecting conditions not to be entirely of the sort I am accustomed to, so I dug out a bottle of ammonia and a couple of rags and set Angus to wiping the entire place down. I changed out of my travel-stained clothes and put on a light blue day dress and matching hat that wouldn't have been out of place on Pall Mall. I then wrapped a length of fake pearls, of good enough quality to appear real on not-too-close inspection, around my neck and completed the costume with pearls in my ears. Ordering Angus to remain in our room until I returned, I set off to explore our new home.

The grand tour took about five minutes.

A gambling parlour looked like a good place to begin scouting out the territory.

I knew better than to hesitate and walked directly into the tent that called itself The Pack Train Saloon.

It was the middle of the day, yet the establishment was busy. Every man in the place looked up as I entered. The roulette wheel clattered to a stop. Hands of cards were dropped and dice lay abandoned.

"Good afternoon," I said. "I am Mrs. MacGillivray and I am here to do business."

"Ma'am." A man came out from behind the bar. "We don't allow that sort o' business here."

"Don't be ridiculous," I said. Through a stroke of considerable fate, I happen to speak with a cut-glass aristocratic English accent. I find that the proper use of the Queen's English reduces Americans and Canadians to bumbling fools. "I will be opening a theatre, a place of respectable stage entertainment. I am in search of premises to rent."

The men glanced at each other.

It did not escape my notice that one particularly sallow-faced fellow slipped out the door.

"If you would be so kind," I said to the bartender, "as to direct me to the real estate office."

"Theatre?" he said. "What sort of theatre?"

"We will perform a selection of stage plays, have musical interludes, some dance performances, a comedian. Accommodation such as this," I waved my hand to indicate the tent and all the men in it, "would be suitable. Until a proper building can be erected."

"You thinkin' of serving liquor?"

I was, but decided it would be best not to let this fellow know, yet. I would be setting up in competition with him.

"No."

"Good," he said. "Cause it ain't legal to serve liquor in Alaska. Ain't that right boys?"

They nodded at the bartender's words. Every last one of them clutched a dirty glass. I eyed the bottles displayed on the plank serving as a bar and on the shelves stacked at the rear. There was even a keg of beer.

"Naturally, I would not be interested in breaking the law," I said.

"Right glad to hear that," a lazy voice said from behind me.

I turned. The sallow-faced man was back, breathing heavily. Beside him stood a heavily-bearded man with well-oiled black hair. He was perfectly dressed in a white silk shirt and satin waistcoat. A diamond pin pierced his tie, and a wide brimmed hat was in his hand.

The men cleared a path, and the newcomer walked toward me, his eyes fixed on my face.

"Ma'am. My name is Jefferson Smith. How may I be of assistance?" He gave me a broad smile. His accent was deep and slow and sounding of warm honey.

"Mrs. Fiona MacGillivray." I held out my hand. Mr. Smith took it in his. His nails were neatly trimmed and clean. He bowed over my hand, and I wouldn't have been entirely surprised if he'd kissed it.

At last, a gentleman of culture and refinement.

I repeated my business.

"Why don't we go to my office and talk in private," Smith said when I'd finished.

That didn't sound like a good idea. "Do you have a place for rent?" I asked.

"You see, Mrs. MacGillivray," he said with a sad shake of his head, very sorry at being the bearer of bad news. "I don't know what things are like where you come from, but here in Alaska, ladies cannot own businesses."

I turned to the bartender. "I'll have a glass of lemonade, please."

He blinked. "I don't got lemonade."

"In that case, I'll have whatever that gentleman is having." I pointed to a large man without a tooth in his mouth or a hair on his head, clutching his glass of mud-coloured liquid.

The bartender looked at Mr. Smith. Smith nodded and I was poured a drink. The glass didn't look too clean, but I hoped the strength of the liquor would kill any infection before it could kill me. I accepted the glass, held it to my mouth, took a quick sniff, threw back my head, and swallowed it all.

Gut-rot. Highly watered gut-rot.

The men stared at me, no doubt expecting me to spit it back up and turn red with coughing. I handed my glass to the bartender. "I'll have another, please. Not so much water this time."

"That'll be fifty cents for the two."

"Quite expensive for flavoured water, I'd say." I pulled the coins out of my reticule and slapped them on the counter. "Mr. Smith, being a newcomer in your fine town, I wouldn't dream of breaking any laws. Fortunately, I am not a lady. Just as the refreshment served here contains no alcohol."

The bartender handed me my second drink. I put it on the counter. "Mr. Smith, gentlemen. Good afternoon." I made my way to the door, and men cleared a path in front of me. When I reached the tent flap, I turned around. Every eye in the place was on me. I had not the slightest doubt that Mr. Jefferson Smith was the big man in this town. "The first evening of theatre will be offered free for everyone. To thank you all for your hospitality."

A wave of men's voices followed me down the street.

* * *

When I returned to what laughingly passed as the best hotel in Skagway, Angus was not there. I felt a moment's panic.

Had I made a terrible mistake, bringing my child here? In England he'd lived at home with me until he was seven, first in the care of a doting nanny and then a governess. On arriving in Toronto, I found him a place in a good Episcopalian boy's school, where he was to be prepared for the life of a proper gentleman. He wasn't entirely an innocent. At one time, I'd been called by the headmaster, who was threatening to expel Angus and his friends for escaping the school at night by climbing down a drainpipe.

But nothing they would have done there could prepare Angus for the Alaskan wilderness.

I took off my hat and looked around the room. Angus had done a decent job of cleaning up. He'd unpacked some of the food and opened a tin of peaches, one of potatoes, and one of corned beef. The tins were half-empty, indicating he'd had some supper.

I hoped we wouldn't have to live on tinned food, served cold, for long. I located a fork and dug into the peaches.

Whether they had some ridiculous regulation in Alaska about women owning businesses or not was neither here nor there. Mr. Smith had quoted me the law in a place where any casual glance showed that the law was something to be ignored.

He was clearly telling me he didn't want me setting up my business.

I had countered by appealing directly to the men, offering a free show. That I didn't have a place to use as a theatre might not matter right now. I could surely find a clearing in the woods, post signs all over town, and hope it wouldn't rain. One or two successful outdoor performances and I'd be getting offers of rental space in no time at all.

I put my hat back on my head and checked my pocket watch. I'd go in search of my son now and contact my new employees tomorrow.

Chapter Eight

"Psst. Angus. Over here."

Angus MacGillivray peered into the Dawson City alley. The buildings on either side blocked the sun, and all he could see were shadows. He heard something rustle and thought it might be a dog. But dogs didn't know his name. "What? Who's there?

A hissing sound. Then, "It's me. Are you alone?"

"Yes, I'm alone."

A shape broke out of the gloom. Paul Sheridan peered around the corners, as though checking that Angus wasn't lying.

"Are you hiding from someone?" Angus asked.

"I don't want to run into your Fly Bull buddy, that's all."

"You mean a Mountie?"

"Yeah. It wasn't nice of you to tell them about me, Angus."

Angus started walking. Sheridan followed. "I don't care about being nice. It was nothing more than my duty to tell the police a known criminal is in town."

"I'm completely legitimate now. I've left Soapy and the gang. I'm here to find gold. Same reason as everyone else."

"Tell them that then, why don't you?"

"I avoid contact with the police whenever possible."

Angus rolled his eyes.

"Oh, yes," Sheridan said, "I understand why you might be suspicious. But I've given up my evil ways."

A horse and cart were stranded in the intersection. Muck came halfway up the cart's wheels. The horse was so thin, Angus could count every rib. The screaming driver flayed its flanks, and spittle and mud sprayed in all directions. Men were gathered to watch, and someone laid a bet on how long it would be before the horse dropped dead.

Angus turned away. "I thought you said you weren't interested in prospecting. You aren't going to find gold hanging around Dawson. You have to go to the Creeks."

Sheridan tapped the side of his nose. "Ah, boy, there you're wrong. Let everyone else go to the Creeks and find a nugget or two, a couple of ounces of dust. Me, I have bigger plans."

Despite himself, Angus asked, "What plans?"

"That's why I need to talk to your mother. I went to collect her for supper last night, but Walker threw me out. I didn't even get to see her. I sent word I was waiting, but Walker never gave her my message. I must have stood in the street for an hour or more. I don't like waiting." His voice turned hard on the last sentence.

Remembering he was supposed to be friendly, he gave Angus a smile that was more of a grimace.

"Why's the bloody town so quiet anyway? Where the hell's everyone gone?"

"It's Sunday. Businesses are closed."

"I'd heard they did that. Didn't actually believe it. You mean men in this town are lily-livered enough to let the Fly Bulls shut their business down for a whole day?"

"Not only business, but any work. A man was arrested last winter for chopping wood for his own stove." Angus debated telling Sheridan that he could also be arrested for using vile language, particularly in the presence of a female or a minor, but he held his tongue. Let the man learn the hard way.

Sheridan shook his head as he digested the news. "Soapy's done for," he said apropos of nothing. "Losing control of the town. Fellows coming in don't want to do what Soapy tells them. Townsfolk are thinking Soapy's bad for business. Miners coming back out are avoiding Skagway 'cause they don't want trouble from Soapy. Business owners don't like that. There's talk they're getting a committee together to force Soapy out."

"Can't say I'm sorry to hear that," Angus said.

"So, being the sensible fellow I am, I figured it was time to strike out on my own." Sheridan pulled a handkerchief out of his pocket and mopped his brow. Last night's rainfall had done nothing to cut the day's heat. "Look, Angus, let's go round to your house now. I'll talk to your mother and tell her my plan."

"Uh, my ma's uh, not home. She's gone for lunch at a … friend's house. That's right, she's having lunch with a friend. A lady friend."

"I'll join her there, escort her home."

"I don't know where it is. Her friend's house, I mean."

"You wouldn't be having me on, would you boy? I don't like to be lied to."

"No, sir. Why don't you tell me your plan and I'll talk to Ma about it. See if she's interested."

Sheridan touched his hand to his chest. He stroked his jacket pocket. "No. You let your tongue slip and the news'll be all over town."

Angus didn't much care. He doubted Paul Sheridan had any great secret, and he was about as sure as he could be his mother wasn't interested in any harebrained scheme the man might come up with. "Suit yourself. I gotta go. Bye."

Angus darted across the street. Mud squelched under his boots and he heard Sheridan shout after him, "I can tell you one thing, boy. You'll want to start packing."

Chapter Nine

The first night we spent in Skagway, I scarcely slept a wink. Bad enough that it was daylight long into what should have been the night, but I kept going over numbers in my head. I'd have to pay my entertainers whether I was charging admittance or not. And probably pay a month's rent on the theatre premises in advance. Plus, find a place for Angus and me to live. We certainly couldn't stay here.

Fortunately, my son was a heavy sleeper, and he'd had a most exciting day. He'd come running up the stairs as I was about to go in search of him, full of chatter about the things he'd seen and the boys he met. Pleased he'd found potential friends, I didn't scold him too severely for going out on his own.

The room next door to us was not being used, shall I say, for sleeping. Every half-hour the door would open·and close, and then open and close again. The floorboards would creak, a man would grunt and a woman would reply. And then the bed would start to shake, sometimes softly, sometimes with enough force I feared for the occupants of the rooms below. The woman would alternately squeal or moan. Then about five minutes of quiet before the bed creaked, footsteps crossed the floor, and the whole process would begin again.

The last customer left before Angus awoke.

I roused the hotel proprietor as soon as we were up and demanded another, quieter, room. As expected, he didn't have any empty rooms, I was lucky to get a room at all, couldn't I see how busy the town was. But if I absolutely insisted, he could move people around. Of course, a quieter room would be more expensive. I bit my tongue and agreed.

The English tradition of the highwayman was alive and well in Alaska in the year 1897.

I went back upstairs and repacked my own sheets.

For breakfast I took us in search of a restaurant, not feeling much like finishing off the cold corned beef. We located an establishment whose sign consisted of a pair of men's trousers, very large men's trousers, with the name written across the seat.

The muck they served at this place was hot, and although it was perfectly dreadful, the coffee held a vague resemblance to coffee.

As Angus was mopping up his beans with a slice of stale bread, I said, "Now that we've arrived safely, would you like to send a telegram to your friends back at school? I'm sure they'd be most pleased to hear from you."

"Telegram?"

"It's quite expensive, five dollars, but I'd like to treat you."

"Telegram?"

"Why do you keep repeating what I say, Angus?"

"Mother, there's no telegraph here."

"Oh, but there is. In my survey of the town, I saw a sign for the telegraph office. Five dollars to send a missive anywhere in the world."

He laughed. "Look around you, Mother. There isn't a boat dock. There are tree stumps sticking out of the middle of the road, we're eating our breakfast in a tent, and everyone is living and doing business out of tents. Do you really think someone has cleared a line though the forest, or laid a cable under the ocean for a thousand miles, and set up a telegraph office before worrying about things like running water or even a government office? I'm sure there's a telegraph machine, and someone to take your money. But there won't be anyone at the other end."

"Oh," I said, feeling rather foolish. I, who should know a thing or two about fleecing unsuspecting innocents, had almost fallen into a trap. My pride was considerably hurt, and for the first time I wondered if I was a match for this place.

As Angus and I stepped outside after our meal, he spotted two young boys squatting on the wooden walkway opposite. They were no dirtier than anyone else in town, but had good teeth and bright smiles. They stood and nodded to me politely.

"Hey," Angus said, clearly delighted. "Those are my friends, Mother. Can I go with them?"

"You may. Perhaps your friends can assist you." I pulled a twenty dollar bill out of my reticule and gave it to him. "I'm going to locate my employees. While I'm doing that, you can move our things to our new room in the hotel. You'll have to hire men to carry the trunks. Pay no more than twenty dollars. Then scrub the room down."

"Sure."

I handed him another bill. "Once that's done, you can take your young friends for refreshment."

He stuffed the money in his pocket, gave me a huge smile, and dashed across the street. I stood for a long time watching the three boys run off. Angus lifted his arms in the air and spun around. He pulled off his cap, tossed it high, and leapt to catch it. Sunlight ignited sparks off his fair hair.

I smiled and went about my business.

One hour later, I was no longer smiling. Not only had the brief flash of sun disappeared and the rain begun again, but

the man who claimed he could tell jokes that would have miners rolling in the aisles had abruptly departed for Dyea. The
three men I'd hired as musicians told me there had been a misunderstanding, and they hadn't *really* accepted my offer. The
woman who claimed to have acted on Broadway — the real
Broadway in New York City — had decided she'd rather not
return to the theatre. The two women travelling together, their
trunk full of dance costumes and accessories, avoided looking
into my face as they told me they'd accepted another position.

I would have slammed the door of their accommodation
on my way out had it not been a tent with flap open to let in a
breeze.

A man leaned up against a tree. He was excessively tall and
very thin and had a cigar clenched between the few teeth still
occupying his mouth. I had noticed him earlier, several times in
fact, as my would-be employees denied they had any intention
of working for me.

"Problems, Miss?" he asked me.

"Yes. As I am sure you know. Take me to see Mr. Smith."

"Smith?"

"Jefferson Smith. Your employer. I wish to speak with him."

"Soapy don't see no one unless he wants to."

"If Soapy is Mr. Smith, he will want to speak with me.
What's your name?"

"Sheridan. Paul Sheridan."

"Mr. Sheridan. Lead the way."

He looked as if he might refuse. Then he looked again, and I
saw him take in my hat, my dress, the earrings in my ears and the
necklace around my throat. He looked into my eyes and studied
my face and then he smiled. "You know my name," he said in
a much softer voice than he'd used previously. "What's yours?"

"I am Mrs. MacGillivray."

"Is Mr. MacGillivray travelling with you, Ma'am?"

"Unfortunately," I said, "Mr. MacGillivray is no longer with us."

He took off his hat, but didn't drop the smile. He held out his arm. I accepted it, and he escorted me through the mud-clogged streets, along the rows of tents, around tree stumps and over logs, past the rotting corpse of a horse, to the building housing "Jeff's Place." It was a saloon in a tumble-down building, wherein was the office of Mr. Jefferson Randolph Smith, also known as Soapy.

Soapy didn't look too pleased to see me, and I suspected a stern talking-to lay in Mr. Paul Sheridan's future.

I got straight to the point.

"I believe there is an opportunity in this town for a theatre. I don't see anyone else offering such entertainment, so I fail to understand why you're blocking my efforts."

"Now, why would I do that, Ma'am?" His office was a back-room behind a bar, not much larger than the square footage of my travelling trunk.

"Perhaps you can tell me, Mr. Smith."

"Call me Soapy, Fiona."

"Mrs. MacGillivray."

"Fiona." He swung his legs off the table. "I think your little theatre might be a great idea. Men like to be entertained. Winter's coming and they tell me it's a tough one around these parts. But you're not thinking big enough, and there I can help you."

"I'm not looking for help."

"Nevertheless, I am offering it." His voice was light and friendly, charming. But his eyes were very dark and his jaw was set. "Now, I envision a theatre out front, pretty ladies such as yourself to draw the customers in. Gambling rooms, a bar. Upstairs rooms for when the men seek private entertainment."

I laughed. "If you want to operate a whorehouse, Mr. Smith, feel free. I will not be competing with you. Good day." I turned to leave.

"Hold on. I didn't ask you here, you came on your own. So you can be polite enough to hear me out."

I settled my face into a listening pose.

"I like you, Fiona. You've got a head on your shoulders and you can make men do what you want. You've practically got Paul there drooling on the floor. It doesn't hurt none that you're about the most beautiful woman I've seen since getting on the boat."

"Enough of the flattery, Mr. Smith. Get on with it."

"This is the way we're going to do it. We'll open a theatre as you said. I can get us a good sized building. You can manage the entertainment, hire them and fire them as you see fit. I think you'll find those folks you called on this morning will be more agreeable when you return in Paul's company. You'll also manage the whores. They usually respond better to a woman, I've found." He ran his eyes down my body as if he were examining a side of beef in the butcher's window. "Some big money fellows are going to be coming this way soon. Not many will get to the Klondike before the White Pass closes, so they'll overwinter here. Then in the spring, all those folks who struck it rich will be heading back out. Men with plenty of money," he looked into my eyes, "will want to get their money's worth. I figure you're it."

"Good day, Mr. Smith." I headed for the door, heart pounding.

"Don't be so quick to turn me down," he called after me. His voice was light, mocking. "I'm not asking you to whore, just to be friendly. You work for me and you can run your theatre as you like. I'll pay a good wage, part of the profits perhaps. This is an expensive town. Not easy to find employment, a woman on her own. With a boy to care for."

I turned to face him. I wrung my hands together and attempted to look hesitant. "I'd like to get the advice of my father. Do you know of any way in which I can send a message to England?"

"Why sure. The telegraph office is next door. Operator's on his meal break right now, but Paul here can help you. Cost is five dollars, even to England. For a bit more, Paul'll stay and wait for your father to reply."

"I'll think it over," I said.

Paul Sheridan followed me back out to the street. "Mrs. MacGillivray, wait," he called.

I stopped, but didn't turn. Sheridan walked around me. "Soapy controls this town," he said. "No one'll do business with you if he tells them not to."

"Surely the police will have something to say about that."

Sheridan laughed. "This isn't England, Mrs. MacGillivray. Or even the Yukon. There's one marshall here, and he does what Soapy says."

"Oh," I said.

"Soapy wasn't really asking you to take up whoring," he said.

"I am sure that will come."

"I can see a fine lady such as yourself wouldn't want to be a whoremistress neither."

"No."

"You need a man to take care of you, Mrs. MacGillivray." The words tumbled out of his mouth. "Fiona. You and that fine looking lad of yours. Marry me and Soapy'll leave you alone. He respects marriage, Soapy does. And ... And ... I think you're the finest woman I ever have seen. Why ..."

"Good heavens," I said.

"Does that mean yes?" His eyes sparkled with joy.

I walked away. Leaving Paul Sheridan standing in the mud of the street, rainwater falling on his battered hat.

Chapter Ten

For the rest of the day, everywhere in Skagway I went, people looked me in the eye and said they couldn't help me. No one had premises to rent. The real estate office man told me every plot in town was sold, although he seemed to be doing a roaring trade with everyone else who stopped by.

I was approached by one gaunt young woman, who scratched constantly at her armpits and crotch and spoke to me with breath like an abattoir. She'd be happy, she said, as I tried not to breathe too heavily, "to come work for you and Mr. Soapy."

I considered Smith's offer.

For about five seconds.

I had been controlled by a man once, and I wasn't much older than Angus is now when I swore I would never allow myself to be so again. I had come to Alaska to make an honest living, to have my son living with me and to be proud of me.

This theatre Soapy was proposing would be nothing but a front for a prostitution operation. If they even needed a front. It seemed like the law didn't much care what Mr. Smith got up to.

When I'd been an apprentice pickpocket, I roomed with a group of whores in Seven Dials, one of London's worst slums. I knew what a foul, exploitative, violent business it is. Illegal, immoral or not, I wanted no part of it.

I was most certainly not going to be a madam for the likes of the woman who had accosted me on the street.

No one in Skagway, probably in Dyea either, would offer me what I needed to set up a business or to find employment. Other than Soapy Smith.

Which meant I would either have to marry Mr. Paul Sheridan, or return to Vancouver.

Neither option appealed to me.

I went back to the restaurant with the sign on a pair of trousers and took a seat to consider what I was going to do now. There would be no trouble getting passage south. Boats were arriving day and night, dumping cargo and passengers and returning almost empty.

I sipped at my tea, which I suspected was more seaweed than leaves grown on the verdant green hillsides of India.

A man came in and took a seat in the corner. He was small and rat-faced, with greasy hair, a mouthful of grey and broken teeth, and skin marked with the memory of childhood acne. He ordered beans and bacon in a rich Glasgow burr, and hearing the sounds of my homeland brought a brief smile to my heart.

"Would ye be Mrs. MacGillivray?" he said to me.

"What of it?" I snapped.

"Just asking," he said. "Ye're the talk o' the town, ye ken."

I humpfed and sipped my tea.

"Ye talk like an Englishwoman but ye've a good Scots name."

"I am a Scotswoman," I said. "I lived on Skye when I was a child."

He pushed his chair back and came over to my table. I looked at his ugly face and saw nothing but a man homesick for Scotland. He held out his hand. "Ray Walker. Of the Glasgow Walkers."

I laughed and accepted his hand. "Why don't you bring your plate over, Mr. Walker, and join me. But I warn you, being seen in my company might not be good for your business prospects. Unless you work for Mr. Smith. Do you?"

"No, Ma'am. I do not."

He dug into his food and I sipped my disgusting tea.

"What are your plans, Mr. Walker?" I asked.

"Heading for Dawson tomorrow, ma'am."

"Prospecting?"

"No. Mining isn't for me. I've a mind to open a bar. Lots of men passing through town, they need someplace to drink."

"I hope you don't run into the likes of Mr. Smith."

"Not likely to. They say the Mounties keep Dawson a law-abiding town. Keep your nose clean, they'll leave a man alone to mind his own business."

I nodded. "Sounds like heaven." I finished my tea, and Ray Walker pushed his empty plate to one side. We stood up and walked outside together. A light rain was falling, making everything even muddier and more depressing than it had been.

I held out my hand. "I wish you luck on your journey, Mr. Walker."

His own hand was rough and scarred. It felt warm and welcoming in mine. "And you too, Mrs. MacGillivray. If I may give ye some advice, Skagway isn't a place for a lady such as yourself."

"So I am beginning to realize."

We both looked up at a shout. Angus and his two companions were running down the road toward us. My son was caked in mud from top to toe. About the only thing recognizable was his big white smile.

I decided, at that moment, I would do whatever necessary in order to keep him with me.

The three laughing boys ran in circles around us.

"Hi, Ma," Angus shouted.

"Ma. Ma," his friends repeated.

"Good heavens," I said. "What happened to you?"

"He fell." One of the boys dropped to the ground and rolled around, presumably imitating Angus. When he stood up he was almost as muddy as my son.

"Are you going to introduce me to your friends," I said.

"Sure. This is Bob and that's Bob."

"They're both named Bob?" I peered at the boys. They had shiny black hair and dark eyes, golden complexions and high cheekbones in round faces. "Oh," I said, "they're Indians."

"Yup," Angus said. "Tiglit. White folks call them Bob 'cause they can't remember their real names. They're cousins or something."

"Mr. Walker, this is my son, Angus. And Bob, and ... uh ... Bob." Ray Walker and Angus shook hands. The Bobs fell back, suddenly shy.

"A pleasure to meet ye, Angus, Mrs. MacGillivray. Good luck to ye. I'm heading to the Yukon tomorrow."

"Wow," Angus said, "are you going prospecting?"

Walker gave me a grin. "In a manner of speaking."

"How are you getting there, sir?"

"I'm taking the White Pass route. They say it's easier than the Chilkoot."

"No," the taller of the Bobs said. "No. White Pass is not good."

"What da ye mean?"

"White Pass is hard. Too hard. Many horses die, many men turn back. Chilkoot better."

"That's not what I've heard," Walker said. "There's a path through the White Pass. The forest has been cleared and a walking path built that's easy for horses to manage."

The boy shook his head.

"Gee, Mr. Walker," Angus said, "you sound like my mother thinking there's a telegraph. When would anyone have had time to cut a path any longer than a couple of hundred yards?"

"I heard ..." Walker said.

"Bob and Bob's parents are working as packers," Angus said. "They're staying with their grannies outside town while their folks are away. They told me. All the Indian packers know the White Path's a death trap."

The boys nodded in unison.

"Chilkoot much better," the taller one said.

"I'd listen to them if I were you, Mr. Walker," I said. "Local knowledge is a valuable thing."

Walker looked dubious. "Perhaps I'd be better staying here a while 'afore rushing off. See what other folks think."

"No," the shorter Bob spoke for the first time. "Rivers freeze soon. Go now, or too late."

"Angus." I spoke very slowly, but my mind was racing. "Have you met any of these packers?"

"Sure. Indians have come from all over looking for work. They'll carry a man's stuff up to the top of the Chilkoot Pass. To the Canadian border. There's a lake at the bottom of the mountain and you can take a boat all the way from there to Dawson."

I looked at Ray Walker. He looked at me.

"Angus and I have three trunks," I said. "And several bags of provisions. Obviously, I cannot carry our belongings all the way to the Klondike. I've brought enough food to last us several weeks, some warm clothes, blankets, sturdy boots. I also have Angus's school books, including the plays of Mr. William Shakespeare. I have excellent dresses, among them a Worth from Paris, as well as hats and accessories."

I did not mention that I had the last of my funds from the sale of Mrs. McNally's jewellery.

"I have food, camping equipment." Walker dropped his voice. "And liquor. Good Scots whisky. Enough for a chap to open a bar."

"And a dance hall, perhaps. Where one could employ respectable entertainers and ladies to dance with the customers."

"I've got a roulette wheel and chips and cards."

A shout came from down the street.

"Mrs. MacGillivray. There you are." Paul Sheridan was running toward us, his long legs churning up mud. "You boys, be off with you." He made a shooing gesture at Angus and his friends. "Don't you be pestering decent white women." The Bobs slipped away. Angus looked confused. His face and hands were streaked with mud and his filthy cap covered most of his shock of overlong blond hair. "Get away boy," Sheridan snapped, "or I'll have you locked up."

"Mr. Sheridan," I said. "You are speaking to my son."

He peered at Angus. Angus's blue eyes blinked back.

"Sorry, boy. Didn't recognize you. Don't you be hanging around with those Indian bastards. Nothing but trouble, the lot of them. Turn your back and they'll steal you blind."

"We can't have that, now can we," I said. My sarcasm escaped Mr. Sheridan.

He turned his attention to Ray Walker. "Is this man bothering you, Mrs. MacGillivray?"

"Most certainly not," I said.

Walker stared at Sheridan until the American flushed and turned away.

"Mrs. MacGillivray," he coughed, "I wonder if I can have a word in private."

"Oh, very well." We crossed the street. Angus and Mr. Walker watched us.

"You shouldn't be associating with Indians," Sheridan said. "It will do your reputation no good."

"Your employer wants me to manage his whorehouse and yet you are concerned with my reputation. Your logic escapes me, Mr. Sheridan."

I might not have spoken, as Sheridan carried on. "And men like that one, Walker. He's leaving for the Yukon, and good riddance. He's small but good with his fists. Mr. Smith offered him a job. He turned Soapy down outright. Soapy don't like that."

"So I gather. As a matter of fact, Mr. Sheridan, I have decided to travel to the Yukon myself."

"You can't be serious! What about my proposal of marriage? Mrs. MacGillivray, I implore you." And to my astonishment, and that of everyone else on the street, he dropped to one knee and took both of my hands in his. "Mrs. MacGillivray. Fiona, I have adored you since ..."

I snatched my hands away. "Get up you fool. You're making a scene."

His legs wobbled as he struggled to stand. With a sigh, I held out my arm and assisted him. The knees of his trousers dripped with mud.

Angus and Mr. Walker were watching us, eyes wide and mouths hanging open. "You tell your mother to forget this talk," Sheridan said, "only fools and easterners go digging for gold."

"We're easterners," Angus said.

"As I'm going to the Klondike in any event," I said, "what would you say is the best route to take?"

Sheridan's eyes slid to one side. "The White Pass, by far. You'll want horses. I can help you find some."

"What an excellent idea. Now, I have to take my son and attempt to find him a bath. Why don't we meet again, say, the day after tomorrow, and you can take me to view these horses."

He touched his hat. "My pleasure, Ma'am. And if, well, if by chance the journey's too hard for you and you want to come back, my offer stands."

"I'm sure it does."

I never did meet with Mr. Sheridan to discuss horses. The following day, with the help of his friends, Angus found six men willing to carry our goods over the Chilkoot Pass. Ray Walker and I met for what passed for tea and discussed a joint business venture. A dance hall and saloon. Each of us owning one half of the business.

I had one more encounter with Mr. Jefferson Smith. We were preparing to board a boat that would take us up the Lynn Canal to Dyea and from there to the Chilkoot. Smith was mounted on a white horse, looking every inch the Southern gentleman.

He swept off his hat as Angus and I approached. "Mrs. MacGillivray. I'm sorry to see you leaving. I'd hoped we could do business. Your grace and beauty would be a valuable asset not only to me, but to the town of Skagway. If I offended you by my crude offer of employment, I apologize. How about we become partners? Equal shares in the theatre?"

I looked at Angus. His sweet open face, his trusting blue eyes.

He believed in me.

"Goodbye, Mr. Smith. I don't expect we will meet again."

We arrived in Dawson in September of 1897. And the long, dark, cold winter settled in.

Chapter Eleven

Spring finally arrived in late May of 1898, the ice on the rivers broke, and thousands upon thousands of people floated down the Yukon River to the mudflats, where the Yukon met the mouth of Klondike and the town of Dawson had been carved out of the wilderness. By summer, despite the hordes of people constantly milling about on the streets, many of whom were out of luck and out of money and wanted nothing more than to go home again, it was not possible for me to continue to avoid Mr. Paul Sheridan.

He was waiting as I came out of the Bank of Commerce on Monday morning.

"Go away," I said. I continued walking.

He fell into step beside me. "Now Fiona, you haven't even heard my offer."

"I have no need to hear it. Mr. Sheridan, I'm pleased you've given up your life of crime. Congratulations. I wish you the best."

"Let me buy you lunch and I'll tell you my plan. You're going to be impressed."

"Mr. Sheridan ..."

"Please, Fiona, call me Paul."

"Mr. Sheridan. I'm off home for an afternoon's rest before returning to the Savoy for the evening. I am not lunching. With you or anyone else."

"I'll walk with you, then."

The last thing I wanted was this ridiculously persistent man knowing where I lived. "No."

"It's no trouble," he said. His smile hadn't faltered in the least. I peered into his eyes, wondering if he might be simple. His smile grew broader.

I caught a glimpse of scarlet on the other side of the street. "There's my escort now." I lifted my hand and waved. "Corporal Sterling, over here!"

Richard waited for a sled pulled by six big dogs to go by, nodded to a woman in a nurse's uniform, her skirt and apron thick with mud, and crossed the street. He touched the broad brim of his uniform hat. "Mrs. MacGillivray. Good day."

I slipped my arm through his. "I'm sorry I'm late. Off we go now. Goodbye, Mr. Sheridan."

Richard gave the man a long look. I tugged at his arm, and he allowed me to lead him away.

"That man bothering you, Fiona?" he asked. "I had a word with him on Saturday. He says he's not here to work for Soapy and I can't run him out of town unless he does something."

"He simply doesn't know the meaning of the word *no*. It's becoming quite tedious. He has some wonderful plan to make a fortune, which he's sure I'll be interested in. I do believe he thinks I'm teasing when I insist I don't want to hear it."

"Let us know if he does anything more than insisting."

"He's harmless." We reached the corner and I snuck a peek behind me. Sheridan was still standing on the sidewalk, like a rock rising out of the sea, while the crowd ebbed and flowed all around him. He waved at me, and I almost jerked Richard off his feet as I changed direction and charged down Queen Street.

Once we were out of Sheridan's line of sight, I did not, however, release Richard's arm. It was a very warm day and the blue sky held no threat of rain. Hopefully, things could dry out a bit before the clouds next opened up.

We arrived in front of my lodgings in due course. Angus and I had taken rooms at Mr. and Mrs. Mann's boarding house. It was a rough wooden building, thrown up almost overnight — as most of the houses in town were. Every scrap of furniture was mismatched at best and broken at worst; the floor creaked and wind blew through cracks in the walls and sought out gaps around doors and windows. The garden was a patch of weeds and dirt, overseen by the neighbours' privy. Steam and heat bellowed from the shed in the back, where Mrs. Mann operated a laundry.

I felt more at home here than I had in my townhouse in Belgravia, where all the furniture was fashionable and expensive and the garden in riotous bloom, with a butler to open the front door and a maid to lay out my gowns and arrange my hair.

Wasn't I becoming a sentimental old fool?

"Do you have time to come in for tea?" I asked Richard. Mrs. Mann was in the laundry shed and Mr. Mann would be at the store with Angus. It was hardly proper for me to entertain a gentleman without other company present, but propriety was never something I cared much about, no matter in what circumstances I was living. "Mrs. Mann always keeps the kettle hot and ready."

"Another time, perhaps," he said with a smile. "I have a meeting with the inspector later and have to get my reports finished."

We bid each other a good day and I went inside.

I removed my jewellery, struggled with the row of tiny buttons on my dress, discarded my petticoat, over-corset, corset, stockings and undergarments, pulled on my night-gown, and crawled into my narrow bed with the lumpy mattress and broken springs for my midday nap.

*   *   *

I was to have the role of matron-of-honour at the marriage
of Martha Witherspoon and Reginald O'Brien. Another first
for me: I've never been in a wedding party. Mainly, I suspect,
because I've never had female friends, not since I was a child.

The best dressmaker in the Yukon had gone out of business
abruptly. Irene Davidson, who'd been friends with the woman,
had swooped in and scooped up the best bolts of cloth before
anyone else could get their hands on them. Where the rest had
gone, I did not know. I kicked myself at being too slow off the
mark: by the time I got to the abandoned shop, all that remained
were some lengths of black homespun and a cotton in a colour
that would make a horse look anaemic.

It was, therefore, to Irene that Martha and I had to go.

Where we would beg for material to make a wedding dress.

Irene and I did not like each other much. Which was of
absolutely no consequence, as long as she was the most popular
dancer in town and I was the boss. We performed our duties and
kept a formal distance. She knew she could leave the Savoy at
any time for a position at any other dance hall, but I paid her an
excellent wage, and the working conditions were no worse than
anywhere else. Things had begun to change recently: I knew
Irene's secret, and she knew I knew. I knew why she had taken
up with Ray Walker, and I did not approve in the least.

That, Irene also knew.

It made for an awkward situation, and I do not care to be
put in a position in which I am unsure as to what is going on.

Ray was visiting Irene when we arrived. Fortunately, all they
appeared to have been doing was drinking tea.

The Lady Irénée occupied a single room in a boarding
house. An unmade bed with an iron headboard and frame took

up a goodly portion of the space. A small table with two chairs around it was in the centre of the room, a large wooden chest pushed against one wall. But there were lace curtains on the windows and a thick colourful rug on the floor, and on the wall, a painting of a pretty blond girl holding a big yellow hat in an alpine meadow.

Ray stood when we entered. "You ladies have a pleasant afternoon," he said. He kissed Irene most possessively, full on the mouth, picked up his hat, and left.

Irene's eyes slid away from mine. Not bothering with pleasantries, she crossed the room in two strides and threw open the lid on the chest.

I pretended indifference, but my heart positively leapt at the sight of crimson satin, pale blue muslin, startlingly white cotton, and navy blue velvet.

"Oh," Martha breathed. "How lovely it all is."

Irene pulled out a bolt of white cotton and then a length of good lace and handed them to Martha. I said the blue muslin would be much more practical (it was considerably less expensive), but Martha was determined to wear a white dress to her wedding, just as Queen Victoria had done.

Martha cradled the cloth as though it were a baby. Her short, stubby, nail-chewed fingers stroked it, not as one would stroke a baby, but a lover.

There would be no quibbling over the price here.

Irene measured and cut the cloth, and then wrapped it in brown paper and string. She then looked at me and, with a smile curling at the edges of her mouth, named her price. I hid a grimace and dug into my reticule. We were not offered tea.

Business completed, we headed back to the Savoy to meet Helen Saunderson, who was going to make Martha's wedding dress. Martha clutched the bundle of cloth to her chest as we walked toward Front Street. I thought it too bad that Martha hadn't been here over the winter; the radiance pouring from her face would have raised the temperature a considerable amount.

Martha and Mouse O'Brien had known each other no more than a few weeks. But things moved quickly in the Klondike. Spring and summer were so short, winter so long and harsh, it seemed as though people needed to pack a whole year into a couple of months. We operated on a different time scale here. I wouldn't be too terribly surprised to travel back Outside and find that ten or twenty years had passed since we'd left Vancouver.

When Ray, Angus, and I arrived last autumn, the town of Dawson wasn't much larger or better built than Skagway, except for government offices and the sturdy Fort Herchmer, operated by the North-West Mounted Police. The town consisted of a few wooden buildings, some planks laid down over the mud, and hundreds of tents. Now, less than a year later, it was a thriving community of close to 30,000 souls, and anything available in the Outside could be found in Dawson.

Although sometimes for an exorbitant price. Such as pure white cotton with which to make a wedding gown.

I gave Helen the afternoon off in order to take Martha home with her, measure her for the dress, and get started on it. The wedding was on Saturday afternoon, five days hence. The dress, and Helen's time working on it, would be Angus's and my wedding gift to the happy couple.

Helen and Martha had just left, Helen chattering away about her own wedding and how her dress had been the best one ever seen in Poughkeepsie, wherever on this earth that might be, when the door flew open and who should be standing there, a big smile on his face and a bouquet of purple fireweed in his hand, but Paul Sheridan.

"Fiona." He crossed the floor in two giant strides. "I'm so glad to see you." He shoved the flowers at me, and I took them without thinking. They were beautiful and the scent was heavenly. "I hope this is a good time to talk," he said.

I sighed.

Both Murray and Not-Murray were working behind the bar. They stopped pouring drinks, and Not-Murray reached under the counter to where Ray kept a good, stout billy club. I signalled to them that it was all right. If Sheridan was so insistent on talking to me, telling me this plan of his, I might as well get it over with.

And then I would once again tell him to go away.

"Very well," I said with an exaggerated sigh. "If you insist."

He beamed at me, and I led the way to a table.

I've been in bars and dance halls in London that would put the Savoy to shame, but very few of them made as much money in a week as we did in a night.

The place had been constructed of green wood, and it groaned in a strong wind. Every night I prayed the second floor balcony wouldn't come crashing down to crush everyone beneath.

I had decorated with what little options were available. A large portrait of Her Imperial Majesty hung behind the bar. Her visage was so sour it was a wonder she didn't poison the whisky stored below. So as to beg favour with the primary nationalities making up the population of the Yukon, we had stuck a Union Jack into the right of the frame and the Stars and Stripes into the left. On either side of the Queen's portrait hung two nudes, one fair-haired, one dark.

Unlikely Her Imperial Majesty would approve. I had very briefly had the acquaintance of her fat, indulgent, womanizing son, Edward, the Prince of Wales, and knew he would most definitely approve.

The walls were covered in heavy red wallpaper with a pattern of gold crowns, making the place look like a bordello. But farmers and miners and labourers seem to think red-and-gold wallpaper equals class, so I'd bought the hideous stuff. Ray and Angus had hung it, covering themselves and everything around them in paste. They hadn't done all that good a job, and strips of paper were beginning to come unstuck from the upper corners. The Savoy was always thick with smoke, not only from cigars but from the kerosene lamps used to provide light, and the wallpaper was already turning a sickly yellow.

The bar itself was sturdily constructed of good mahogany and ran the entire length of the room. We were required by law to provide safe drinking water, and a big barrel of it stood in the corner. A few tables and chairs were scattered throughout the room, although most of the men seemed to prefer to stand at the bar.

Better to hear the gossip, I suspect.

Men can be so naive — which makes it all the easier to fleece them. They crowded around Barney now, buying him drinks, begging him to tell them stories of Snookum Jim, Taglish Charlie, George Carmacks, and the day they discovered gold on Bonanza Creek. As if hearing Barney tell the story, again, would mean they'd have a similar story to tell someday.

Few, if any, of them would. The best claims had been staked before word of the strike reached the teeming, depression-plagued cities of the south. It was men like Barney, old timers who'd wandered the north for years, who made it rich. Whereupon most of them quite simply proceeded to spend it all in a series of sprees that would shame a drunken sailor. Barney had gathered together sixteen of his biggest gold nuggets and had a belt made for a dancer at the Horseshoe. She'd accepted the gift, thanked him with a kiss on the cheek, and gone home to her husband.

A year later, all Barney had left was his reputation. He spent his nights, and most of his days, propping up bars in dance halls up and down Front Street, trading stories for drink.

I gestured toward a round table in the centre of the room. Three cheechakos — newcomers — were seated there, celebrating their arrival in the Klondike. They were dressed in what they probably thought of as mining gear, but the clothes were spotlessly clean, their hands pink and uncallused with neatly trimmed nails. They'd probably not even come over the passes, but paid for passage on a boat from St. Michael.

They were planning on heading out to the Creeks tomorrow.

They would be in for a very rough surprise.

It was not my place to disabuse them of their dreams. No doubt on the way back they'd need to drown their sorrows in more whisky.

"We will sit here," I said to Paul Sheridan. "Gentlemen, if you please."

They grabbed their glasses and began to rise.

"No!" Sheridan almost shouted. He clutched his hands to his chest. "I can't have anyone overhearing."

The three would-be-miners remained frozen, trapped in the act of standing.

"Mr. Sheridan," I said. "I have agreed to listen to your plans. If this isn't a convenient place, then I have business to which I must attend."

He leaned his head toward me. I bent forward also. "What I have to tell you, Fiona, would have this entire town in an immediate uproar were word to escape." He patted his jacket pocket and gave me a wink. "I have something to show you, and it must remain unknown."

"Very well. We will go upstairs to my office." I gestured to the three men to resume their seats, caught Murray's eye and pointed to the ceiling. He nodded.

I led Paul Sheridan to the back of the saloon and upstairs to the second floor. I could almost hear the necks of the men standing beneath the stairs creak as they tried to get a peek at my ankles. Angus had tested the view and told me nothing could be seen.

Not that I mind men looking at my ankles, why, I've even been known to swirl my skirts enough to display a flash of lower leg. But I've found that, as the part owner of this dance hall, it's preferable to maintain an aura of mystery and unavailability.

Keeps them hoping.

We operate neither a hotel nor a restaurant, but we keep a couple of bedrolls and wash basins in the rooms on the second floor in the event a big spender needs a place to rest up before spending again. Helen Saunderson has a small kitchen in a corner of the broom closet behind the bar, in which she can quickly whip up bacon and beans and bread should a gambler make noises about going in search of something to eat. A gambler who is losing, that is. One who is winning is welcome to find sustenance elsewhere.

Today, the rooms were unoccupied. Our footsteps echoed on the uncarpeted floor. I unlocked the door to my office and gestured to Mr. Sheridan to proceed. I did not shut the door behind me.

I settled into the chair behind my desk and edged open the drawer where I kept a billy club of my own.

Not that I expected to have to use it. I would not have brought Sheridan up here if I had. I sensed he meant me no harm; he only wanted to declare his undying love for me and wait for me do so in return.

But some men, as well I knew, have a way of turning violent when thwarted.

He leaned over my desk and pushed a jar of pencils aside. Then he pulled a bulky piece of paper out of his jacket pocket. With great ceremony, he unfolded the paper and spread it out. It was about two feet square, the edges curled and torn, paper fading into shades of yellow.

No words were on it. Just a mess of black and blue lines, a bunch of small triangles, and a big circle, which might once have been red, near the top right corner.

Sheridan stared at the paper, his eyes alight. "You're the only person I've ever shown this to," he said in whisper.

"Is this an art work of some sort? I've heard there's experimental art happening in Europe, but I've never seen a ... painting quite like this."

He laughed. "This is no painting. It's a fortune. My fortune. Our future."

"It is?" The man really was out of his mind. I'd attempt to have a word with the doctor, the real doctor, and see if something could be done.

"Look closely," he said. "Tell me what you see."

"I see lines. Scribbles. A red dot."

He tapped one dirty finger on the bottom left where two blue squiggles intersected. "The Yukon. The Klondike. They meet here, just like this."

"Oh. I see now." Ray had a map of the Yukon, and as we made plans in Skagway to set out for Dawson he had shown it to me. I recognized the angle of the two rivers, but nothing else was at all familiar. If it were a map, it was a useless one. It didn't even show the trail to the Creeks.

"Most interesting." I opened another desk drawer and pulled out my ledger. "Thank you for showing it to me. Now, if you don't mind, I have some work to catch up on."

"I haven't explained. This is Dawson." He tapped the joining of the rivers. "And this," he said, his finger moving slowly across the page, going north east until it reached the dot, "is the most valuable place on earth."

"It is?" I peered at the once-red blotch.

"There's a valley, here. Where hot springs flow. Because of the layout of the valley, it's very deep and surrounded by high mountains as straight up as a wall. The hot water from the springs is contained in the valley. It's as warm as California. All year around. Palm trees grow and the water's warm enough for bathing and all manner of crops will thrive. And flowers." He pointed to the fireweed I'd plopped into a jar. "Big lush flowers, orange and red and brilliant. Of course, being so warm there's plenty of game to be had."

For a moment, he almost had me. I leaned closer, imagining this valley of riches.

Then I remembered where I was: The Klondike. Where dreams died in the face of reality. And who I was: Fiona MacGillivray, gamekeeper's daughter. My father loved to tell me tales around the peat fire in our neat white croft on a dark winter's night. The old Scottish legends of the Green Isle and the Princess of Land-under-Waves. He always finished the stories with a kiss on the top of my head and a reminder that we were simple folk, and many a man had been ruined chasing after fairies.

"Sounds perfectly lovely," I said to Mr. Sheridan. "Although I suspect someone is taking you for a fool."

I doubt he even heard me. "I haven't told you the best part, Fiona."

"You haven't?"

He leaned over. I put my head closer. He did have a way of seeming to share a secret that was somehow alluring. I shook my head and leaned back in my chair.

"The greatest gold deposit on earth." He tapped his finger.

"Which is one of the reasons the warm air stays in the valley, even in the middle of winter. This mountain acts as insulation. It's gold. Almost pure gold. Gold Mountain."

I looked into his eyes. They were as bright as with a fever.

And it was a fever, of a different sort. Gold fever.

"Are you telling me this is a map to this Gold Mountain? A treasure map?"

"Exactly." He straightened and threw his arms into the air. "I knew you'd understand, Fiona. Soon as you're ready we'll be off."

"We?"

"Angus can come, of course. We won't need many supplies, just a few days' worth to see us safely there. I'm going to be a king. King of Gold Mountain. And you, my beloved Fiona, will be my queen."

Chapter Twelve

When it came to delusion, the three clean-cut, hopeful miners below had nothing on Paul Sheridan.

The beautiful, warm valley I might almost believe, but the mountain of pure gold was nothing but another mad fantasy.

I laughed.

He grinned at me, misunderstanding. "Sounds perfect, doesn't it?"

"Regretfully, I am not planning to travel at this time. Good day, Mr. Sheridan." I picked up my pen.

I should have known he wouldn't take the hint.

The fellow was a lunatic.

But he was wise to keep the map secret. Plenty of men seemed to turn lunatics at the very thought of gold. He ran his fingers across the paper.

My curiously got the better of me, and I found myself, rather than showing him the door, asking Mr. Sheridan where he obtained this map. His eyes focused on the paper and he lovingly traced a line with his finger, from the point where the two blue lines intersected — Dawson — up toward the red dot.

He'd befriended a man in Skagway, he said, over the winter. The man was from Bavaria and had been in possession of the map for many years, but he didn't know where to even begin looking for the legendary Gold Mountain. That is, until he'd seen a drawing of the Yukon in a German newspaper and recognized the coordinates immediately. He had spent all his money getting to America, crossing the continent, and buying the required year's supplies. He didn't want Soapy to hear of the map, of course, but he and Sheridan had struck up a friendship, and so he told Sheridan about its existence.

Sheridan's glance slid to one side. The German had died, knifed in bar fight in Skagway. With his last breath, he told his good buddy Paul where the map was hidden. Then he let out his death rattle, a sound terrible to hear, and expired in his friend's arms.

Sheridan was not a very good liar. He'd either been responsible for that death rattle himself or had simply stolen the map.

If the latter, he'd done the German a favour. Save the man disappearing into the wilderness with nothing but a foolish dream to sustain him. I wondered if Sheridan had told his boss, Soapy Smith, about the map and if Soapy treated it with the derision it deserved, or if Sheridan thought he was pulling one over on Smith.

I could sit here all day arguing with Mr. Sheridan as to the validity of his plan. Better, perhaps, to keep my opinions to myself. I put on my regretful face and told him I had pressing matters to attend to. I would, of course, consider his proposition.

He re-folded the paper with great care and returned it to his pocket.

"Today's Monday," he said. "I have a few purchases to make, and then we can be off. Can you be ready on Thursday?"

"Martha and Reginald's wedding is Saturday. I cannot possibly fail to be in attendance. I am the matron-of-honour. Why don't you go ahead of me," I suggested. "Make me a copy of the map and I'll follow."

He looked so shocked, I might have suggested he publish the map in the Klondike *Nugget*. "There's only one copy of this document in existence, Fiona. I intend to keep it that way." He tapped his chest. "This paper doesn't leave my person. Never. We'll leave Sunday morning. I'll be round to your place to get you and Angus at eleven. Be ready."

He gave me a wink and said, "I'm trusting you with this secret, Fiona. Be sure not to tell anyone, including Walker, where're going."

At last he stood up. The colour rose in his face, and he shuffled his feet. "I'm glad I've found you, Fiona. I'll make you very happy. You'll be more than my queen. You'll be my wife. Thank you." He headed for the door, but just as I began to exhale with relief, he turned. "We don't want gossip floating around town before we leave, so I'll keep my distance. Let Walker think he's scared me away from the Savoy. Until Sunday. Be ready." He left, closing the door behind him.

What a bother. I'd make myself scarce on Sunday when he tried to collect me. He might not take no for an answer, but he was waiting an extra three days for me as it was. He'd be most anxious to head off and become King of Gold Mountain.

If he came to the Savoy on Monday, I'd tell him to go away.

I can be just as naive, sometimes, as men expecting to find gold nuggets hanging from the trees like apples.

* * *

"Angus, I'm glad I ran into you."

Angus looked up from sorting men's trousers. "Where else would I be?" he grumbled.

Paul Sheridan grinned. "Not liking the job, are you?"

Angus felt a tug of loyalty for Mr. Mann. "It's all right."

The sun was high in the sky and the river mud was stinking. The woman who owned the next tent over, selling ladies' undergarments, lightly used she claimed, had taken out her lunch before going to help a customer. Flies settled on her food.

Sheridan glanced to each side. The two women were examining a corset with a broken rib and haggling over the price. A group of cheechakos walked past, laughing and talking loudly. Mr. Mann had gone to inspect a prospector's goods and there were no customers at the store. No one was paying any attention to them.

Sheridan leaned over the counter. Angus leaned forward.

"Can you keep a secret, boy?"

"Of course I can."

"Promise."

"I promise."

Sheridan leapt back at the sound of Mr. Mann's booming voice shouting, "Fool. Wans whats hes pays in Seattle for goods. Ha, Ies tell him. Ha." Mr. Mann pointed at the mining equipment stacked on the counter and piled at the back of the tent. "Then takes back to Seattle and gets yous money back, I says. Ha." He eyed Sheridan. "You wants help?"

"I'm here to talk to Angus. What time do you get lunch, boy?"

Angus began to say he'd had his lunch. That wasn't true, but he didn't want to waste time on Paul Sheridan. Mr. Mann said, "Goes and haves lunch now. Store not busy."

Angus had no choice but to reach under the counter for the package Mrs. Mann had made up for him.

Sheridan said, "We don't want to talk where we can be overheard. You know someplace quiet, Angus?"

"Not in Dawson."

Sheridan looked a bit taken aback at that. He shrugged and said, "We'll have to keep our voices low then."

Angus led the way down the waterfront to where things were fractionally less frantic. He found a large boulder, stopped, and began to unpack his lunch. Truth be told, he was starving and glad of the opportunity to get an early lunch, even if he did have to spend it with Paul Sheridan. He hoped the man wouldn't want to share.

Sheridan helped himself to the largest of the two bacon sandwiches. He ate quickly, his eyes constantly surveying their surroundings.

Angus took the remaining sandwich with a sigh. Sheridan stuffed the last piece in his mouth and reached for a slice of raisin cake. He picked the pieces of fruit out of the cake and tossed them on the ground as he began to talk.

"I'm going north, Angus, looking for gold. Your mother's agreed to come with me, and she won't want to leave you behind. Be ready to leave first thing Sunday morning. You won't need to take much. No more than a week's worth of food, a few clothes, tent and a bedroll. I have my own tent of course; I won't intrude on your mother until we're properly wed."

Angus loved raisins. He eyed the little black specks scattered across the ground. He had no doubt whatsoever that his mother was not planning on leaving town in the company of Mr. Paul Sheridan and heading north toward nowhere. If nothing else, the moment they'd stepped out of the boat that brought them from Lake Bennett, Fiona had fallen to her knees, heedless of the mud and the skirt of her travelling costume, and sworn that she would never, ever, leave civilization again.

If she was stringing Sheridan along for some reason, Angus wasn't going to enlighten the man. "Sure. But I think you ... uh, I mean we'll need a heck of a lot more food. I don't have a rifle, and can't shoot anyway, so we can't count on hunting. Can't ask people we meet on their way to the Creeks to give us food, most of them will only have enough for themselves."

"We're not going to the Creeks, Angus."

Curious, despite himself, Angus said, "Where exactly are we going?"

Sheridan looked around. No one was paying any attention to the tall thin man and the tall blond boy sharing lunch over a boulder. He reached into his jacket pocket. "Now, Angus, I'm trusting you with this because you're your mother's son. What I'm about to show you is the probably the most valuable piece of paper in these United States, if not the whole world."

"This isn't the United States," Angus reminded him.

Sheridan didn't hear. He ran his tongue across his lips. "I got this from a French fellow. He was kicked in the head by a horse on the White Pass trail and as he lay dying in my arms he told me to take the map and find ... Gold Mountain!"

Angus would have laughed if not for the fire in Sheridan's eyes, almost frightening in its intensity. Sheridan went on to mumble something about a mountain made of pure gold and the hot springs within which ensured the valley was warm and comfortable all year long.

He told Angus of his plans to be king of this undiscovered kingdom with Fiona as his queen. "Which means that you'll be a prince."

"Grand!" Angus pulled out his pocket watch, his proudest possession. He'd heard the old-timers' stories of a land of warmth and riches. And he'd heard their derisive laughter. "Will you look at the time? Mr. Mann will be wondering where I've gotten to." If he left now, he'd have time to run home and beg Mrs. Mann to make him more lunch.

"I sense," Sheridan said, "you're a mite skeptical. That's good. Don't believe everything a man tells you. Here, let me show you."

He pulled a bulky square of paper out of his pocket. With his other hand he swept the remains of Angus' lunch onto the ground. Then he spread the paper out. It looked like a map, but without much detail. Sheridan pointed out the spot where the two rivers joined and drew his finger up, tracing a black line to a faded red dot near the top. It had no scale, but judging by the size of the rivers as they'd been drawn, Angus estimated two or three hundred miles to the red dot. This man was planning on setting out, on foot, for a three-hundred-mile journey almost due north with a well-bred city lady and food for a week?

"Are we uh ... taking packers?" Angus asked.

"Certainly not. Can't risk word getting out. No one must know of this, Angus. At least not until I've collected enough gold that I can hire an army to protect our land."

"This uh ... valley where it's so warm? Won't the natives have discovered it long ago?"

"Indians have no work ethic, Angus, and no sense of discovery or adventure. They won't have bothered to climb the mountain to find the valley."

Angus doubted that. Sheridan was beaming at his map as a mother might gaze at her new baby. Angus studied it. He saw nothing more than squiggles that were probably supposed to be rivers and a few triangles that might indicate mountains.

"We'll start by following the Klondike River east," Sheridan said. "Before long it meets up with this river here." He pointed to a smaller blue line, running north. It in turn led to a thin black line, heading north east. "And then the trail, which will take us almost the entire way to our destination."

"If there's a trail, how come no one else has followed it?"

"Indian trail. Completely unknown to the white man."

"I don't know, Mr. Sheridan. Seems to me you're taking quite a chance heading off into the wilderness hoping to hook up with this trail. What if you can't find it?"

"I'll find it. Or rather, we'll find it. My friend told me, as he gasped out his last breath, that the Indians use this trail to take them to their sacred burying sites, so they keep it well maintained."

Angus didn't bother to mention that it was unlikely any of the native tribes travelled hundreds of miles carrying their dead.

Sheridan began folding the map. He ran his fingers across it, lovingly, and tucked it into his pocket. "Now remember, Angus, not a word to anyone."

"You can count on me, sir."

"Be ready Sunday morning. If you have any favourite books, bring them. It'll be a bit lonely in the valley I'm afraid. At least 'til my workers and their families start arriving. You'll want school books too, so you can keep your education up."

"Right."

"I'll teach you the practical things in life. Such as how to hunt — you'll want to supply your mother with fresh game. Which reminds me. Where might I find some cartridges for the rifle I bought the other day? Can't hunt without ammunition. "

"I saw some last week at Mr. McBride's shop. It's at the east end of Bowery Street. Close to the water."

Sheridan touched his hat and strolled away.

Angus decided that rather than plead with Mrs. Mann to fix him another sandwich, he'd go to the Savoy. Mrs. Saunderson could be counted on to have something tucked away in her tiny kitchen. Then he could ask his mother what on earth she was doing encouraging the man.

Chapter Thirteen

I spent most of the week worrying about what to wear to the wedding on Saturday. My clothes were either dance hall–owner evening gowns or day dresses suitable for appearing in the streets. I did not want to look as if I were trying to upstage the bride, nor as if I were heading off to the shops. My only suitable dress was a white muslin two-piece with rows of fine tucks across the sleeves, but I could hardly wear white if the bride was in white.

It would have to be my green satin gown. The neckline was high, unlike most of my evening wear, covering the throat. Because the neckline was so high, I could be outrageously daring and go bareheaded in that outfit, with nothing but a green ribbon to hold my hair back. I didn't have a hat to go with the green satin.

Most certainly I could not go to church without a hat.

Hadn't I come to Dawson to get away from such formalities? I settled my face into a sulk. Pooh!

If I became Queen of Gold Mountain, I would dictate that women could wear britches whenever they liked. Wouldn't that be lovely?

I would also outlaw unkempt beards and unwashed hair and hand out free toothbrushes.

I realized I was smiling. Perhaps I wouldn't settle merely for being Queen Consort of Gold Mountain. I'd get rid of the self-anointed King and take charge myself.

All of which did nothing about fixing my current dilemma: what to wear to Martha's wedding.

Nothing for it but to find a suitable hat. The pale green satin gown is beautiful, the colour of ice on the North Atlantic Ocean, with long slim lines and big leg-of-mutton sleeves. I'd never liked it much and had finally come to understand why. I'm black-haired and dark-eyed and that particular shade of green doesn't suit my colouring. The late much-lamented seamstress had told me to dress in dramatic blues and reds. I could also get away, she said, with blacks and whites.

Any hat that would match the green satin dress would look simply awful on me.

Of course, when it comes to my appearance, awful is a relative term.

I took gold dust out of the bag in my bottom drawer, weighed it in the small scales kept on my desk for that purpose, wrapped it in a scrap of paper, noted the amount in my ledger, tucked the dust into my reticule, and set off to buy an ugly hat.

As I walked to the hat shop, a woman's sudden scream caused me to whirl around. A child had dashed on·to the road, into the path of a horse cart. The woman who'd screamed grabbed her little one by the arm in time to pull him to safety. Over the heads of the crowd, I caught a glimpse of a tall man darting into an alley.

Today was Thursday, and I'd left it late to finalize my wedding costume. Since that ridiculous conversation on Monday, whenever I'd ventured outside, I'd caught glimpses of Paul Sheridan following in my wake. No doubt the man thought he was being surreptitious lurking in shop doorways, hiding behind draft horses, and covering his face with a newspaper should I glance in his direction. I'd considered speaking to Richard Sterling about the matter, but as long as Sheridan kept his distance there wasn't anything the police could do. Anyway, the man would be on his way to Gold Mountain soon enough. Highly unlikely he would ever return.

The milliner had nothing in pale green, thank heavens. After much debate and even more haggling over the price, I left the shop with a cream velvet hat that turned up on the left side, decorated with a contrasting black ostrich feather (if it was from a real ostrich I'd eat it), a clump of grapes, and a wide cream ribbon. It had a long lace train I didn't fancy, so I had the shop owner tuck it up behind with a few impromptu stitches.

When the last minute adjustments were finished, I left the shop, thinking that after the wedding I might make some adjustments of my own — get rid of the grapes and add flowers, perhaps a more colourful ribbon — when Graham Donohue, the newspaperman, stepped into my path.

"Shopping, Fiona?"

I lifted the box. "A new hat. For the wedding."

"I'm sure you'll look positively spectacular in it."

"I hope not," I said, hiding a smile. "It's not my role to look spectacular, but to ensure the bride does so."

"Yeah. Anyway, Fiona, speaking of the wedding, I've been meaning to ask if I may have the honour of being your escort to that affair."

"I'm going with Angus."

"Come on, Fiona, say yes. We rarely ever get the chance to spend time in each other's company lately, what with you always working and all. If you won't allow me to be your escort at the wedding, how about we do something on Sunday? A stroll perhaps, followed by tea."

I stopped walking. We were almost at the Savoy, standing on the stretch of boardwalk outside the small bakery operated by my neighbours the Misses Vanderhaege. Like so much in Dawson, calling the place a bakery was a considerable exaggeration. They sold waffles for twenty-five cents each and undrinkable coffee.

I was about to remind Graham that we had tea less than a week ago. Instead, I said, "Sunday. Excellent idea. Why don't you come for a late breakfast? Say around ten o' clock."

Graham's eyes almost popped out of his handsome face. "Breakfast?"

"I've decided to start a new fashion. Rather than wait until tea time, I will entertain in the morning. Mr. and Mrs. Mann will be home from church by ten." And if for some reason they were delayed, I'd have Graham to chase off Sheridan should the fool become overly persistent. Much better than spending the day hiding out in Ray Walker's lodgings, which had been my original plan. I've never been to Ray's lodgings, but I knew he lived in a men's boarding house. I could only imagine the place would be quite foul: cramped and dirty, with the smell of unwashed men and stale liquor and too much cigar smoke.

I do not entertain on Sundays, my only day of rest. I usually wash my hair, drying it in the sun if it is nice out, or by the stove if not. Perhaps in the late afternoon I'll put on a suitable afternoon dress and go for a walk, to catch some of the news. I spend six days week being charming and friendly and beautiful. I do not wish to do so on the seventh. Except for being beautiful. That I can always do.

Just this once, I would make an exception to my routine.

I took a quick peek around. The streets were busy with the usual packs of wandering layabouts, respectable women going about their family's business, the occasional less-than-respectable woman looking for her own business, miners either heading for the creeks or returning from them, pack horses and donkeys, dog-trains, and feral dogs. About 90 percent of the people were men, and there were very few children.

"Are you expecting someone, Fiona?" Graham asked, also surveying the streetscape.

"No," I said brightly. "No one. Until Saturday, Graham."

"And breakfast on Sunday," he said in a voice designed to carry.

I gave him a smile and took my new hat home.

Chapter Fourteen

Saturday was a glorious day. The sun shone warm in a clear blue sky, but a pleasant breeze kept it from getting overly hot. I was at Martha's hotel before noon, supposedly to help her prepare for her grand event. Never in my life had I assisted a woman to dress. Fortunately, my role was strictly a formality, for Helen had created a beautiful, yet entirely practical, wedding gown. It was in two pieces, and each piece could later be altered slightly and matched with a skirt or blouse of colour to create two new outfits. The expensive lace was attached with large, well-spaced stitches so it could be removed. Used for a christening gown, perhaps, Martha said as her cheeks flamed.

She was no beauty, Martha. Tall and sturdy with a large bosom trapped beneath a rigid corset, she had a nose like a bird's beak and small dark eyes. Her cheeks were too round, her chin too small, and her complexion too ruddy to be fashionable. An Englishwoman of a respectable but impoverished family, she'd travelled to the Klondike in the guise of a writer, hoping to pen a book to provide her with much-needed income. At the advanced age of thirty-three years, she (and her family) had given up hope she would ever marry, and it had become necessary for her to make her own way in the world. Instead, she had found Reginald O'Brien.

Which was just as well. I had seen samples of her writing and thought it unimaginative rubbish. Martha managed to make the Klondike sound as rigidly boring as afternoon tea at Buckingham Palace.

We were not friends. As I've said, I have no women friends. Angus was much closer to Martha than I. He'd been her assistant when she'd been dashing about town making notes of everything she saw and generally getting in everyone's way. Angus could hardly be a bridesmaid, and Martha had no one else to ask.

She chattered and fussed and twitched constantly as she dressed. Her hat was a small neat affair, and the train came only as far as her shoulders. I had lent her a pair of gold earrings, which toned down the over-red face fractionally.

She looked, I was surprised to see, absolutely lovely.

Angus was waiting for us in the hotel lobby. He jumped to his feet as Martha and I descended the stairs. His jaw dropped open, and his eyes bulged. "Miss Witherspoon," he cried. "You look ... very nice."

Martha smiled. "Thank you, my dear boy."

Angus looked nice also in a clean jacket and new white shirt, highly starched. His face was scrubbed, his blond hair was combed, and he'd slicked the unruly cowlick down with a touch of oil. I myself do not care for oil in a man's hair and told him to go easy on it.

A small crowd had gathered outside the Richmond Hotel, hoping to get a glimpse of the bride. They broke into applause when we exited. Someone, probably Angus, had swept the boardwalk.

The carriage Mouse O'Brien had hired to take Martha, Angus, and me to the church was waiting when we exited the hotel. "Carriage" being a bit of an exaggeration: it was a wooden cart pulled by an aging horse. But the horse had more meat on its bones than many around town, and it had been brushed to a shine, with white ribbons braided through its mane. The cart had only one proper seat, where the driver and a single passenger could sit. Angus assisted Martha to climb up while I held her skirts and tried to keep the white cloth away from the none-too-clean undercarriage. In the open back there were two bales of hay, covered by blankets. Once Martha was seated, hands folded neatly in her lap, eyes alight and face burning with embarrassed pleasure, I eyed my own chair with some degree of trepidation.

"Mother," Angus said, extending his arm. I don't know what we would have done if it had been raining. I lifted the skirts of my green satin gown to shocking heights, clutched the bunch of cloth in my right hand, gripped Angus's arm with my left, wished I had a third to hold onto my hat, and hoisted myself up. For a moment, I balanced precariously on the lip of wood running along the outside of the cart, but my son pushed against my bottom (I hope it was my son) and shoved me over the edge and into the back of the cart like a sack of feed.

I attempted to retain some shreds of dignity and settled into my make-shift chair, adjusting the long strand of fake pearls around my neck — equally fake pearls were in my ears. Angus leapt up beside me, and the driver yelled to his animal to proceed. The crowd cheered. I began to lift my hand to wave, but Angus grabbed it and shook his head, reminding me I was not the centre of attention on this day.

Helen met us as we alighted from the cart outside St. Paul's Church, ready to adjust Martha's garments should such be required. Helen had earlier festooned the ground with petals of blue larkspur, yellow buttercups, and purple fireweed.

Reginald O'Brien's nickname was intended to be satirical. He resembled an ox more than a mouse. He neared seven feet tall, and his shoulders and thighs were massive. But he was soft-spoken and unfailingly polite. He dressed well and was fastidious about his grooming. Today, he'd outdone himself. He looked resplendent in his black trousers and grey frock-coat, red waist-coat with heavy gold chain, crisp white shirt, and black tie secured with a gold stickpin. His boots were polished to a high shine, and not a speck of dust marred the grey hat with a band which matched his waistcoat.

He stood by the front door of the church beside Reverend Bowen and Richard Sterling, handsome in dress uniform, who would serve as the groomsman. Mouse's face lit up when he caught his first glimpse of his bride bouncing along in the horse cart. He settled his face into solemn lines before stepping forward and helping her out of the cart. Angus leapt down and assisted me.

The wedding party shifted and we arranged ourselves. Helen slipped into the church to take her seat.

Mouse and Richard entered first, followed by me, and then Angus and Martha. Angus was acting the role of Martha's father, somewhat unusual considering that he was twelve years old, but Martha had been insistent.

St. Paul's Church was full. Martha knew no one in town except for Angus and me, but Mouse knew everyone, and the forthcoming nuptials had been the talk of the Savoy all week. We'd closed for the afternoon in order that the staff could attend the ceremony. Sergeant Lancaster, my erstwhile suitor, was present, hair thick with oil, seated in a group of Mounties including Inspector McKnight. Graham Donohue had had a haircut, and Mr. and Mrs. Mann were dressed in their Sunday best. Ray Walker sat next to Irene Davidson, her arm tucked into his, at the end of a row of dance hall girls looking as bright and colourful as hollyhocks in an English garden. Barney and many of his bar-mates were in attendance. Some of them had even gone to the trouble of washing their face and hands. Jake, the head coupler at the Savoy, was at the back, with

the bartenders Murray and Not-Murray. Belinda Mulrooney
was in attendance, dressed as always in a prim starched navy
blouse and dark skirt, her hair in a severe bun atop her square
face. Belinda's Fairview Hotel would be opening in a couple of
weeks, and it was going to be the biggest and most luxurious in
town. Big Alex McDonald, whom they called the King of the
Klondike, was seated in the row behind Belinda, tugging at his
tight shirt collar. They were business rivals, never friends, and
the rivalry could get extreme at times.

To be honest, I'd worried about Martha. She was making
a big step, committing herself, body and soul, to a man she
scarcely knew, in a place far from home and family. But as
I looked around the crowded church, I realized that this was
now Martha's home, and we, a rough-and-tumble collection of
miscreants and adventurers, were her family.

I took my place at one side of the altar and peeked at Mouse
standing stiffly opposite. His chest bulged with pride, his face
glowed with happiness. And I knew that Reginald O'Brien truly
loved the annoying Englishwoman.

* * *

Mouse had rented the top floor of the dance hall for his wedding party. He wasn't rich, but he'd done better than most on
the Creeks and, quite by accident, had found a small productive
claim. He gambled, but never played more than he could afford to
lose. He liked the dance hall girls, but didn't try to get them drunk
or ask them to meet him after hours. He was fond of champagne,
but only bought one bottle at a time and shared it freely with his
dance partner and people in adjoining boxes or tables. He was a
giant of a man, and today he resembled a mischievous schoolboy
at his birthday tea.

After the bridal party had been settled in the upper level, Mouse stood up, leaned over the balcony, and announced that for the next five minutes all drinks were on him.

As could have been expected, the rush for the bar was instantaneous. Word spread up and down the street, and the saloon got so crowed, Ray had to order his men to guard the front door lest folk be trampled to death.

Ray and I stayed for a glass of champagne, Mumm Extra Dry, quite delicious, and a toast to the happy couple. We slipped away as Helen and Not-Murray were clambering up the stairs, bearing platters of sandwiches and sliced meat. Mouse had spared no expense: a boiled egg was served to each of his guests, and a bowl of almonds sat on every table.

It had been a lovely wedding, but for Ray and me, it was now just another Saturday night in Dawson, and we had a business to run.

When Angus came down to tell me Mr. and Mrs. O'Brien were leaving, Ray and I met them at the door to say goodbye and extend our best wishes. Mouse would be heading back to the Creeks on Monday. He'd rented a small house on Seventh Avenue, where Martha would live. Even though her writing skills were non-existent, I'd suggested she continue collecting stories, as any news (no matter how poorly written) from the Klondike was eagerly devoured in the Outside, but she had recoiled as if I'd struck her and said that, naturally, once a married woman, she would never offer her husband such an insult as to do a job of work. She did not consider that her proposed collection of tips for women coming to the Yukon was a job, merely a service to help others.

Unlikely Martha would again come into the Savoy. It was not a suitable place for a married woman. Chances were, even though she was now clinging to me and whispering in my ear that we would always be friends, I'd not see her again, other than around town or in the shops. I considered making a ribald joke about the joys of the wedding night, but that would spook the poor thing too much. Now that the formalities of the wedding were over and she and her husband were heading off to their home and bed, she looked nothing but terrified.

I wondered if, in the absence of her mother, I should explain something of what was to be expected. But I held my tongue. She'd find out soon enough. As I had.

I felt sorry for Martha suddenly. As I struggled to get out from her embrace, I whispered, "Relax and have fun."

She pulled back, eyes as round and white as a horse smelling fire. Without another word, she dashed for the street, leaving a startled husband to follow.

Ray lifted one eyebrow and looked at me. I chuckled, told Angus it was time he was heading home, and went back inside.

Chapter Fifteen

Saturday night, we close at two minutes to midnight for the Lord's Day. Every week there are incredulous Americans who think that arguing with Murray will persuade him to keep pouring drinks, or having a winning streak at roulette will mean Jake will keep the game going, or having finally snagged a dance with their favourite percentage girl will mean the musicians will keep playing.

But the Mounties are ruthless, and no matter how much of a bribe we've been offered, and it's sometimes a considerable amount, we would never agree to lock the doors and draw the drapes (not that there are any) and keep the party going.

Ray had lost patience with a fellow who was arguing that he'd only gotten off the boat three hours ago, and what the hell else was a man supposed to do in this god-forsaken town, and thrown the man into the street. Many a man had learned too late not to scrap with the diminutive Scot.

So strict was the law that even Ray and I dared not linger after midnight to so much as sweep the floor or count the night's takings. I carried the money upstairs to lock it in my desk drawer. When I came down, only a couple of the performers and Ray were still in the front room.

"Wasn't that a beautiful wedding, Mrs. MacGillivray?" Ellie, the oldest of the dancers, said.

"It certainly was," I replied. I was still wearing my wedding attire, complete with new hat.

"Not as nice as my wedding though," Maxie put in.

"I didn't know you'd been married," Betsy said.

"Oh, yes. So sad." Maxie touched a handkerchief to her eyes. "George was his name. The dearest man who ever lived. Absolutely adored me, he did. He died of consumption only two weeks after our wedding. I've been asked many times since, of course, but no man can measure up to my dear George."

Ellie rolled her eyes. If the conversation was about a barn cat, you could be sure Maxie had once owned the biggest and smartest barn cat that ever lived.

"Wonder when there will be another wedding," Ellie said, with a noticeable glance at Irene, standing close to Ray.

Ray beamed and puffed up his chest, just a bit. Irene threw Ellie a look that would curdle milk, and Betsy glowered.

Which reminded me.

"Betsy, if you will stay for a moment, please. Good night, ladies. Ray."

Betsy had not been happy when Irene took up with Ray, nor at the speed with which Ray threw her over. Her resentment was beginning to affect her work. Perhaps suspecting I'd be preoccupied with the wedding guests in the balcony and not paying quite as much attention to the activities on stage as usual, she'd almost tripped Irene earlier tonight. They'd been acting out the climax of Macbeth. Irene played MacDuff (earlier she'd been Lady Macbeth, wandering the stage in her night-gown), with Ellie as the Thane of Cawdor, while Betsy and a couple of the other girls waved wooden swords and pranced about in their bloomers, shouting encouragement. As Macbeth said the immortal words: "Lay on, MacDuff, and damned be he who cries hold enough," somehow Betsy's sword found itself between

Irene's knees. MacDuff stumbled, but managed to keep herself upright. The men in the front row, who'd seen what happened, roared their disapproval. Irene stopped dead, lowered her sword, turned to face Betsy, and gave her a look that would melt the ice on the Klondike River in February. Only when Betsy slunk behind the other actors did Irene resume the play. By that time, the men were stomping their boots on the plank floors and hooting.

If Betsy wanted to remain in my employ, she'd better keep her resentment to herself.

The girls filed out. Maxie wanted to talk about her wedding to the doomed George, but Ellie cut her off, beginning a story about the time Big Gertrude married a donkey on the stage of a dance hall in Leadville, Colorado. Ellie was the oldest, by far, of the performers, and the younger girls loved to hear stories of the places she'd worked and characters she'd known.

Ray and Irene followed. The door was swinging shut behind him when I remembered something. "Ray, did you lock the back door?"

He half-turned. "Don't think I did." He started to come back, but Irene pulled away from his arm. "I'm tired," she said. "I'm going home. Good night."

Ray looked at me. Then he looked longingly at Irene, heading off down the street.

"Very well," I said with a martyred sigh. "I'll get it."

My partner scurried off and disappeared into the shuffling crowd. The night was warm, and the fresh air flowing down from the mountains felt good on my face and in my lungs. I took a few deep breaths and moved to shut the door. Then I remembered the sulking Betsy and turned to face her. She tried to keep her head up and her look defiant, but after one sharp glance from me, her eyes slid away. She studied the pattern in the boards at her feet. "We've had words before," I said. "I believe I told you if there was one more occasion, I would let you go."

She mumbled something that might have been, "I didn't do nothin'."

"You almost tripped Irene."

"Was an accident. You told me not to be friendly with Mr. Walker, well I ain't bein' friendly no more, now am I? So you got no call to let me go."

Perhaps I was still in a mellow mood after the wedding. And the two glasses of Mouse's excellent Champagne for which he'd paid full price. I said, "This is your last warning. Beware, Betsy, I want no more trouble. Now get off home and be smiling and presentable on Monday."

"Yes, Ma'am." She bolted for the safety of the street. I headed for the back and did not hear the door click shut as Betsy left.

The windows were small and dirty, but some light seeped into the room. I knew every inch of the place intimately, so it wasn't necessary to bother relighting a lamp.

The gambling room had no windows, but my feet could find their own way into the dance hall without the aid of my eyes.

My footsteps echoed on the bare boards. It wasn't often the Savoy was a quiet, still place. The shadows were as long as the silence, and I felt a knot of quiet satisfaction in my stomach. This was my Empire. I wondered if the Queen felt the same sense of pride looking at a map of a pink-coloured world, alone in her study in Balmoral.

My mind wandered to Martha's wedding. She'd been so happy. I myself have never had a wedding. Angus believes I'd been married to his father, but MacGillivray was my own dear parents' name.

I reached the back door and pulled my keys from the deep pockets that had been sewn into my skirts.

"Ready to go?" A voice came from behind me. I almost leapt out of my skin.

I whirled around. All I could see was a shape, a very tall thin shape standing at the doors to the gambling hall. Paul Sheridan. Deep in contemplation, I hadn't heard him behind me. Foolishly, I'd left Betsy to close the front door.

"Good heavens," I said in my sternest dance-hall owner voice, the one I copied from the governess who'd ruled the schoolroom of my childhood. "You can walk quietly. What do you mean coming up behind me like that, Mr. Sheridan? It is after hours. The Savoy is closed."

"It's Sunday."

"Precisely. Which is why we're closed and you must leave immediately. If the Mounties come along and find you here, they'll think we're conducting business and they'll shut the Savoy down."

Curses! I'd forgotten all about pesky Mr. Sheridan and his crazy notions. I hadn't seen him since buying my hat on Thursday, and his plans had completely slipped my mind.

"Sunday," he repeated. As my eyes became accustomed to the lack of light, I could see his face. His mouth was set into a firm line.

"We're leaving today."

"So we are. But I have not yet slept and I've had an exceedingly busy day. There was a wedding, you know."

"You looked beautiful."

He'd been watching me. A shiver crawled up my spine. Sheridan filled the doorway leading through the building to the safety of Front Street. I put my hand on the door behind me, feeling for the knob. This exit led to the back alley. "You said you'd collect me at eleven in the morning."

"I heard you."

"Heard me what?"

"Talking to that man, the American. You invited him around for breakfast this morning. Ten o'clock you said."

I tried to laugh, but the sound caught in my throat. "It's going to be a quick breakfast."

"Don't lie to me, Fiona," Sheridan shouted. The sound cracked through the empty dance hall like a gunshot. He took a step forward and then another. The veins in his neck bulged. "That waffle shop next door's a nice place to watch the comings and goings in the Savoy. I heard you make plans with that man, and I knew you don't intend to be ready for me at eleven o'clock. We're leaving now. A horse and wagon's waiting next street over."

My fingers found the doorknob. I tried to turn it, but my hand was slippery with sweat. "Very well. I'll go for Angus and meet you back here." I wiped my hand on my skirt and tried again. This time the knob moved. It didn't make a sound.

"Do you think me a total fool?" Sheridan shouted.

I refrained from saying "yes."

"We'll go without Angus. The boy wants to come, but he'll have to wait here. If I let you go you won't come back to me, will you Fiona?"

"You got that right," I said. I pulled the door open and ran out. Boots pounded on the loose wooden floors of the dance hall. I pulled the door shut behind me, but felt resistance and let it go. I looked in either direction. Across the alley, the mortuary was to my right, the dry goods shop to the left. Needless to say, there would be no one there at this time on a Sunday morning. I'd hoped to find a group of drunks sharing a bottle, a couple who couldn't wait to get to a room, or best of all, a patrolling policeman.

The alley was deserted. The door to the Savoy flew open. I headed left toward York, the shortest route to the street.

Sheridan yelled at me to stop. I've learned a few things in my day, including how to fight a man. If I had to, I would turn and stand firm. Despite the earliness of the hour, the streets were busy and I could reach them in seconds. I felt a tug at the back of my dress, heard satin rip. I screamed, trying to attract attention.

"Goddamn you, woman. You're coming with me," Sheridan roared.

I reached the corner of the building. I heard a man laugh and a dog bark. I'd worn evening shoes to Martha's wedding and not bothered to change into the practical boots I'd recently purchased to wear at work. My foot slipped in a patch of mud, and I stumbled forward. Off balance, I crashed into a wagon wheel leaning up against the wall and went down.

I hit the ground hard, but instantly rolled onto my back, braced myself on my forearms, and grounded my feet to propel me back up. Sheridan stood over me. He looked rather startled to see me on the ground. I pulled my left leg up and launched the foot straight into his knee. He screamed in pain and staggered backwards. I tried to get myself to a seated position, from which I could kick out while screaming my head off and hoping for someone to come, but the ridiculous leg-of-mutton sleeves of my dress had snagged on something. I grabbed a handful of fabric and pulled. It tore and I was free, but too late. Sheridan was back. His eyes shone with a red rage, and a line of spittle dripped from the corner of his mouth. He fell on me, his knees digging into my stomach, knocking all the breath out of me. I lifted my hand to my head and sought a hat pin. Long and deadly sharp, a hat pin makes a formidable weapon — some small degree of compensation for being forced to fight in a long dress, corset and petticoats, and shoes with high heels. I jerked my hand back and the pin came with it. I drove it upwards aiming for Sheridan's eye. Anger made him quick and he grabbed my hand and twisted. I clung to the pin but felt my arm being gradually pushed toward the ground. I saw the blow coming but could do nothing to get out of the way. He punched me full in the face with his free hand. Propelled by the impact, my head snapped back and smashed into the ground.

And all the world went dark.

Chapter Sixteen

Angus MacGillivray had had a grand time at the wedding, so important in his new shirt and oiled hair, giving away the bride! He'd even had a small glass of champagne at the reception after. He hadn't liked the taste much, but the bubbles in his glass were fun. Of course, he told Mr. O'Brien it was excellent stuff.

Angus had never asked his mother about her wedding. She didn't like to talk about his father, who died several months before he, Angus, was born. She didn't have a picture of him, but she said he was tall and blond and blue-eyed, and Angus looked a great deal like him. Then she turned away, swallowing her words, and asked if he was ready for tea. She'd given Angus his father's watch recently, and he carried it proudly everywhere he went.

Tonight seemed like a good night to sit her down and find out what he could about his father and how his parents had met and the years of their marriage.

He said good night to the Manns — Mrs. Mann flushed beet red from her single glass of champagne — and went to his mother's tiny sitting room to wait. Her book was on the table, her bookmark close to the end. It was called *Anna Karenina*. He sat in the room's single chair. There were two photographs on the table: one of himself as a baby and another of the two of them at a park outing when Angus was young enough to be dressed in a sailor suit with a stupid hat.

A painting hung on the wall. He'd been with his mother down at the waterfront when she'd seen it. She told him it was of the Black Cuillins, the mountains on Skye where she'd been born. He imagined his father striding manfully across the bare hills, his head high, his back straight, his step firm. Angus's mother waiting for his father, all girlish giggles and sideways glances. He shook his head, picked up the book and began to read.

The next thing Angus knew, someone was banging on the door, his neck ached, the book was on the floor, and the light streaming in the window came from the east.

He stumbled to the front door and opened it.

"Morning, Angus," Graham Donohue said. His cheeks glowed pink from a recent shave, his hair was still wet, and his moustache neatly combed.

"What time is it?" Angus said.

"Ten o'clock." Donohue stepped forward as though he intended to enter. Angus stood firm.

"What brings you here at this hour?"

"I've come for breakfast. Didn't your mother mention it?"

"Breakfast? My mother doesn't eat breakfast on Sundays, much less invite company." Saturday night was the only night of the week Fiona got a full night's sleep. She often didn't rise until late afternoon.

Angus narrowed his eyes and stared at Donohue. At one time, he thought his mother might marry Mr. Donohue, and he'd take them to America. Angus hadn't been sure if he either wanted Mr. Donohue as his father or to go to America, but then he'd found out the man frequented prostitutes. From that moment on, Angus was determined to keep the newspaperman away from his mother. "Mrs. Mann's gone to church and my mother doesn't cook. There's nothing to eat. Goodbye." He began to shut the door. Donohue stuck his foot in it.

"I know it sounds strange. I thought it somewhat unusual myself. But she did invite me to breakfast and she did say ten o'clock. Really, Angus."

Angus relaxed his grip on the door, thinking. It did seem odd, but Donohue had no reason to lie. Easy enough to check, and if Fiona was woken on a Sunday morning without reason, it would be Donohue's scalp she'd be after.

Anything that made his mother angry with Graham Donohue was, in Angus's opinion, a good thing.

"I'll go and ask her," Angus said.

"Thank you." Donohue stepped into the hall.

The Mann's house wasn't much larger than the common room in Angus's school back in Toronto. Four rooms plus the kitchen and a privy in the back yard. The Manns' room was at the back, beside the kitchen. Angus and his mother each had a tiny bedroom at the front of the house, and Fiona enjoyed a private sitting room where she could, in theory, entertain visitors. That she never had any visitors didn't really matter. She loved sitting there, curled up in a big chair with the horsehair stuffing escaping, reading. Fanning herself absentmindedly in summer or wrapped in a colourful quilt beside the iron stove in winter.

Angus tapped lightly on his mother's bedroom door. No answer. He knocked harder and called out, "Sorry to bother you, Mother, but Mr. Donohue's here. He says he's been invited for breakfast, is that right?" No answer. He felt Donohue behind him.

"Step back, Mr. Donohue," Angus ordered. "I'm going into my mother's bedroom." He'd have been embarrassed to realize just how much he sounded like Fiona.

Donohue gave way, about the width of a hair, and Angus slowly opened the door while attempting to use his body to block the man's view. The room was neat, the bed made, blanket and pillows in place.

116   Vicki Delany

Angus took a step forward and Donohue followed. It took no more than a second to ascertain that Fiona was not hiding behind the door or concealed in the closet.

"What on earth?" Angus said. "She's not here."

"That bed hasn't been slept in."

They jumped as the back door opened. Footsteps sounded on the bare wood of the hall, and Mr. Mann's baritone grumbled something in German.

"My mother," Angus shouted. "She's gone. Did you see her last night, Mrs. Mann? Sir?"

Mrs. Mann raised her hands to her face. She threw a worried look at her husband. "No. We were tired after the wedding and went to bed early."

"Fetch the police, Mrs. Mann, please. Quickly."

"Not again," Mr. Mann said with a shake of his head as his wife fled. "Okay. Yous goes to Savoy, Angus. Ies checks seh waterfront. Likes seh last times." He followed his wife.

"Tell the Mounties to meet me at the Savoy," Angus shouted.

"You suspect something," Donohue said.

"Last time Ma disappeared, we waited too long before starting a search. But it's this breakfast invitation that worries me. So completely out of character something must be up. And I'm afraid I know what it is." Angus thought back to the conversation with Paul Sheridan while they ate Angus's lunch over a boulder by the Yukon River. Sheridan was determined to follow his treasure map and equally determined that Fiona and Angus would accompany him. Angus asked her why she was encouraging the man, and she replied that Sheridan wasn't prepared to take no for an answer, so she'd given him the answer he wanted. She'd stay out of his way and he'd soon give up and head off into the wilderness by himself. If necessary, she added, she'd drop a hint that she was considering outfitting an expedition of her own. That would get him out of town fast enough; he was terrified someone else would reach his mountain first.

Angus had his doubts about that. He'd seen the fire in the man's eyes as he talked not only about Gold Mountain but also about making Fiona his queen.

But he'd kept his misgivings to himself.

That had, obviously, been a mistake.

He ran out of the house, Donohue hot on his heels, shouting, "Are you going to tell me what this is about?"

"Later. I know ... but I don't have a bloody clue how we're going to find them."

Chapter Seventeen

Angus expected to have to break into the Savoy. His mother had shown him how the lock didn't completely catch, and if you gave it a sharp shift to the right as you turned the handle, the lock would pop free. He wondered on occasion about some of the things his mother knew. Unlikely she would have left the faulty lock in place if she hadn't intended it to be that way. Did she install the lock herself, giving her access if she needed it?

He'd think about that another day.

Right now, the door was not locked, and it swung open as Angus touched the handle.

He sprinted up the stairs to check the office and the spare rooms on the second floor. It was possible, although highly unlikely, she'd simply sat down and fallen asleep.

But all was dark and empty. The only sounds were floorboards groaning under his feet and Graham Donohue searching below.

The newspaperman shouted, "Angus. Here. Quickly."

Angus hit the stairs so fast his boot slipped, and he tumbled in a mess of windmilling arms and legs toward the bottom. He grabbed the banister and managed to keep himself upright, and then he ran through the building to the dance hall, where Donohue stood by the back wall.

"Door was standing wide open," Donohue said. "And look." He pointed outside. The light in the alley was never bright, but at this time of the morning it was good enough to see a clear imprint of a woman's shoe in the mud. A larger boot print was beside it.

"Mother would never leave the front door unlocked and the back standing open. Anyone could come by and help himself to the whisky."

Donahue looked up from the footprints and caught Angus's eye. The boy could see the reflection of his own worry in the newspaperman's face.

They turned at the sound of voices in the saloon. "Out here," Angus shouted.

Corporal Sterling was first, followed by a constable who didn't look much older than Angus himself. Mrs. Mann, puffing heavily from her exertions, brought up the rear.

"Mrs. Mann says your mother's missing?" Sterling said. He was dressed in uniform, as was the young constable, hats straight, buttons done up. Mrs. Mann must have found them at the detachment.

"It would seem so," Donohue spoke before Angus could. "Looks like she ran out the back door, and I'm about to go out and have a look."

"Step back, please," Sterling said. "Mrs. Mann would you ..."

The woman put her arm around Angus's shoulders. He shook her off. He felt panic rising and tried to force it down. "We're wasting time." He was embarrassed at the shake in his voice.

"Looking for evidence is never a waste of time, Angus. Wait here." Keeping his eyes on the ground and placing his feet carefully, Corporal Sterling stepped into the alley. Angus felt his heart pounding in his chest and the weight of Mrs. Mann's arm on his shoulders. The Mountie was back in seconds. "Alley's clear," he said. "But the mud's all churned up. I want to take a closer look, but first, Angus, do you have any idea where your mother might have gone?"

There was another shout and more footsteps as Mr. Mann joined them. "Wees not seens her at seh waterfront. None of seh boats haves left since yesterday afternoon." Two scruffy looking fellows followed in his wake.

"What on earth is going on here?" Ray Walker shouted. The buttons on his shirt were done up incorrectly, only one of his boots laced, and he wasn't wearing a hat. He also had a retinue of followers. "Joe Hamilton here," Walker said, with a jerk of his thumb to the man close behind him, "came round to tell me the Mounties are crawling all over the Savoy and someone's been asking if Fiona got on a boat?"

"Is there a party?" A woman's voice said. It was Betsy, one of the dancers. "Why Maxie and me, we's walking out this morning and here's the door open and people coming in." She peered at the group, growing by the minute. "It's Sunday but must be all right if'n the Mounties are here."

"Walker," Sterling said, "you'd better lock the front door before the rest of the town gets here."

Ray Walker passed his key to Joe Hamilton with a jerk of his head, and the man scurried off.

"Angus," Sterling said, "you were about to tell me what's going on."

Maxie and Betsy settled themselves onto a bench. Maxie tidied her hat, and Betsy arranged her skirts carefully around her legs and kept her eye on Ray Walker. He ignored her.

Hamilton returned at a fast clip, not wanting to miss any of Angus's revelations. He was followed by Old Barney, the bartender Murray, a fresh-faced young cheechako Angus didn't recognize, two grizzled sourdoughs, and Anna Marie Vanderhaege from the bakery, wiping her hands on her flour-covered apron.

Walker pointedly held out his hand for the key. Hamilton passed it over with obvious reluctance.

"Almost got myself locked out," Barney said with a chuckle. "That would never do. What's your ma gone and done now, boy?"

One of the sourdoughs coughed and spat a lump of bloody phlegm into his filthy hand. He wiped the hand on the seat of his pants. His eyes were red and dripping mucus, and he didn't have a tooth in his mouth.

"Don't tell us Mrs. MacGillivray's in trouble again," Miss Vanderhaege said, clearly hoping to hear just such news.

Angus looked at Corporal Sterling and Ray Walker, trying to ignore the press of people. "Paul Sheridan. We told you about him, remember, sir? Part of Soapy Smith's gang from over in Skagway."

The words Soapy Smith and gang moved through the crowd.

"I remember. I spoke to the man myself. He said he wasn't with Soapy any more."

"That was true. He left Skagway because he has this map, a map he says will take him to," Angus looked around the room, everyone leaning closer to hear better, "a valley where it's tropical all year round, even though it's north of here, because of the hot springs." Angus decided best not to mention the mountain of gold.

Barney snorted. "Not that damn fool story again." Long unwashed hair and unkempt beards shook as the other sour-doughs indicated their agreement. "Every couple o' years, as long as I kin remember, someone comes lookin' for that valley. Bet he told you the hills are solid gold too, right?"

Angus nodded.

"You ever seen a hot springs, boy?"

"I don't think so, sir."

"Water's hot all right. Man kin have a nice bath outdoors middle o' winter. But one foot away from the water, the snow's as deep as a moose's ass. Beggin' your pardon, Corporal, ladies."

"That's neither here nor there," Sterling said. "Continue, Angus."

Barney found something of interest in his back teeth and began excavating for it.

Angus said, "He's got this map and he wants my ma and me to come with him. To live in this valley."

Ray Walker slapped his forehead with his hand. "Is the man insane?"

"That's what I'm afraid of," Angus said. "He told her we would leave Sunday morning. Right about now actually. But she didn't come home last night and ..."

"I left her here," Walker said. "Alone. Never thought a thing about it. Even if this was a rough town ye ken, and it isn't, Fiona never needs protection. We closed up and I forgot to lock the back door. Remembered when we were standing on the stoop out front. She came back inside to do it and I left. I'm sorry, Angus. So sorry."

That was about the longest speech Angus had ever heard Ray Walker give. The man's accent was so strong, particularly when he was stressed or worried, Angus could barely understand one word in two. But he got the point. As did Sterling.

"You couldn't know, Walker," the Mountie said. "Don't blame yourself." Angus could see by the anguished look on his mother's partner's unwashed and unshaven face that he did.

Walker suddenly whirled around and glared at Betsy. "No, that's nae right. I dinna leave her alone. You stayed behind because she wanted a word."

Betsy squeaked. "I didn't do nothin'. She wanted to tell me I'd done a great job in the play and she's thinkin' o' givin' me a speaking part."

Maxie laughed.

"I doubt that very much," Walker said. "What have ye done with her?"

"What!" Betsy leapt to her feet. "Now see here ..."

"Enough!" Sterling bellowed. "Sit down, Madam." Betsy sat so hard the bench rattled. "And tell us what happened after Walker left."

"Like I said," she sniffed, "Mrs. MacGillivray had a word with me. And then I left too. Couldn't of been more than a minute or two behind Mr. Walker and the rest."

"Was anyone with her when you left?"

"No."

"Did you see anyone approaching the Savoy?"

She twisted her hands and then lifted her chin and looked directly into Sterling's eyes. "No. I saw no one."

The words hung in the room, and Betsy snuck a peek at Ray Walker.

"I'll talk to you later," Sterling said. "Right now, I need all you people ..."

"What seems to be the problem here?" Sergeant Lancaster stuck his head through the back door. "Goodness me. Word came to the Fort that there's trouble at the Savoy, so naturally I volunteered to investigate."

Sterling suppressed a groan. "Please come in, sir. And watch where you step. Is anyone else out there with you?"

A burst of female laughter answered him, and three women who worked out of the cribs on Paradise Alley peered around Lancaster's bulk into the room.

Sterling finally lost his patience. "Oh, for heaven's sake. This is a crime scene, not a lady's garden party. McAllen, get outside and block the entrance to this alley. Not one more person is to come this way under threat of arrest. Watch where you step. You," he bellowed at a lady with painted cheeks and hair far redder than found in nature. "Do not move. Sergeant, get in here so those ladies can get their feet out of the evidence."

"Oh, evidence," a second woman said. She peered at the ground around her, looking for such a thing.

"I don't care for ..." Lancaster began, but the red-headed woman pushed him aside and came in. She was comfortably padded, fat almost, with small brown eyes in a face the colour and consistency of uncooked pastry. Cheap rings were trapped in the flesh of her pudgy fingers, and wiry grey hairs protruded from her chin and upper lip. Her companions followed. They were both younger, and one of them might have been pretty, if not for the eye that drooped to one side and a slack mouth that dripped drool. A wave of cheap scent accompanied them. Lancaster followed meekly.

"Bar open?" one of the prostitutes inquired of Ray. He growled in answer. McAllen went through the door sideways, head down, cheeks burning, taking great care not to brush up against the women's skirts.

Sterling rolled his eyes and sighed. "Mr. Mann, go to the Fort, if you will. Find Inspector McKnight and request more men to secure this area. Walker, let him out and be sure to relock the door. I'm going outside and anyone who follows me, male or female, will spend the rest of the month chopping wood at the Fort. Do you understand?" He swept the room with his eyes. Angus followed his gaze. Most of the people had begun to realize that this was not an impromptu party. Even Old Barney was looking worried.

"Sir," Angus said, trying to keep his voice steady. "I'm coming with you."

Sterling studied him. "Very well. But keep your footsteps inside mine."

* * *

It was a sunny day and the light in the alley was good. The print from a woman's shoe had been trodden on by Sergeant Lancaster, but Sterling had seen it before it was destroyed. The three prostitutes had confused matters, but he should be able to distinguish their footprints — coming into the Savoy — from the set he was interested in — leaving the Savoy. "Shut the door behind you, Angus," he said. "We don't need everyone and their dog helping."

Angus did as he was told, shutting off the wave of excited voices. "What do you think's happened, sir?"

"I think that she isn't here, in this alley, and that's good." Sterling pointed to a line of footsteps. "See how far apart the prints are and how deep? She was running. Those bigger prints, they were following her, running also. They overlay the lady's print in places, but the lady's shoe prints do not overlay the larger ones. I'm not saying someone was chasing her, mind, anyone at all might have come this way after the lady put down those prints. As we've seen, the doors of the Savoy, Sunday or not, get a lot of traffic. Nor am I saying the footprints belong to your mother."

"Who else's would they be?"

"Who else indeed."

Constable McAllen stood on the boardwalk at York Street. Sterling noted with approval that the man wasn't watching him but faced the street, eyes on the people trying to get a peek into the alley, arms outstretched to keep them back.

Sterling walked carefully, thinking and observing before putting each foot down. Angus was silent behind him, the only sound the boy's heavy breathing. They reached the corner of the building where the alley met York Street. The ground was

churned up, the woman's footprints disappearing into the mud.
Something had lain here, thrashing about by the look of it. That
something had been large enough to be a person. An abandoned
wagon wheel was propped against the wall of the Savoy, a scrap
of cloth caught on a rusting nail. Satin, in a green as pale as sage.

"My mother's dress," Angus said.

Fiona had worn the green satin dress to church and had
still been wearing it when Sterling said his goodnights and left
the wedding party. Her hat, of a sort any respectable matron
might wear to church, had toned her dance-hall owner costume
down enough so that she looked the role of bridesmaid perfectly.
Sterling shook off the image of Fiona peeking out from beneath
the raised brim on one side of the hat and giving him a smile as
soft and innocent as a schoolgirl. The edges of her mouth had
turned up, and he thought he might have seen the flash of a
wink before she turned her attention back to Reverend Bowen
droning on.

Sterling dropped into a squat. He reached out one hand
and brushed his index finger across the scrap of fabric. Then,
aware of Angus's intense stare, he coughed, shook sense back
into his head, and studied the area around the wagon wheel.
Angus shifted behind him, allowing a shaft of sunlight to hit
the ground. It flashed on a sliver of metal half-buried in the
mud. Slowly and carefully, Richard Sterling lifted it up. About
six inches long, sharpened to a fierce point, a fake pearl mounted
on the opposite end. A hat pin.

"Recognize this?" Sterling asked Angus.

"My mother has one like that. Most women do, don't they?"

"Yes." But most women didn't wear such a lovely green satin
gown.

He studied the ground. There had been a fight here.
Someone, almost certainly Fiona, had fallen or been knocked

to the ground. His stomach clenched and a red mist descended behind his eyes.

"Sterling!" He started at the shout.

Inspector McKnight and Mr. Mann were standing with McAllen. Two constables were with them. "What have you got?"

Sterling pushed himself upright. "You can come, sir. I've seen all I need to."

McKnight and his men walked toward them.

"You," Sterling said to one of the constables. "Guard the corner at King Street. I don't want every ghoul in town stamping all over this alley." The man gave him a nod and trotted off.

"Let's go back inside," Sterling said.

Everyone in the dancehall jumped as the door opened. Joe Hamilton hastily stuffed a deck of cards into his pocket, Betsy stopped complaining about her sore feet, and one of the prostitutes took her hand off the knee of one of the cheechakos. Sergeant Lancaster's tale of when he'd been the champion boxer of Winnipeg, told to a yawning Mrs. Mann, died on his lips.

Without laughing, cheering, foot-stomping miners, or badly played music, flickering kerosene lamps, and colourful costumes, the dance hall reminded Sterling of the building where his father, a pastor, held meetings. Stern and unadorned. Bare wood and long, deep shadows.

But most of all, without Fiona MacGillivray, black eyes constantly moving, neck and back straight, perfume subtle, gown and hair immaculate, the room seemed empty and sterile.

He shoved the sentiment aside.

It was just a room. A cheap room in a cheap frontier dancehall.

"Do we need all these people listening in?" McKnight asked.

"No. Walker, unlock the door. Everyone's to leave except for Walker and Angus."

"No! I stay." Mr. Mann said very firmly.

"I guess that's okay."

"I'm not going anywhere until I find out what's happened to my dear friend," Mrs. Mann said, her chin extended and her tone matching her husband's.

Everyone began shouting. No one made a move to follow Sterling's orders.

"You can't arrest us all, Corporal," Barney said. "We're here 'cause we care about Mrs. Fiona and we're gonna help. Ain't that right, boys?"

The men muttered their agreement.

"We could be here all day," McKnight said. "Very well, carry on Mr. Sterling."

"Mrs. MacGillivray appears to have been kidnapped," Sterling said.

"Not again!" McKnight groaned as everyone started talking at once.

"Be quiet," Sterling shouted above the din. "Or I'll empty the room."

The voices died down.

"That woman. For the life of me, I cannot understand how one female can so consistently get herself into trouble." McKnight glared at Angus as if his mother's conduct was all his fault.

"I say, sir," Angus began. Sterling cut him off.

"She was here last night at midnight. You left," he looked at Ray Walker, "out the front door?"

"Aye."

"And you," he asked Betsy, "you left through the front door also?"

"Yes, I did."

"Whereupon Mrs. MacGillivray appears to have walked through to the back to lock the door leading onto the alley. Did she lock the front door after you, Betsy?"

"I don't think so."

Sterling gave her a long look. Then he said, "For the moment we'll assume she did not. Someone entered through the unlocked front door and followed her through the building. He confronted her as she reached the back. I surmise she attempted to flee into the alley, and the man chased her. She got almost to York Street before he reached her. There was ..." Sterling was suddenly aware of the wide-eyed boy watching him. "I'm sorry, Angus, but I believe the man caught her and," he coughed, "hit her and knocked her to the ground."

The room erupted. Lancaster looked as though he were about to have a heart attack. Murray pounded his fist into his hand, and Barney spat on the floor. Maxie gasped and Mrs. Mann moaned. One of the men tittered and Joe Hamilton waved a fist in the fellow's face. The red-headed prostitute leaned against the cheechako to steady herself. The cheechako put a comforting arm around her. Betsy said, "I didn't think ..."

Sterling had to take a deep breath to steady his nerves. The thought of a lady such as Fiona being assaulted by a brute of a man.... She'd probably never seen an act of violence in her life. Other than the time she was knifed and tied up in the wilderness for the bears and wolves to get her. Or when a lunatic threatened to cut Martha Witherspoon's throat, and Mouse O'Brien was shot trying to rescue her.

"What happened after that, I can't tell. There are too many tracks on York Street for me to follow, particularly if the man in question had a horse and wagon, which was probably the case."

"Do we have a suspect?" McKnight asked.

"I believe we do, yes. Angus, tell the inspector the story."

Angus stepped forward. He described Paul Sheridan and repeated the story of Gold Mountain and the valley as warm as California.

Barney spat on the floor once again. Sterling saw the two cheechakos exchange glances and the men who'd followed Mr. Mann from the waterfront stand a bit straighter.

"Was this the person you let into the Savoy, Betsy?" Sterling asked.

"He was comin' in as I was goin' out." She lifted her chin, realizing she'd been caught in a lie. "*She* shoulda locked the door if she didn't want people trailin' in. I was so pleased, you see, at being offered a speakin' part in the play, I wasn't paying much attention. Anyway, ain't for me to be chasing customers away. Maybe she'd arranged to meet him once everyone were gone."

"Why you ..." Walker said.

"Leave it," Sterling snapped. "We must assume this fellow Paul Sheridan has taken Fiona MacGillivray against her will and they are on their way to ... wherever this place is he wants to find."

McKnight read something in the boy's face. "Angus, do you know ..."

"I'd suggest we adjourn to the Fort, sir," Sterling interrupted. "Nothing more can be accomplished here." The last thing this town needed was Angus revealing details of the supposed location of the fabled Gold Mountain. Barney and the old timers knew the story was rubbish, but from the look on the faces of the city boys and the dock-workers, it wouldn't take much to have them all rushing into the wilderness. Gold had a way of making men plumb crazy.

"What do we do now?" Murray shouted.

"Go home," McKnight said. "It's Sunday and these premises are closed. Leave this matter in the hands of the North-West

Mounted Police, where it belongs. If you learn anything about the whereabouts of Mrs. Fiona MacGillivray or of this Sheridan, come to the Fort and make a report."

Angus's eyes filled and the boy struggled not to let the tears fall. "That's it? That's all you're going to do for my mother?" Mrs. Mann touched his shoulder and he shrugged her off.

"I'm forming a search party. Who's with me?" Joe Hamilton yelled. Some of the men shouted their agreement and stepped forward. Mr. Mann raised his hand, avoiding his wife's angry glare.

"Don't be ridiculous," McKnight said. "You all go haring off into the wilderness you'll be lucky to find your way back, never mind bring Mrs. MacGillivray with you."

The cheechako signalled to his friend. The man unwound himself from the red-headed prostitute and the two men slipped away. The woman pouted. Several other men saw them leave, and a rush for the back door began.

McKnight continued talking as his audience got smaller and smaller. "If Mrs. MacGillivray has gone, against her will or not, with Sheridan, we can only hope the man has enough sense to turn around when he realizes this Gold Mountain's a pipe dream."

"If you won't do anything, then I will," Angus stretched to his full height. "Mr. Hamilton, I'm with you."

"Angus," Sterling snapped. "No one said we're going to do nothing. Calm down. Hamilton, if I need you, I know where to find you. Walker, you and Angus come with me. I have some ideas. Everyone else, this place is closed. Get out or you'll be arrested."

The women began to leave. Miss Vanderdaege gave Angus a quick hug and a peck on the cheek. Sterling saw the red-headed prostitute start to do the same, but her hand lingered on Angus's chest and he growled, "Kate, one more charge and it's a blue ticket for you."

She snatched her hand away. "I ain't doin' nothin' Mr. Sterling," she whined. "Just figured the boy needs a hug, what with his ma being missin' and probably dead. Or somefin' worse."

Angus swallowed heavily.

Having scored a direct hit, she gave Sterling a smirk full of malice and left the dance hall. Her two companions scurried after her.

The Mounties did not have the facilities or supplies to accommodate prisoners. There were only two sentences handed out in the Yukon: a term spent chopping wood for the NWMP's ravenous stoves, or a blue ticket, banning the miscreant from the territory permanently.

One of these days, Sterling thought, he'd find an excuse to see both Kate and her Madame, Joey LeBlanc, run out of town.

"Anyone else want to stand here and argue?" he said.

Mr. Mann took his wife's arm. "Comes Helga, home now. Yous needs help, Sterling, I gives it."

"Thank you."

Betsy lumbered to her feet. "Are you sure the streets are safe, Corporal?" She shivered in terror and opened her eyes wide. "Mr. Walker, would you be so good as to walk a girl home. I'm that frightened."

"No," Walker said.

"I'll protect you, Betsy," Maxie said with an unladylike snort of laughter. She turned with a flounce of her skirts and stalked out, trailing mud behind her. Murray grinned and he and Betsy followed her.

Soon only Ray Walker, Graham Donohue, Angus MacGillivray, and the police were left.

McKnight coughed. "Well done clearing the room. Good job, Corporal. I suggest that we... uh."

"Angus," Sterling said. "Am I right that you've seen this map of Sheridan's?"

"Yes, sir. I have."

"Donohue, you've always got paper and pen on you. Give a blank sheet to Angus. Start drawing what you remember."

Chapter Eighteen

I was a few days short of my eleventh birthday when my parents were murdered and I ran for my life. My father had been groundskeeper on a great estate, and he and I had walked the Black Cuillins of Skye together since I took my first steps. The Earl had eleven sons and one lonely, shy daughter, and I was being educated in the big house in order to provide her with companionship. Neither of my parents had stepped foot out of Western Skye in their lives, and my father never understood why anyone would possibly want to, but I knew something of the wider world. I dreamed of one day travelling to London, to Paris or Rome, perhaps even to New York.

I found the wider world far sooner than I wanted.

I ran from our neat white-washed croft, the bloodied bodies of my parents, and the man who had killed them. I hid in the wilds for three days, knowing he'd kill me if he found me. It was November and the Highland nights were cold and rain fell hard. Eventually, the scent of food cooking over an open fire lured me down from the hills.

I moved slowly through the trees. I'd thrown off the uncomfortable shoes I wore in the big house and was in my bare feet. I knew how to move in the wilds without making a sound.

A cart was pulled into a clearing beside a swift-moving creek, swollen with rain water. A sway-backed horse hobbled nearby chewed a patch of grass and lifted its head at my approach. It let out a soft whinny. I stood still until it lost interest and bent its big brown head back to its meal. Firelight flickered through the bare branches of the trees, water gurgled as it rushed over rocks, and people spoke in loud voices. A man shouted and a woman laughed. It was a nice laugh, I thought.

There are not many trees on Skye, and what there are tend to be small and scraggly, but the campsite was in a grove of alders. A large iron pot was suspended over the fire, emitting clouds of fragrant steam. My mouth watered.

"Come forward child," a woman's voice said.

No one had moved and no one had looked in my direction.

"The fire's warm," she said, "and the sloorich's ready."

The voice belonged to a woman squatting beside the pot. She held a large wooden spoon in her hand. She lifted her eyes and held out the spoon. "Stew. Hot and good."

I stepped into the circle of light. Nine people watched me. No one moved, no one spoke. No one smiled. I knew they were Travellers, Gypsies. My father was charged with sending them on their way if they tried to set up camp on the Earl's property when they weren't needed, or giving them work at berry picking time.

The woman reached behind herself and found a bowl. Not looking at me, she dipped her spoon into the cauldron and slowly poured a long line of stew. I smelled rich broth, cooked vegetables, spices. She held out the bowl. "Eat, child."

My manners fled and I dashed forward. I grabbed the offering. It was almost too hot to eat but I spooned it up quickly.

"Good?" she said when I paused for breath.

I nodded.

"Then sit."

I squatted on the ground.

"What's your name?" A man asked. His accent was very rough and the words broken. He was seated closest to the fire. The only one of them in a proper chair.

I hesitated. He had a large beard and long unkempt hair the colour of smoke rising from the fire. His eyes were cloudy and the skin on his face folded over and over itself. His hands were scarred and thick with calluses, the knuckles swollen with arthritis. He was missing the thumb on his right hand. He smelled as if his teeth were rotting inside his mouth.

"I am called Fiona and I thank you for the dinner, ma'am, sir," I said, remembering my manners at last. "It was most delicious." I pulled my handkerchief out of my skirt pocket and dabbed at my lips.

The old man's bushy eyebrows lifted in surprise. He threw a glance at the woman. She studied my face for a long time and then leaned over to put a log on the fire and as the flames shot up I could see she was as grey and well-worn as he although her brown eyes were bright and clear.

"What're you doing out by yourself?" a younger man asked. "Are you lost?"

"No," I replied, "I am not lost."

"A runaway then," he said.

I did not speak.

"You can eat with us tonight," the old man said. His voice rumbled deep in his chest. "Sleep in the tent. Tomorrow I'll decide."

I thanked him. The woman began passing around bowls of stew. Sloorich, she explained to me. Everything into the pot with a lot of potatoes. A girl close to my age, dressed in a plain brown skirt with faded yellow blouse, shifted over on the log where she was sitting. She patted it, indicating that I could join her.

I smiled my thanks and did so.

Her hair was matted and dirty, but her face and hands were clean. She told me her name was Moira and pointed out the others. As well as the old man and woman, there was a younger woman, three boys older than I, one of whom stared openly at me, and two small girls, poking each other in the ribs and giggling at I knew not what.

The old woman handed around bowls of stew.

The men and boys were in working-man's overalls and caps. Their collars and cuffs were shredding and stained with grime, but like the girl, their faces and hands were clean for eating. The two younger girls wore once-white dresses and pinafores. Their hair was a mass of blond curls, and one had a red ribbon looped through it and tied in a bow at the top.

I jerked awake as I almost fell off the log. The old woman smiled at me. "Come," she said, getting to her feet. "Sleep."

She led the way to a tent. It was very small — cloth bent over branches with an open doorway. She gestured for me to enter and I crawled inside. The floor was soft with straw covered by a sheet, and a pile of blankets was stacked against the wall. I lay down.

"Thank you for your kindness," I said. "I'll be off in the morning."

The blankets were rough wool and smelled of much use and infrequent washing, but they were warm, and I felt safe for the first time in three days.

Whereas I'd fallen asleep sitting up, with a bowl of stew on my lap, now that I was lying down I was awake, watching flames dance against the tent walls, listening to the people talk. They pitched their voices low, but the night air was still, and I could hear. The old man said, "Morning, go to the house and listen. Say nothing about the girl."

I woke when the first light of the sun touched the tent. I knew where I was right away and what had happened to me. Something was pressed up against my back, and my face almost touched the tent walls. I rolled over and sat up. The tent was full of bodies.

I'd thought all the blankets were for me and had wrapped myself up warmly. I was now aware of the cold and damp under the one shredded covering I'd been left.

"Mornin'," Moira said. Two brown eyes peered over the rim of her blanket. The covers shifted, and I could see that the rest of the tent was occupied by the younger girls, still sleeping.

We crawled out of the tent and went into the bushes to take care of what needed to be taken care of. The ground was thick with frost, and clouds hung so low I couldn't see the surrounding hills. "Do you sleep in tents all year?" I asked Moira.

"Aye."

"Don't you get cold? What do you do when it snows?"

She looked at me as if that were a very stupid question. "We brush it off, of course."

When we got back to camp, the adults were up. The old lady, Jean was her name, was stirring the embers of the fire back to life and Yuri, her husband, was lighting his pipe.

The girls came out of their tent and the three young men out of another. The oldest of them, nineteen or twenty perhaps, ran his eyes up and down my body in a way that reminded me of Alistair Forester regarding my mother. I shivered and turned away. Jean handed each of the boys a hunk of bread, and they set off without a word.

If they were going to the big house to ask about me, I did not want to be here when they returned.

But I'd have time for breakfast.

We ate porridge that was not as good as my mother made and bread neither toasted nor served with butter or jam. When I finished eating, I pulled my handkerchief out of my pocket and dapped at my lips once again. It was a nice handkerchief, lovely stiff linen, pure white, trimmed with blue lace, and my name was flamboyantly embroidered in one corner. It had been a birthday gift from Euila, the Earl's daughter and my school-mate. Euila, I thought, would be shocked to see how filthy it was now.

I was feeling quite grubby after three days and nights in the same clothes, but judging by the garments these people were wearing, they didn't do laundry all that often.

I put my handkerchief away and got to my feet. "Thank you for your hospitality, sir, madam. I'll be on my way now." Where I would go, what I would do, how I would survive, I had absolutely no idea. The Earl, who'd spoken politely to my mother, who'd shared a dram with my father while they talked about salmon in the rivers and stags on the hills and slipped me shortbread from the kitchen, was seriously ill and no longer left the house. The second son, Alistair, was in charge.

Alistair had killed my parents, and he knew I'd seen him do it.

"Sit," Yuri said. He slurped watery porridge through one side of his mouth while his pipe remained clamped in the other.

"I don't want to impose."

"We won't send ye were ye dinna want ta go, girl. Now sit."

I sat.

The boys soon returned. The one named Jock, whom I did not care for, thrust a thumb in my direction and said, "The daughter of the house isn't missing."

Yuri looked at me. His eyes were covered by a white film, and I wondered how much he could see. Enough, I had no doubt.

"I could have told you that," I said with a sniff.

"You have a mouth on you, girl," Jock said.

"Quiet," Yuri said. "Who's she then? Dressed like that, speaking like that?"

"We didn't have to walk far to hear the news," one of the younger boys said. His eyes bulged as if there were eggs stuffed behind them, but his smile was shy and kind. "Everyone's talking about it. Fire in a croft on the estate. The groundskeeper and his wife and wee daughter run off. The Earl's son's saying MacGillivray was caught poaching to sell for himself."

Old Yuri stroked his beard and asked me one question only: "What's your father's name, girl?"

"Angus MacGillivray," I replied, lifting my head high. "Our ancestors were at Culloden."

"Time we were moving on," Yuri said, and the women and young men and girls rushed to break up camp.

I lived with Yuri and his family for two years. Although Jean was Yuri's wife, the younger woman, Mary, often slept in his tent. Travellers, I learned, did not bother with the conventions of Scottish society, and things such as marriages were rarely formalized.

Jock and Donald and Davie were the sons of Yuri and Jean. The two little girls were the daughters of Yuri and Mary. Moira was the daughter of Jean's sister. Her mother was dead and her father in jail.

Yuri and Jean had to be a lot younger than they looked, if their oldest child was not yet twenty. I soon came to realize Travellers led a hard life indeed. They and their parents and their children had been born in a tent in the woods, and they'd lived every day of their lives outside, sun or snow, always on the move as they followed work and the seasons.

The family were plain-featured, with long, strong faces resembling horses, crooked teeth and sallow complexions, either spotty or scarred. They were short and thin, probably due as much to poor diet as to family characteristics. My mother, dressed in her homespun clothes, bending over a peat fire, had been more beautiful than any of the fine ladies from London or Edinburgh who visited the estate, trailing scores of servants and trunks full of good clothes and glittering jewellery. She'd had clear skin, thick black hair, high cheekbones, delicate hands, and dark eyes rimmed with long lashes. I took after her.

Yuri immediately realized that with my plumy upper-crust accent (beaten into me in Euila's schoolroom) and my looks, I could be profitably put to beg.

It became my job to stand on street corners, looking sad and beautiful, and tell well-dressed passersby my tragic story in my perfect accent. When my beloved father had been tragically killed, his heartless family threw my mother — of whom they never approved, because although she was minor aristocracy, her family was moneyless — into the street. She was dying of consumption, I went on, and had no one but me to bring in money for food and medicine. I would touch my beautiful handkerchief to my eyes and look stoic and brave. When my family was destroyed, I'd been wearing an altered, cast-off day-dress from Lady Forester, which probably cost more than Yuri's family would see in a year. Jean looked after it with great care and it, along with my handkerchief, was put aside to be used only as my begging outfit. Jock or Donald or Davie would stand on the other side of the road or around the corner in case some well-meaning lady wanted to take me home. I made a lot of money.

Yuri was afraid I'd start taking on their speech, and retribution would be harsh and sudden if I slipped in a word of Scottish or said ye instead of you.

One night, sitting around the fire, watching sparks leap into the trees, I asked Jean if she ever feared the tents would catch fire. Yuri lifted his stick and hit me across the back of the head. I fell to the ground with a cry and he kicked me soundly in the ribs.

He didn't have cause to hit me often, but when he did he made sure never to strike my face. That would be bad for business.

Travelling families generally keep to the same routine year after year, making a circuit of towns, farms, and camping sites. Generations return to the same farms, moving with the seasons, picking berries or harvesting the neeps. When times are good and work finished, they gather at established campsites — dozens of families, maybe hundreds of people — to exchange the news, see new babies and growing children, drink whisky, and sing around the fire in the soft summer light.

Whether Yuri's family did this before I arrived I do not know, but now they kept themselves apart. We left Skye immediately and spent the winter travelling Scotland. It was hard work, living on the move. It could take hours to put up the tents, as holes had to be dug into the sometimes frozen ground to secure the shelter against the winter winds. The poles were cut from trees, hazel or ash usually, which were able to be bent. I'd lived in a croft house, but I could never get warm enough in the tent. Not once I realized I had to share the blankets with three other girls.

I made enough money for the family over the winter that come spring, they'd been able to buy a strong, healthy horse from a farmer, get rid of the sway-backed nag, and replace the cart with a handsome wagon for the adults and the girls to sleep in. The wagon was a real luxury in more ways than one: Jean and Mary no longer had to walk alongside the cart. They took turns riding in style beside Yuri as he clamped on his pipe and flicked the horse's reins.

In the world of Travellers we were rich.

In spring, with the horse pulling the wagon containing most of our goods, we walked out of Scotland and headed south through England.

There was little point in setting up near farms and hoping for work in the fields — no English farmer would give me coins because I spoke well and told a sad story — so we camped near the larger towns and cities. While I begged on street corners and one of the boys guarded me, Jean and Mary and the girls would go hawking. Selling things door to door, flowers they'd collected from the fields, trinkets they'd picked up on our travels, objects they'd made, such as scourers for cleaning pots, colourful shawls, or painted wooden decorations. Sometimes they'd read palms or tell fortunes. Yuri and his sons would knock on doors asking for work, things to be fixed, trees to be cut down or trimmed.

At first I thought I would never get over the death of my parents, but as time went on and the seasons changed, and we left behind the harsh beautiful highlands I loved, I found hours could go by without thinking of them. I stopped dreaming every night of Alistair Forester drenched with my mother's blood. After about a year, Moira told me I was no longer tossing and turning and crying out in fear in my dreams.

I never felt love from my new family. Jean was kind to me, and she fed me and ensured I had a place to sleep, but she never wrapped me in her arms or held me tight. Yuri was quick to discipline me for incidents of what he saw as disrespect or failure to do my job. I was as much a worker for his family as was the new horse, and I received just as much affection. Mary, the younger wife, disliked me intensely and was quick with a punch or kick if I didn't move fast enough or she thought I was talking back. Only later did I understand she feared that when I got older I would be invited into Yuri's tent.

Moira and I had little choice but to become friends. Girls of an age surrounded by adults, older boys, and younger girls. But I suspected she was jealous of me and never put my trust in her.

Davie and Donald pretty much ignored me, and I them.

Jock, however, watched me constantly. He was a small man, but he was strong. He'd slap my bottom or make a grab at my breasts, tiny as rosebuds, or grab me around the waist and ask for a kiss and not let go until Yuri growled at him. He pretended, in front of the others, it was all in fun, but I knew better. His laughter was forced and his smile did not reach his dark eyes.

One day he hid in the bushes while I was returning from the privy and jumped out as I passed. He wrapped his arms, strong from hard labour, around me and bent my head for a kiss. When I resisted, he knocked me to the ground with a growl. But he tripped and I was able to get to my feet and flee.

Jean gave me a long look when I came running out of the trees, the back of my dress covered in dead leaves and dirt, followed by a grinning, swaggering Jock.

We arrived in Oxford, and I was sent into town with Jock to do my job while the others made the rounds of hawking and seeking odd jobs. I did particularly well that day and had collected the incredible sum of ten pounds from an elderly don, who was almost brought to tears by my heartbreaking story of indescribable woe. Which I described at great length. I handed over all the money to Jock, as I was expected to, and we made our way out of town toward camp.

As we were passing a pub, Jock shoved me into an alley. I lost my footing and staggered backwards, falling into the dirty ground. Before I knew what was happening, he was on me, one hand reaching up my skirt, clawing at the delicate skin on the top of my legs. His mouth came down hard on mine and his thick tongue thrust between my lips. Something long and hard was pressed up against my thigh and I knew Jock was scrambling to undo his trouser buttons.

I bit down, hard, onto his tongue and felt blood spurt into my mouth. Jock yelled and punched me in the face. Once, twice, three times. Stars moved behind my eyes. I raked my fingers down his face and screamed.

"You there. What do you think you're doing?"

The weight lifted off me as Jock lumbered to his feet. "Piss off," he growled.

"I don't care what you get up to with your whore, but you won't be doing it next to my premises. Get off with you. Why, she's just a child."

The man was very large, red-faced and round-bellied, with enormous white whiskers. He turned to Jock and his face filled with anger. "I'll have the police on you, lad." He stepped toward me and held out his hand. "Are you all right, child?" He pulled me to my feet.

I straightened my dress, nodded, and wiped blood from my nose. I said in an accent that was pure crofter's daughter. "Aye, sir. I thank ye for the kindness, sir."

"She's my sister," Jock said with a growl, "and I don't need the likes of you interfering if she needs disciplining."

He grabbed my hand and we ran, the man's shouts following us.

Once he was sure we were not being pursued, Jock dropped my hand. "Not a word o' this, you hear?"

I stared into his eyes, black and hard as chips of coal. "I'm not afraid of you."

"You should be. You will be."

He left me standing alone on the street corner, my day's earnings in his pocket.

I made my own way back to camp.

Jean cried out when she saw me. I must have made quite a sight with my face bruised and bloodied, my dress torn and dirty. I said something about a tough trying to take my money, and she dipped a clean rag into the can set to boil for tea and wiped at my face gently.

Yuri asked me where Jock had been while I was being assaulted, and I said I didn't know. He studied me through milky eyes and a cloud of smoke and read the lie in my face.

I didn't hear Jock return to camp, but he was at breakfast the following morning. Deep scratches ran down his right cheek, and he blustered about fighting off three men in a pub. An unlikely story, as even I was well aware Travellers were not welcome in pubs. If they did fancy a pint, they were expected to be out by three o'clock when the locals arrived. Yuri said I was to go hawking with the women today and ordered Jock to stay behind once the others had left to find work.

When we returned that evening, Jock's eye was black and purple and almost swollen shut, and he walked as if his ribs were hurting him. The knuckles on Yuri's right hand were bruised. Neither man said a word about what had happened, and no one asked.

I was off the street for a week while my bruises faded and the cuts healed over, and I knew Yuri was angrier with Jock at the signs of violence on my face than the attack itself.

From that day on, Jock regarded me with a smouldering anger, but he did not try to touch me again.

Jean took me aside after supper the night of the attack. We went around to the far side of the wagon. She pulled something out of the folds of her dress. It was a knife in a battered leather sheath. "Our Jock is not a good man. He's my son and I'm sorry, but that's the way of the world sometimes and there's nae help for it. You need to watch out for yourself, Fiona. Take this." She pressed the sheath into my hand. I gripped it, and pulled the knife out slowly. Firelight reflected off the blade. It was very sharp.

"Davie will show you how to use it. Keep it with you always."
Yuri called for tea, and she slipped away.

Davie was as opposite a man from his brother as two people
could be. He was shy and spoke in a low voice with his bulging
eyes fixed on the ground. He was always kind to me and seemed
genuinely fond of his cousin and two half-sisters. He was the
youngest and smallest of Jean's three boys, and the two older ones
treated him with a sort of casual contempt; it was not unknown
for him to come to meals with a bloodied nose or blackening eye.

He taught me well. How to keep the knife concealed but
available instantly when needed; to ensure the sheath was always
smooth inside so the blade wouldn't stick. He showed me how
to thrust and how to parry, to stab deep and hard, and to use it
to block an incoming blow. After the incident with Jock, Yuri
assigned Davie to watch over me while I begged, and we usually
stopped somewhere private on the way back for a lesson. The
day I accidently cut his forearm, he laughed and said I needed
a teacher no longer. I'm sure Yuri knew what was going on, but
nothing was ever said between us.

Moira saw the knife when I laid it beside my head at night
or took off my clothes to bathe in a summer stream. Like the rest
of the family, she said nothing about it. I told the younger girls
it was for peeling tatties and neeps.

We tramped the length and breadth of Scotland and England,
and after two years we set up camp outside London for the first
time. I was excited about seeing the great city. Euila's governess,
Miss Wheatley, had been a proud Englishwoman and had gone on
at enormous length as to how London was the centre of the world.
She'd described all the wonders to be found there: Buckingham
Palace, Westminster Abbey, St. Paul's Cathedral, High Park, Pall
Mall. As much as I hated Miss Wheatley, her enthusiasm was so
great I'd always wanted to see the city.

We set up our tents at the rim of a Travellers' camp. There were about ten other families and we girls were very much looking forward to songs and talk and laugher around the communal fire.

Yuri puffed on his pipe and watched the boys erect the tent. It was late November, so the boys worked hard to protect the tent against harsh winter winds. It had been six months since that afternoon in Oxford when Jock tried to rape me — I had no doubt that had been his intent — and if anything, his anger at me was only growing. I was thirteen now, my body taking shape into curves, my long gangly limbs coming under some sort of control. Jock was over twenty. He was short and scrawny but hard-muscled after a life outdoors and days full of manual labour.

On occasion his mother tried to talk to him about marrying soon, and he would growl and tell her to shut her mouth. He watched me across the flames of the cooking fire, and if I happened to look up and catch his eye, he would draw the pad of his index finger very slowly across his thick lips and give me a slow wink that had my spine turning to ice.

Mary was always making comments and tossing out suggestions, actively encouraging Jock to court me. She told me Jock would be the head of the family one day, and if I was his proper acknowledged wife, I'd have status in the travelling community. They were hoping, she told me, to find a husband for Moira, and I would have to either marry Jock or leave. I didn't think they were going to keep me on forever did I?

Considering that I made more money than all the rest of them put together, I did think they were going to keep me forever.

I didn't know how I felt about that. It was probably just the way things were going to be.

Who knows what would have happened, how my life would have turned out, had Jock been a bit kinder, not so openly vicious when no one else was around. I was only thirteen years old, and although Yuri's family fed me and housed me, I was emotionally alone in the world. I might have been persuaded by charm and good manners.

Instead, I feared him.

He had a cruel streak and directed it not only at me. Since the day he'd attacked me and had been punished by his father, he turned his hostility onto the younger ones. He tripped little May one day as she was passing the fire. She fell forward, hands outstretched to break her fall. Fortunately, Davey was there, and quick-witted, as he grabbed May's arm and wrenched her away from the open flame.

We never did get to join the dancing and singing around the communal fire that night outside London. As Donald turned to pronounce the tent ready, Yuri gave a strangled cry and fell forward.

He was dead before he hit the ground.

When the funeral was over and the other travelling families had returned to their own camps, Jock got to his feet and stood before our fire. We sat silently, waiting for him to speak.

He looked everyone in the eye, one after another.

"I'm head of this family now."

Murmurs of agreement.

"Mum and Mary, you'll move into the tent with the girls."

"Aye," Mary said.

"And you," he said to me, "will move into my tent. Tonight. Get your things."

Moira studied her feet, May and Polly shifted. Donald laughed and Davie grumbled. "You got something ta say aboot that?" Jock asked him.

"No."

"See ye don't. What are you waiting for woman? I said now."

I got to my feet, very slowly. I felt the weight of the knife in my belt. I looked at the faces around the fire. No one was looking at me.

"No," I said.

I heard breath being sucked in. Jock approached me. He was not much taller than I, yet he was fully grown and I had several more inches to come. "You'll do what I say, girl, or you'll feel my fist."

"What a charming proposal," I said, exactly as Miss Wheatley would have addressed him. "Nevertheless, I am forced to decline. I will not be your wife. I will not sleep in your tent."

He glanced at the faces around the fire. No one moved, no one said a word. Jock lifted his arm and swung his hand, palm open, at my face.

Jean yelled, "No," and Moira screamed. One of the girls began to cry.

I read his intent long before he even began to move. I danced out of the way and the blow went wild. He cursed me. The knife was in my hand, blade out, without conscious thought. When Jock came at me again, I was ready. The blade gleamed in the firelight before it sliced into Jock's arm.

He yelled in shock and stared at his arm. The cut wasn't deep, but deep enough. Blood leaked through the cloth of his shirt.

I spoke to the women, but focused on Jock, his eyes wide with surprise and shock. "Time for me to be moving on, I believe. Ladies, I bid you a very good day."

I had almost nothing in the way of possessions: a couple of skirts, a blouse, a hairbrush and some ribbon. A knife.

I dared not go into the confined space of the wagon to get my things.

I walked away from the traveller's camp, heading toward the lights of London, far in the distance. An orange glow in the night sky.

I did not look back.

Chapter Nineteen

My head hurt. I was lying on something very rough, and something was digging into the small of my back. A horse whinnied not far away, and I could hear the wind moving through the trees and water rushing over rocks. A twig snapped and a man mumbled.

For a very brief moment, I thought I was back on Skye, that it was the first morning I'd been with the Travellers and they were breaking camp, readying to move on. But I caught no scent of oatmeal bubbling over the fire, heard no chattering women ·or laughing children, and did not smell heather or grouse or the barren hills of the Highlands. A cool breeze blew against my cheek, a breeze that had drifted through boreal forests of pine, spruce, and birch. It brought with it the scent of scrub and decaying vegetation and fresh water racing for the frozen sea.

Taking care not to move, I opened my eyes. I was looking up into a tree, a rather scruffy, stunted old pine. The sky above was blue, and white clouds drifted overhead.

I heard the strike of a match and a muttered curse and then turned my head, very slowly.

A man was about ten feet away. His back was to me, and he crouched over a pile of twigs. He struck another match and a puff of wind playfully blew it out before it could touch the wood.

Beyond the man and the fire pit, a brown horse munched on grasses at the banks of a river, its tail constantly moving as it flicked flies away.

I felt something land on my hand, a fly or a mosquito, but I didn't move. I took inventory of my body. I was lying on my back, a rough blanket tucked around me. My right cheek was throbbing and the back of my head hurt. I wiggled my toes and felt blood flowing through my legs. I was not wearing shoes. I remembered a fight, falling down.

Then I remembered it all.

It was Paul Sheridan trying to light a fire in the wind. The sun was high overhead. Other than the wind and the trees and the horse and Sheridan, not a sound could be heard. We were nowhere near town, where the racket never ended, nor the Creeks, where people were coming and going at all times, day or night, nor the Yukon River where an armada of boats crowded with excited people headed for Dawson.

I had not the slightest idea how long I'd been unconscious or where we were.

I felt a sting in my hand and knew the mosquito had bitten me. Still, I didn't move. I could probably get to my feet without disturbing Sheridan, his head bowed, intent on his task. I'd make a noise getting to the horse, and the animal itself would react. It didn't have a saddle and wasn't standing near a convenient boulder. Difficult to mount, and even if I did get on, almost impossible to control. There were three packs stacked beside a tree, fastened shut. My new hat rested on top of one. I could see nothing I could use for a weapon. A rifle leaned up against a tired old spruce, but it was on the far side of Sheridan. He'd get to it before I could.

About all I could do would be to quietly get to my feet and hope to make cover of the trees before he noticed my absence.

And then what?

I had absolutely no idea where I was or where I should go. I didn't have a knife or a gun. I was in stocking feet, wearing an evening gown. By the feel of it, my hair had broken away from its pins, so it was unlikely I even had a hairpin to hand.

Nevertheless, I would try. Surely we couldn't be too far from town, and the Indians around here were not hostile. Once I was away from Sheridan, I'd yell and scream as I walked, and someone would find me.

Hopefully a person before a wolf or bear. Or Paul Sheridan.

I kept my eyes on the man, now trying to make a windbreak of his body while striking a fresh match, and tensed my arms and legs. I rolled slowly onto one side, but as I lifted my head, a pain as sharp as if a hatpin had been driven through it had me taking a gasp.

Sheridan looked up. "Ah," he said, "You're awake. Good. I was starting to worry." He rose to his feet with a groan.

I pushed myself up. The trees wobbled and I closed my eyes. When I opened them again, the trees were standing still and Sheridan was smiling. "Hungry? Let me get this fire going and I'll have the coffee on and fix us something to eat."

"I don't want coffee, nor food," I said. "Unless it's in my own home." I walked toward the horse, keeping my head high. Something was wrong with these woods: the trees were faded and blurry around the edges. "I hope this creature knows the way back to town. Where's the saddle?"

"No saddle," Sheridan said. "We came by cart, but it won't be taking us any further." He looked over my shoulder and I turned. At a bend in the river, a makeshift contraption lay on its side. It was about the size of a barrow a gardener might employ, with a single wheel at the back and excessively long poles lashed to the front. The wheel hung at an unhealthy angle. "I made something for the horse to pull, thinking you'd prefer to ride as long as you could. Didn't expect it would get far. Least you had someplace to sleep. It'll be the rest of the way on foot, I'm afraid. The horse'll carry the bags."

"Mr. Sheridan." I placed my hands on my hips. "I am returning to town, thank you very much. You may accompany me or not."

"Fiona, why are you being so difficult?" He threw up his hands, and genuinely looked confused. "I've told you my plan. I'm gonna make you the richest woman in the world."

"I'm going nowhere without my son."

"Well, I'm right sorry we had to leave without him, but that was your fault, you know. If you'd come along like I told you to, Angus would be here, wouldn't he?"

I couldn't argue with that. Then again, there didn't seem to be any point at all in arguing with Mr. Paul Sheridan. I shook my head, trying to look defiant while refocusing my vision. Slowly, Sheridan merged back into one person.

"I'll send word for the boy," he continued, "soon as we've arrived and I've staked the claim to the mountain and valley."

"Mr. Sheridan," I said, opening my eyes wide and touching my hands to my chest. "You must understand. I appreciate your offer very much, I am honoured to have been chosen to be your ... companion." I was not going to say queen — that would be almost *lèse majesté*. There is only one Queen in the Empire. "However," my eyes filled with tears, "I am not yet ready to remarry. You see, Mr. MacGillivray has only been dead less than two years."

He studied me. And then, to my surprise, he broke into laughter. "You really are a piece of work, aren't you?" I blinked. "Oh, yes, the dainty English lady with your nice dresses and accent and charming smile. But you were quick enough and clever enough to get yourself out of Soapy's reach lickety-split. I've seen you in the Savoy, listened to talk around town; everyone knows it's you who's in charge, not Walker. Tell you the truth, Fiona, you almost had me convinced. I learned the hard way outside the Savoy Saturday night. You fight like a man. Didn't learn that from your governess, did you? I'm sorry I had to hit you, but you shouldn't have fought me. Now I'm gonna get this damn fire lit and make us coffee. And then we'll be on our way. Got it?"

"Mr. Sheridan ..."

"Paul."

"Mr. Sheridan. All that may, or may not, be as you say. But I'm not going with you. I wish you the best on your journey." I lifted my skirts.

"How far you gonna get, you think? You've had a blow to the head and been unconscious for a long time. Can you see properly? Or are you trying to make everything stand straight? I see how you keep squinting and shaking your head. Do you know where we are? Do you know which way's town? Go running off helter-skelter you won't get far. For all your manners and business sense, I doubt you can live off the wilderness."

He wasn't entirely right about that. I'd walked the wilds of Skye with my father, and lived with Travellers for two years. That, however, had been on the sheep-filled hills of Scotland and among the neat hedgerows of England, where one was never more than a few hours walk from some village or hamlet or just a crofter's cabin. Not much my father or the Travellers taught me would be of use in the wilds of the Yukon. And Sheridan was right about one thing. If I moved my head too quickly, my vision swam, and that hatpin was there, ready to stab me behind the eyes.

Would Sheridan kill me if I tried to get away?

I looked into his face and did not know.

No matter. The man had to sleep and he couldn't watch me constantly. I'd wait until my head cleared and bide my time.

Besides, surely someone would come looking for me.

Wouldn't they?

I let some of the anger fade from my face.

"Good girl. Now you sit right there, where I can see you while I get this fire going."

He'd gathered rotting logs and piled them into a circle in the clearing. The wind was strong, coming straight across the river.

The river. If I followed the river, it should take me ... somewhere. I had no idea what river this was or in what direction it flowed. For all I knew it would only take me deeper away from civilization. Hadn't I heard somewhere that the rivers here flow north to the Arctic? I couldn't remember. Miss Wheatley had not instructed us in geography. I cursed the oversight.

"Mr. Sheridan," I said. "You need a windbreak. Even if you get that fire lit it will not last long. Collect rocks from the riverbank and place them in a circle. Inside the circle you can place your kindling. The logs you're using are too big. Use twigs and dead needles. Put the logs on once the flames have taken. Didn't anyone teach you to make a fire?"

"Not out-of-doors," he said.

I'd suspected as much. His speech wasn't too rough and his hands were uncallused. He'd been brought up in a city, and had no doubt always made his living by following the orders of Soapy Smith or his ilk.

Following my instruction — I was certainly not going to do the work myself — before long he had a cheerful blaze going. He walked over to the packs and pulled out a tin coffee pot and frying pan. I eyed the packs. They were rather small for taking two people into the wilderness.

"How much food did you bring?"

He opened the corned beef using the little key attached to the can, dropped a spoonful of lard into the pan, and tossed the beef on top.

"Enough. I can hunt," he nodded to the rifle, "to supplement our rations. Anyway, we'll be there soon enough." He tapped his chest. "The map's been right so far. Tomorrow we follow this river, then cut inland. Couple hours 'till we get to the old Indian trail and straight all the way."

I didn't bother to hide a sigh. The man couldn't light a campfire, but he thought he could hunt for our food?

In that I would not be able to assist him: I have never handled a firearm. I eyed the rifle.

How quickly could I learn?

Chapter Twenty

Angus MacGillivray sucked on the end of the pencil and studied the sketch. He was aware everyone was gathered around, leaning over him, willing him to finish the drawing. He added a line. Back in school, he'd loved geography best of all the subjects, learning how to read a map and the wonders of the world it opened up.

"I'm pretty sure that's it, sir," he said.

Everyone in the room leaned back in disappointment.

"Why, it could be anywhere," Sergeant Lancaster said.

"Not really," McKnight replied. "You can see where the Klondike and the Yukon Rivers meet. Here's the Klondike moving off due east. I have a map of the territory in my office. We might want to compare."

"And then what?" Graham Donohue said. "The rest of this map is nonsense. It doesn't show Grand Forks or the trail to the Creeks or Forty Mile or anything recognizable. There must be more to it, Angus. What are you forgetting?"

"I'm not forgetting anything. This is it. The map Mr. Sheridan showed me."

"Man couldn't find his way to his ass following this map," Donohue said.

"That Mr. Sheridan is labouring under an illusion is not in question here," McKnight said. "I've heard the stories. There are hundreds of them. Gold beyond imagining. A valley where fruit trees grow and rivers never freeze. No one can ever explain why, if this place is so special, even the Indians haven't found it by now."

"It's hidden. Secret," Lancaster said. Angus looked up at the man. His eyes were unfocused. "Part of this world yet not." Lancaster, Angus knew, had been a champion boxer in his youth. He suspected the sergeant had been hit on the head a few too many times. He'd recently proposed to Fiona. She politely turned him down, but the man continued to live in hope.

"Nonsense," Donohue said. "Pure fantasy told to keep men warm around the stove on a winter's night. That damned fool's taking Fiona straight into nothing."

"They say," Lancaster continued, "only the pure of heart can find it."

"That eliminates Sheridan then," Ray said. "And Fiona too, begging your pardon young Angus."

Sterling hadn't said a word. He ran his eyes over the map and rubbed at his chin. Whatever was at the end of this map — fantasy mountain or not — if Fiona MacGillivray was being taken there, he would go after her. And he would not return without her.

"McAllen," he said at last. "You've been down the Klondike. How far?"

"No more than thirty miles, Corporal. There's nothing there but trees and more trees."

"North of the river?"

"Don't know, sir. We were exploring the south bank some. Not the north."

Sterling tapped the paper with his finger. A smaller blue line led away from the larger one. Going north. "Do you know what's here?"

McAllen peered at the map. He shook his head. "Hard to judge distance on that map there. That's what, five, seven miles up? I don't remember anything of significance."

"I'd like to have a look at the map in your office, sir," Sterling said to McKnight. "There must be some reason this spot's marked."

McKnight and Sterling held each other's eyes. Angus didn't breathe. "Good idea," the inspector said at last.

"I'm going with you," Angus said.

"No, son. Not this time. I need to move fast."

"If not with you then I'll go by myself," Angus said. "I will. I have the map in my head, remember."

"No," Sterling said.

Angus's ally came from an unexpected direction. "Take the lad, Corporal," McKnight said. "He's proven himself to be a good man. They say you're a tracker, Sterling, but moving fast might not be wise. It's easy to miss signs in haste. McAllen, you'll accompany them."

"Yes, sir."

"I'm going too," Donohue said.

"Why?" Sterling said. "So you can write it down and send a report to your newspaper? That's no help to us."

Donohue stretched himself, as though trying to reach the Corporal's height. He fell very short. "Mrs. MacGillivray is my friend and I intend to find her."

Ray snorted. "Fiona's my friend also, as well as my partner, but I ken it won't be doing her no good a Glasgow lad stomping though the wilderness." He gave Angus what he probably thought was an encouraging smile. It did not have the desired effect. "I'll stay behind. Run our business. Keep everything in order for when she gets back."

"Sort your party out, Sterling," McKnight said. "Report to me before leaving. Anyone attempting to reproduce this map will be brought up on charges or given a blue ticket. In the meantime, Constable Fitzhenry...."

The officer standing guard at the back door, whose neck had stretched a good couple of inches as he strained to get a glimpse of the map, snapped to attention.

"You and Campbell ask around, see if anyone's seen this Sheridan fellow recently. It's entirely possible the man's still in town and has nothing to do with any of this."

"Yes, sir." Fitzhenry headed for the door.

Sterling reached for the scrap of paper, but Angus snatched it up. Sterling held out his hand. "If the Inspector says so, you can accompany us. But you don't forget for a minute who's in command."

Sheepishly, Angus passed the map over. Sterling took one more look at it before folding it and putting it in his pocket.

"You'll need a warm jacket, change of clothes, extra socks, bedroll, and food for several days. Meet me at the Fort in one hour."

"Yes, sir."

"Donohue, if you insist on coming, you'll need supplies also. One hour or I'll leave without you. Mr. McAllen, the same. We'll start at the mouth of the Klondike and follow the river. I'm not rushing blind into the wilderness. If I can't find a trail to follow, we'll turn back. Is that understood?"

Chapter Twenty-One

Sheridan opened a can of potatoes and one of corn, and we ate them cold with corned beef fried in too much lard. I wasn't hungry, and my head spun if I turned it too abruptly, but I knew I should try to eat something. Sheridan munched happily and chatted about his plans for our future.

He eyed my unfinished plate. "Can't let food go to waste. I've only brought enough for the trip."

I passed the remains of my meal over, and he dug in with enthusiasm.

Before coming to the near-Arctic, if I'd thought about it at all, I would have assumed the sun hung high overhead all day. But it didn't, of course. It moved in a circle from east to west, from low on the horizon to a mid-point overhead and down again. Further north, they tell me, the sun does not set at all at this time of year. Here it dipped below the horizon for a short while and a trace of light shone below the horizon in the dead of night. You could tell the time of day in the Yukon by looking at the sun as well as any place else on earth. It wasn't much different from the north of Scotland where I'd been a child. I knew the movements of the sun at this latitude.

It was afternoon, I guessed. I didn't know how long I'd been unconscious, but hopefully no more than a few hours, so it should have still been Sunday. I'd fought with Sheridan outside the Savoy at midnight on Saturday. Perhaps twelve hours had passed since that unfortunate encounter. The river beside us wasn't very wide. Not the Yukon, certainly. I tried to envision Ray's map, which I'd seen in Skagway. The Klondike River came from the east and ended where it met the Yukon, but I had no way of knowing if it narrowed before that. I'd seen the map too long ago, and not paid much attention at any rate.

If I had the slightest idea where we were, I would bide my time and simply leave when the fool had his back turned.

Unfortunately, I did not have the slightest idea where we were.

I reluctantly came to the conclusion that for the time being I was better off with Mr. Sheridan than leaving him. As well as being lost, I was not sure of my physical state. If I fell, reinjured my head perhaps or twisted an ankle, I could lie alone in the bush until I starved to death.

Once he'd scraped both plates clean, Sheridan announced it was time to be on our way.

"I'm sorry, Fiona, but you'll have to walk. I don't have a saddle for the horse. I'd hoped the cart would get us further than it did. I saw a picture in a book of the way Indians travel and figured it might work if I added a wheel. Should of known that if the Indians were too backward to use a wheel, their darn cart would be useless."

I refrained from mentioning that perhaps Indians knew when and where to use this contraption and when not to. I hadn't seen them with anything of its like navigating the rough mountain passes.

"Never mind, we won't be travelling very fast, not over this ground. Pack up the dishes, will you, my dear."

I considered refusing. I wasn't his maid. But I bit my tongue. I'd pick my battles as and when I judged it would do me the most good.

He untied the horse and led the reluctant beast over to the saddle bags. I tossed the frying pan and coffee pot into a pack and Sheridan loaded up the horse.

It was a pathetically small amount of equipment for two people in the wilderness. No doubt the horse was delighted, but I was not.

"I will need," I said in a tone as though I were the Queen's secretary discussing a pending visit to some luckless earls' country estate, "a change of clothing and sufficient toiletries for the journey."

"Well there, Fiona," he said, giving the straps under the horse's belly a good tug, "if you'd been ready for me this morning like I suggested, you'd have brought what you needed, now wouldn't you?"

Couldn't argue with that.

Perhaps I should have met Sheridan at my lodgings on Sunday morning after all. With two steamer trunks full of dresses, shoes, corsets, undergarments, nightgowns, coats, toiletries, reading material, a jewellery box, tea set, travelling writing-table, sheets, cushions, pillows, a full length mirror, hat boxes. Not to mention Angus's belongings. Surely then the man would have left us behind.

I'd made a series of serious errors in this matter. I've always found it so easy to convince men they should do things the way I wanted while leaving them to believe it was their idea all along. Was I getting soft, losing some of my skill at manipulation? Was that a natural result of having a son who seemed totally impervious to any suggestions I might make?

"May I at least have my shoes back?" I asked.

He pulled my footwear out of the pack and tossed them to me.

The heels were about two inches high, there were no straps, buttons or buckles. A dainty green bow decorated the instep.

Perfectly suitable should we happen across a lady's croquet party taking a break for tea. Otherwise, scarcely much better than going barefoot.

Nevertheless, I put them on.

"Be sure and extinguish the fire," I said. "You don't want to set the woods ablaze."

He kicked a bit of dirt into the circle of rocks, and so we set off. One scraggly horse, one determined American, one most reluctant daintily-shod and evening-gowned Scotswoman. Sheridan talked as we walked, encouraging both the horse and me. The horse was not much happier about this expedition than I. Sheridan went first, leading the beast, and I trotted along behind as we followed the path of the river. The riverbank was rocky, steep in places. Thick clumps of red willow, dwarf willow, and Labrador tea grew right down to the water.

I'd decided my best option would be to slow us down so that searchers could catch up to us, in the event someone — anyone — was coming after me. However, subterfuge on my part was scarcely necessary. I estimated we were moving at the speed of a particularly indolent snail. At this rate, Angus would be a grandfather by the time we reached our destination. There was no trail. We rounded aspen and birch trees, clusters of poplar saplings, and more clumps of dwarf willow. We climbed boulders, fought for footing amongst loose dirt, stones, and fallen branches. We slipped on tussocks and hummocks, and our feet sunk into spots of rich loamy soil. Attempting to clamber over a boulder rather than go around, I lost my footing and plunged ankle-deep into the water. It was freezing cold and I yelped. Sheridan gave me a poisonous look. The horse snatched at sedge growing on a tussock and ripped off a mouthful.

I sat down on the rock. It was damp and cold. "Mr. Sheridan, I can go no further. This whole expedition is a total waste of time and effort. We will only get lost and blunder about in the wilderness until we starve or break a leg."

"The going gets easier up ahead a bit."

"Don't be ridiculous, you fool. You've never been here. You have no idea what's up ahead." Suddenly I was furious. Too angry to attempt to be charming and subtly persuasive. I was nothing but tired and sore and, to be honest, getting very frightened.

We were heading into nothing, being led by a madman.

"I don't like being called a fool," he said.

"Then don't act like one."

He walked over to the horse, and for one brief moment my heart lifted and I thought he was going to turn us around. Instead, he plunged his hand into a saddlebag and came out with a knife. He faced me, the knife held up in front of him. It wasn't a particularly big knife, nor was it a very sharp one.

But it was big enough. Sharp enough.

"I am going to Gold Mountain, Fiona. Now, you can come with me and stop your goddamned complaining. Or you can stay here. With this knife buried in your belly. Which will it be?"

I hesitated. I doubted that Sheridan would kill me.

Could I take that chance? If I ran for it, he'd catch me with no trouble at all. He eyes were very dark and tight lines radiated out from his mouth. An angry man could do a lot of damage he'd later come to regret.

I got slowly to my feet. "Very well," I said. "Provided you put that knife away." He ran one finger slowly up the flat of the blade, his eyes fixed on my face. Then he grinned and shoved it back into the pack. "You might be tired now, Fiona, but you'll thank me for my perseverance one day." He waved his arm gesturing for me to proceed. "Ladies first. You should be able to stick to the riverbank for a bit."

I passed him and the horse. I'd keep walking until I could find a chance to escape safely. But I most certainly would not stop complaining.

We didn't stop to eat or to rest. When I complained that I was hungry and thirsty, Sheridan said I should have eaten when I had the chance, and paused only long enough to hand me a container of water. It was very hot and the sky was clear. At least the mosquitoes were taking a nap.

In his enthusiasm, Sheridan, leading the horse, had passed me on a straight stretch. Unfortunately, he kept looking over his shoulder to tell me to hurry up, and I had no opportunity to slip quietly away.

Several hours passed in this manner before Sheridan stopped so abruptly the horse crashed into him, and I into the horse. The river had dwindled to a creek, and the creek was dwindling into a stream. We'd reached a point at which the edges of the watercourse were largely dry while a trickle of water drifted down the middle. Sheridan clambered down the steep bank and beast and woman followed. The river bottom was very soft, but in most places the ground had dried and wasn't too muddy. We didn't have bush to push through and made much better time from then on.

We travelled until well into the evening. Mosquitoes gathered in clouds, delighted at the convenient arrival of dinner. My feet were dragging, my arm was mechanically sweeping the black ostrich feather on my hat across my face to keep the bugs off. I was almost asleep on my feet, but Sheridan moved steadily, his steps strong and determined, head down. Every once in a while, he'd pull out his map and consult it without breaking stride. The man must be exhausted. He wouldn't have slept last night, busy as he'd been kidnapping me and dragging my unconscious body out of town.

Ambition and determination had taken control of him.

At last Sheridan stopped once again. He pulled out his map and studied it while I sunk gratefully onto the soft river bank. A new group of mosquitoes instantly descended. The horse munched at grasses beside me and flicked his tail. I pulled off my shoes and studied my left foot. A blister was forming on the back of my heel and another on the little toe. At the moment, they were only an irritation. Tomorrow, walking would be very painful indeed. I could not walk on rocks and pine needles barefoot.

"We'll stop here for the night," he said.

I looked around. "Stop where?"

"Here. There's a patch of clear ground over there where we can put the tent."

"This is a watercourse. We can't sleep on a riverbed, you fool."

He blinked. A mosquito settled on his cheek but he didn't brush it away. "Why not?"

"In case it rains in the night and all that rainwater decides to come this way."

He glanced at the sky. "Doesn't look like rain."

I rolled my eyes. "Do as you will, but my tent will be set up there, on the bank under that tree."

The expression on his face indicated that he might argue, but then the stubborn set to his shoulders fell and he said, "I knew you were the woman for me, Fiona. You're quite right. Don't ever be afraid to contradict me. I want our marriage to be a true partnership."

I refrained from making a comment.

Chapter Twenty-Two

Richard Sterling followed the excited barking of dogs as he crossed the parade ground of NWMP Fort Herchmer. The Union Jack in the centre of the square snapped briskly in the strong north wind. Men stopped what they were doing to watch him. News had travelled fast, as it always did in the Yukon. Fiona MacGillivray was a well-known woman. She was generally liked, although she did have enemies. Ironically, it seemed as if she was in this mess because of someone who wanted to be her friend, not an adversary.

Sterling glanced up at the sky. The wind was strong but the clouds were not heavy and he didn't smell rain on the air. Rain now would be a disaster, destroying his best hope of finding a trail to follow. He'd met Paul Sheridan once. His impression had been of a city fellow, small-time crook, and gang-member. Not someone used to the wilderness or to physically covering his tracks. He hadn't even come over the Chilkoot, but by boat from St. Michael. And Fiona? She'd travelled the Chilkoot trail, up the Golden Stairs, on a makeshift boat down the Yukon, but by Angus's account she hadn't even been able to prepare their meals. Nevertheless, she was a highly resourceful woman and Sterling expected — hoped — she'd have enough of her wits around her to leave signs of their passage.

If she were still alive. No one had dared mention, in the crowded back room of the Savoy, that she might not have survived Sheridan's attack.

Richard Sterling pushed the thought aside. She was alive and he would find her.

He pushed open the door to the NWMP kennels, and the animals set up a round of joyous barking. The dog-keeper was leading a large white dog out of its cage. "Here she is," he said, "I figured you'd want Mrs. Miller again."

Sterling shook his head. News travelled faster by mouth in the Yukon than it did by telephone in the cities.

The long-haired dog wagged her tongue and wiggled her bottom. Sterling crouched down. "You're right there," he said to the man. "Best pack dog in the Territory." He gave Mrs. Miller a scratch between her ears and then ran his hands over her body, particularly down her legs.

"She's in good shape. I'd know otherwise."

"Just checking." Her name was Mrs. Miller, after the prune-faced wife of an inspector in the NWMP. Mrs. Miller, the canine one, at seven years old was no longer young, but she was clever and could cheerfully walk a long way bearing a heavy pack. "Good old Millie," Sterling said. The man took saddle bags down from a row of hooks on the wall and tossed them over the dog's back. He handed Sterling a small canvas bag containing strips of dried fish, her food.

"Thanks." Sterling took the offered lead and left. Mrs. Miller trotted happily behind.

At least she, Sterling thought, *is looking forward to the journey.*

"Good luck," the dog handler called out.

Next stop was the kitchens, where he asked the cooks to pack him five days' worth of food. He would take supplies only for himself and McAllen. The civilians would have to bring their own. Next stop was the barracks. He tied the dog to a railing and went inside to pull his bed roll off his bunk and dig spare clothes out of his trunk. The non-commissioned officers' barracks were empty and he was glad of it. He didn't want to waste time while advice and useless good wishes were offered.

Back outside he untied the dog. About forty-five minutes had passed since he'd left the Savoy. No sign of Donohue or Angus yet. Angus, he didn't mind taking. The boy was smart and quick although somewhat impulsive. Donohue on the other hand. What did he have to offer? If he wasn't coming along to write it up for his newspaper, then it was to get into Fiona's favour. Sterling didn't realize he'd growled until he saw the questioning look on Millie's face.

McKnight stood behind his desk, the surface almost invisible under mounds of papers and books, when Sterling knocked and walked in. The office was a mess of papers, winter clothes, spare boots, and wood — chopped, stacked, ready for the stove. A Winchester rifle rested on the table next to the bookcase.

"Let's have a look at young Angus's sketch again, shall we." McKnight took the map off the wall and spread it across his desk, the papers underneath creating mountains and valleys. It was an up-to-date map of the Yukon mining district. Unfortunately, everything north of the Klondike River was marked "unexplored." Sterling unfolded his own map. The two men studied them.

"This line here," McKnight said, "might be this river. I can barely make out the name. What's it say?"

"Thomas Creek."

"Is it this blue line on Sheridan's map, do you think?"

"I think, sir," Sterling said, "it's irrelevant if it is or not. Chances are good Sheridan expects to come across a river feeding into the Klondike from the north, so he'll take the first one he comes across that white people haven't reached yet. If the Gold Commissioner doesn't know what's there, then no one else does. Except the Indians and they don't need to make maps. Least not ones we can read."

McKnight peered myopically though a thick layer of glass. The man must be as blind as a bat, Sterling thought, without his spectacles. The inspector stroked his moustache. "You're in the boss's favour at the moment, Sterling. But favours come and go. You want to take care you don't get ahead of yourself. And get busted down. Again."

Sterling felt his gut tighten. "I'll remember your advice. Sir."

"See that you do. Now, I'm sending you on this excursion, better to say I'm letting you go, because the NWMP has to be seen to be doing something to affect the return of one of the town's most prominent citizens. Do you expect, honestly, to accomplish anything? Why not just wait until Sheridan sheepishly returns to town?"

"In many cases, I'd agree with you," Sterling said, trying to sound reasonable. It was no secret he and McKnight didn't get on: they'd butted heads too many times. "But I sense a madness in the man. To attack Mrs. MacGillivray, provided that's what happened, and carry her off." He shook his head. "She's not a, shall we say, compliant woman."

"No."

"My fear, if I may say so sir, is that they'll get lost. Unlikely Sheridan has much, if any, experience surviving in the wilderness and Mrs. MacGillivray ..."

"Is a lady, of course. Completely out of her depth."

"If they get lost, they might not be able to find their way to town or to the Creeks if even the man decides to turn back." Sterling thought of the Yukon as it had been before the rush. As most of it still was. A vast space teeming with life, if you knew how to look for it. To city eyes it seemed as empty and inhospitable as a desert. "The Indians around here are not aggressive. If they come across any lost people, they'll be more than happy to bring them to us expecting a reward. But Sheridan might not know that. He's an American and they've been fighting Indians down there until not so long ago. He'll try to avoid them."

"Do you honestly think you can find them?"

"I have some skill in the bush, yes. If they make it as far as the tundra? I've never been there, but tracking is tracking."

"You can tell me some day where you got this skill. But for now ..." McKnight stopped at a knock on the door, shouted, "Enter," and Constable Fitzhenry came in. He gasped for breath, his face was flushed, and Sterling knew the man had news before he even opened his mouth. "Sheridan left his lodgings Saturday night. Cleared out all his things and told the landlady he'd not be back. He'd originally taken the room until Thursday, then changed it to Sunday and left on Saturday."

He paused to take a breath and McKnight asked, "Did he say anything about where he was going?"

"No, but he kept hinting he'd be back some day, rich as a king of the Orient, he said. She paid him no mind. They all say that, don't they?"

Sterling and McKnight nodded in unison. Fitzhenry continued, "She told me something interesting. Sheridan bought a horse last week. The landlady said it was a miserable creature. And then," he paused for effect, "he made a wagon."

"A wagon?"

"More of a cart, she said. With one big wheel at the back and two poles about six feet long at the front, and a leather harness of some sort."

"Like a travois?" Sterling asked.

"What's that?"

"The Plains Indians use a travois. Fastened to the back of a horse or dog, it pulls a load. Like a wagon without wheels." Being a white man, Sheridan probably thought he was improving on the native design by adding a wheel. Not realizing that a wheel was a liability, not an advantage, where there were no roads. Even the best designed travois was not meant to penetrate bush or manoeuvre over hills and gullies.

"I don't suppose anyone saw this horse and travois in town on Sunday?" McKnight asked.

Fitzhenry shook his head. "I don't know, sir. Shall we ask around?"

"What an excellent idea, considering we are attempting to locate the person who made this vehicle," McKnight snapped.

Fitzhenry flushed. McKnight waved his hand and the young constable fled.

"I like the sound of that," Sterling said. "A horse and a wheeled contraption will leave a clear trail."

"Better get on with it then," McKnight said. "You're to take that." He gestured to the rifle. It was a Winchester Carbine, polished to a high shine, a box of cartridges beside it. Sterling raised one eyebrow. "Let's hope you don't have to use it. At best it might provide some food if you're out longer than expected."

Sterling picked the weapon up. He balanced the weight in his hands, laid it against his cheek, and stared down the barrel. He looked at McKnight, nodded, and headed for the door. The inspector's voice stopped him and he turned back. McKnight coughed. Sterling waited. McKnight cleared his throat and said, "Good luck, Corporal. Take as much time as you need."

"Thank you, sir."

Donohue and Angus were seated on the steps beside the dog. McAllen leaned against a post, but he snapped to attention when Sterling came out of the office.

Mouse O'Brien was with them, pack on his shoulders.

Sterling groaned.

Angus let out a low whistle when he saw the rifle.

"Mouse, what are you doing here?" Sterling said, fearing he knew the answer.

"I heard the news, figured you needed some help."

"I don't need any more help and I'm not leading any more city folks into the wilderness."

"Sure you do," Mouse said. "You got a lot of stuff for that one little dog to carry."

"Thought you'd want to spend the time with your new bride. And aren't you going back to the Creeks tomorrow?"

"Mrs. O'Brien." Mouse tasted the words on his tongue. "Insisted that I come. A man's first duty, after his country and his family, is to his friends, she said."

Sterling did not want to argue any more. Best get moving before anyone else came to join them. Next it would be Mrs. Saunderson and the dancers.

He eyed the packs at the men's feet.

"It's grand that you've got Millie," Angus said, rubbing the big dog's head. "She'll find Ma, won't you girl?"

Millie barked her agreement.

"The dog is the property of the NWMP and will carry McAllen's and my supplies," Sterling said. "Donohue, O'Brien, you and Angus are to carry your own. Do you understand?"

Donohue said, "Yup," and Angus nodded enthusiastically.

"That's why I've come," O'Brien said. "I can take some of Angus's things."

"You all brought food? Enough for five days at least?"

"Yes."

"That should do. If we need more, hopefully we'll come across some game." He stroked the rifle butt, then reached into his jacket and pulled out the map. "Angus, you're in charge of this."

"Thank you, sir."

McAllen had stopped at the kitchen to pick up the provisions and cooking supplies. They packed the dog's saddle bags as best they could with food, pans, a coffee pot, and a tiny travelling stove. Sterling would carry his bedroll and spare clothes. And the rifle.

Donohue rechecked the contents of his own pack.

"If we're ready, let's go," Sterling said. "Angus, you can walk with Millie."

"Okay," Angus said, taking the dog's lead. "I've been thinking about this Gold Mountain. You don't suppose there's actually something to it, do you, sir?"

"No, Angus, I do not. There's enough strange and wonderful things in this world without making up stories. I suppose there might be a gold deposit, after all there's gold around here, isn't there? But if there is, it's highly unlikely to be marked on a map Paul Sheridan picked up in his travels."

Sterling led his small party across the parade square. Mounties and civilians came out of the barracks and offices to watch them pass.

Chapter Twenty-Three

Sheridan unloaded the horse and secured it with a long rope to a black spruce at the edge of the clearing, whereupon it immediately began munching on the soft buds of a nearby willow. The buds snapped easily off the tree, and the horse seemed content. Sheridan rummaged around in the bags, eventually emerging with a tent, bedroll, and blankets. But first he took the knife out of the pack and stuck it into his belt. He then pulled an axe out of another pack and chopped down two small poplars to serve as tent poles. I watched suspiciously as he struggled to erect the tent. It looked quite small.

Supper was, once again, fried corned beef. This time served with a can of pears for dessert. The pots and plates and cutlery hadn't been washed from our earlier repast, so I ventured to the middle of the trickle of water and gave them a rinse.

As soon as we'd finished the totally inadequate meal, Sheridan announced it was time to sleep.

He read my mind and said that, as he feared he didn't yet have my complete trust, I'd have to be secured while he slept. Once again, I considered resisting and bolting for it, but that would probably lead to a scuffle with Sheridan that might further damage my head or perhaps get me knifed. I'd thought about making a grab for the rifle, but considering that I didn't know how to use the thing, he'd be on me before I could figure it out.

My head had felt almost normal most of the day, and the lancing pain had settled into a dull ache. My vision had cleared once I'd had something to eat, but nevertheless if I did manage to get away, I was not happy at the prospect of wandering through the bush alone and disoriented.

With a considerable degree of ill-grace, I lay down in the tent and allowed the man to tie my arms in front of me. He apologized constantly, kept checking that the bounds weren't too tight, and asked if I was comfortable.

Finally, he settled down and closed his eyes, and fortunately he kept his distance, what little distance there was in the hot, stuffy tent, smelling of mould and unwashed men. He'd taken the rifle to bed with him. It was tucked inside his bedroll, close to the far tent wall, his arms wrapped around it. He'd returned the knife to the smallest pack, which he tucked under his head for a pillow.

He fell asleep almost instantly. The man had a snore that would wake a hibernating bear.

I was hideously uncomfortable. The tent had no floor, and small pebbles and scratchy pine needles poked through the single inadequate blanket wrapped around me. I was very cold.

It was getting light when I awoke. Yesterday, using what miniscule bit of geographic knowledge I did have, I determined we were travelling almost due north by watching the path of the sun as the day progressed.

That was not good. North meant farther and farther away from civilization.

I'd kicked most of the blanket off in my sleep. The rope Sheridan had used to bind me was so long, I'd been able to get moderately comfortable, as comfortable as one can be sleeping on rough ground while tied up. I'd slept in worse conditions, but I'd been considerably younger.

When Paul Sheridan awoke, I was attempting to stir the embers of the campfire back to life. He crawled out of the tent, blinking and scratching at the cluster of mosquito bites on his face. "What the...?"

"Most uncomfortable," I said. Thinking perhaps that I'd simply lie where told to, and not wanting to tie me too tightly, he'd left the rope so loose I had no trouble at all unpicking the fat knots.

"You stayed," he said, as comprehension dawned. Followed closely by sheer joy.

"So it would appear. I'm not eating any more of that dreadful beef. I found bacon and powdered eggs in the packs. We'll have that."

He dashed behind a bush to relieve himself. When he returned, I was pulling on a pair of thick men's socks with leather heels, which I'd also found among his possessions. Unfortunately, I had not found a revolver or a spare knife suitable for threatening to cut a man's throat. Judging by the trouble he'd had chopping down a tree about the width of my thumb, the axe would make a most inefficient weapon.

"What are you doing?" he said.

"I won't be able to walk in my shoes any farther." I wasn't lying about that. My left foot in particular had a couple of very bad blisters. They were plump and oozing blood. Blood caked the inside of my shoe.

"I'm starving," he said.

We ate a quick breakfast of burned bacon, runny tasteless eggs, and coffee so thick and vile I considered spreading it on the blisters on my feet. I have never claimed to be able to cook.

Chapter Twenty-Four

Sterling and his group passed through the eastern end of town to the Klondike River, where they turned to follow the river upstream. No point in looking for tracks with all the horse, dog, cart, wagon, and foot traffic around here. A patch of flatland dotted with white canvas spread open beneath the steep hills of the river bank. Children and dogs ran between the tents, and adults relaxed in the sunshine, visiting neighbours and enjoying a day of rest. They all stopped what they were doing to watch the search party pass.

"Afternoon," Richard Sterling said to a cluster of men sitting on recently felled logs and puffing on pipes.

"Afternoon, Corporal." The eldest man had a pure white beard and a mane of hair. His eyebrows were grey and so long they stood up as if waxed. "Young Angus. Off after Mrs. MacGillivray are you?"

"Word travels fast," Sterling said. Millie plunked her bottom in the only patch of soft grass for miles.

"That it does. Johnny here was tellin' us something earlier you might want ta hear." He nodded to the youngest of the men, who, full of self-importance, rose to his feet and stood perfectly straight as though called upon at school to recite the alphabet.

"My wife, she don't sleep too good." Colour flooded into his face. "She's expecting any day now and can't get comfortable.

So I was out having a smoke, see. And I seen the strangest thing coming down the path."

"What time was this?"

The young man shrugged. "After midnight sometime. Before sun-up."

"Carry on."

"Man with a horse pulling a funny kinda cart. Sort of a half-cart with only one wheel at the back and long poles tying the cart to the horse."

Sterling's heart began to beat faster. He kept his face impassive.

"Was a woman with him?" Angus shouted. "Was my ma with him?"

"Be quiet, boy," Sterling said. "I'll ask the questions."

"But ..."

"I said be quiet. You want to go back to town, say so now."

"No, sir." Angus's face fell into a pout.

"Tell you the truth." The man paused, looking at the men around him, drawing out the story, enjoying his moment in the limelight. Sterling gave him a look. "Yes, there was a woman." He held up one hand, "I didn't see her face. She was lying in the cart. With a blanket over her. Only knew it was a woman 'cause she was wearing a dress and had pretty little feet."

"Describe the dress," Donohue shouted. "Was it green?"

Sterling feared he'd made a mistake allowing a bunch of civilians to tag along.

"Green, yeah. Pretty green, sorta like ..." the young man looked around, searching for something green with which to compare. Here, in what a year ago had been the Yukon wilderness, he couldn't find anything the right colour. "Green," he said at last.

Angus couldn't restrain himself. "It must be my mother. We're wasting time." He jerked Millie's lead and started to move off. Donohue followed.

Sterling let them go. "This woman. Was she ... awake?"

The man shrugged. "Can't say. She weren't moving, not that I saw. I figured she was a drunken whore being carted off by her pimp or a customer. None o' my business. Sorry, Corporal."

Sterling and Mouse O'Brien exchanged glances. No need to say that Sheridan might have been taking a dead Fiona as well as a live one out of town.

"Can you describe the man?"

"He was walking beside the horse, leading it. Tall, taller than the horse's head but right skinny, just a bag of bones. He didn't say nothing to me, and I didn't say nothing to him. Like I said, none of my business what a man's doing with a drunken whore. Might even o' been his wife, all I knew."

"Thanks," Sterling said. "Any one got anything to add?" The men shook their heads.

"Hope you find 'er, Corporal," the bearded one said.

Sterling did not reply. Angus and Donohue were up ahead, moving fast, as if they expected to come across Fiona around the next bend.

Well beyond the tents and cabins that made up the town of Dawson, the forest had been stripped of lumber for building, but eventually all signs of humanity faded away and the wilderness returned. Aspen and birch, pine and poplar closed in around them; the underbrush was thick, and the forest floor covered with leaves, branches, and twigs. Traces of woodsmoke from town faded, to be replaced by the scent of mulch and rotting humus. Birds flew overhead or called from the tops of trees, small animals rustled in the undergrowth, and Millie's ears lifted for no reason the men could discern.

Sterling moved slowly, eyes fixed on the ground. He'd ordered the others to stay behind him, particularly an impatient Angus and eager Millie. They were on the north bank of the river. The path to the gold fields was south; no one had reason to come this way.

Before long, he found what he'd scarcely dared hope he'd find: hoof prints. Boot marks were beside them, and the jagged line of a wheel being dragged across rough ground. The weather was on his side. It had rained a couple of days ago, sufficient to make the ground soft enough to take prints, not too muddy to make the going difficult. Nevertheless, the trail was hard to follow, crossing rocks, stepping into the river, rounding trees, circling back on itself.

Sheridan would have a minimum of twelve hours on them, more if he'd left town immediately. Which was probably the case. The longer he kept Fiona subdued, the more likely someone would come across them or she'd kick up a fuss that could not be ignored.

Say they'd left shortly after midnight when Walker and Betsy had seen her last. It had been close to four in the afternoon before Sterling and his party followed. He should be able to move faster on foot than Sheridan, with horse and cart and reluctant woman. But Sheridan presumably knew where he was going, whereas Sterling had to search for tracks. If he hurried, as Angus kept insisting, and lost the trail, he'd waste a lot of time getting back to it.

He was positive now that Fiona was alive. If Sheridan had killed her and was taking the body out of town to dispose of it in the wilderness, he would have done so by now. But the weight of the cart seemed to remain the same, and they had not come across any signs of the ground being disturbed or the cart unloaded.

They were heading east, following the north bank of the Klondike River. The going wasn't easy: no one came this way. A bit of a deer track cut through the bush, which no doubt Indians also used. Wisely, Sheridan had stuck to that. Get turned around in the deep bush and a man might never find his way out again. According to the map as Angus remembered it, Sheridan would be heading north soon.

Sterling heard it before he saw it: water rushing over boulders in a hurry to meet up with the larger river. Another few steps and they came across a small river coming south, spilling into the Klondike.

"That's odd." He thought back to the big map in McKnight's office. It showed Thomas Creek, a small river not far out of town, which they'd crossed some time ago, and then Twelve Mile Creek, which should be a good bit further east.

"Let's have another look at that map," Sterling said to Angus. The boy came over and unfolded it. Everyone, including Millie, gathered around. "This is the river," Sterling moved his finger down what they'd assumed to be the Klondike. "And right here," he tapped on a small blue line, "seems to be this creek. But it isn't on the gold commissioner's map. I'd assumed Sheridan's map was nothing put a mess of squiggles. Maybe there's something to it after all."

"You mean there really is a gold mountain?" Donohue said.

"I mean nothing of the sort. It's possible whoever drew this map was here at one time. Trappers and prospectors have been in the wilds for twenty, thirty years or more. Just seems odd that the official map doesn't show this river. Wait here. I'm going to have a look up ahead."

Angus looped Millie's lead around a dwarf willow, Mouse O'Brien pulled out his pipe, and Graham Donohue collapsed to the ground with a groan.

Sterling placed every foot with care. The banks of the river were not steep here, and the rough trail came close to the water. The cart tracks entered the water and disappeared. Sterling cursed. He walked along the bank, eyes on the ground. If he couldn't find where they came out, he'd have to decide which way to go. Carry on following the Klondike, or turn and go north beside the unnamed river. It would have to be north: Sheridan would be following his map. He found no sign of anyone's passage for about a hundred feet. Then Sterling spotted a branch snapped off a young poplar. It was a fresh break, the exposed wood clean and white. Beneath the tree, the earth was churned up, doubtlessly by feet scrambling for purchase. Another few steps and he found the print of a shod horse. Sterling let out a breath and turned to shout at his followers. "I've got it. This way." He didn't wait for them to catch up. Better if one by one they gave up and returned to town.

He heard running feet and the sound of Millie panting. "Did they teach you to track in the Mounties, sir?" Angus said. "Will you teach me?"

"No, and perhaps. When I was a boy we lived in the Carrot River Valley in Saskatchewan. Not many white families around, so my friends were mostly Cree. They taught me a lot — to hunt, to track game." He was quiet for a long time. He did not say, "To be a man."

"That must have been grand, sir," Angus said.

"It was. When I was young." In his mind's eye he saw a flash of long shiny black hair, liquid eyes, white teeth, and golden skin. Her name was Many Birds, and he had not thought of her for a very long time. Richard Sterling shook his head and noticed a scrap of grey wool caught on the branch of a black spruce, at about the height of a horse's back. He lifted it gently away from the tree and showed it to the others without a word. From a blanket, probably. It was reasonably clean and dry. It hadn't been there for long.

The shadows were getting long, and it would soon be necessary to stop. No point trying to track a man in the near-dark.

Lose the trail, and he could waste precious hours trying to find it again.

They were tired now, not talking much, stumbling on the rough ground. Once they'd left the noise of the bigger river behind them, Sterling had become aware of another sound. A sound that didn't belong here.

"McAllen," he said, not breaking stride or lifting his eyes from the ground. The young constable trotted up.

"Someone's following us."

McAllen's head whipped around. "I don't see anyone."

"Nevertheless, they're there. When we round that bend up ahead I want you to duck into the woods. Wait and see who it is. If it's an Indian party, leave them alone and catch us up. If it's someone from town, who has no reason to be here, shout out for me."

Sterling kept walking, slowing his pace. O'Brien, Donohue, and Angus caught up before he reached the curve of the river. They rounded the bend and McAllen slipped behind a tree. Sterling hissed at the others to keep moving.

Two minutes passed, and then he heard McAllen shout, "Stop. You're all under arrest."

Sterling ran back. Voices rose in argument.

"We're not doing anything wrong. Just out for a walk." Joe Hamilton had his hands in the air. Two men who'd been in the Savoy in the morning were with him. They carried thin packs on their backs and gripped stout walking sticks.

"What the hell are you lot doing here?" Sterling growled.

"Nothing," Hamilton said. He looked at his companions. "Right boys?" The man's mouth was a mess of broken and rotted teeth and it stunk to high heaven.

"Figured you'd need some help rescuing Mrs. Fiona," one of Hamilton's companions said. His hat was worn and dusty, most of the buttons were torn off his jacket, and Sterling could see bare flesh through the thin fabric in the knees of the man's trousers.

"Well, I don't. Go back to town."

"Don't know the way."

"Follow the river."

"You can't stop us from going where we want, Sterling," the third man said. He glared at the Mountie. Hamilton's face was as guilty as a schoolboy caught laughing in church, the second man was embarrassed at being caught, but this one was defiant. Joe Hamilton might think he was dashing to Fiona's rescue. His companions were hoping to get to Gold Mountain first.

"Actually," Sterling said, "I can. You're interfering with a servant of Her Majesty in the performance of his duties."

"We didn't mean any harm, Mr. Sterling. We'd like to help, that's all," Hamilton said, with an attempt at a smile.

"Go ahead," the other man said, "arrest us." He looked around. "Don't see no jail. Guess we'll all have to troop back to town together. Leaving poor Mrs. Fiona in the hands of that villain."

"Look here, Ralph Green," Mouse O'Brien said, "I'm not having any of your nonsense." The big man stepped forward, hands clenched. He loomed over Green, whose cockiness suddenly deserted him. "I'll take you back to town myself, if I have to. And," he added, "you won't be walking." Mouse lunged forward with a growl. Green jumped back.

Mouse dug in his pocket and pulled out a drawstring bag. "Here," he said. "Go to the Savoy tomorrow and report to Walker that we've found her trail. Have a drink on me while you're there." He handed a gold nugget to Joe Hamilton and a smaller one to the second man. He looked at Green. "You going with them, Ralph?"

"Guess so." Green held out his hand. Mouse dumped a nugget into it. Green looked at the gold, and then stared pointedly back at Mouse. He kept his hand outstretched. Mouse put the bag away. He sighed heavily and started taking off his jacket. "If that's what you want."

"Okay, okay. We're going." Without another word Green headed back the way they'd come.

"Thanks, Mouse." Hamilton touched the brim of his cap. The second man grunted.

When the three men had disappeared around the bend, Sterling said, "The NWMP doesn't bribe men to obey the law. But thanks anyway."

"Joe Hamilton means no trouble. Everyone in town knows he worships Mrs. MacGillivray. But that Ralph Green. If he cares about rescuing your ma, Angus, then I'm your Aunt Fanny."

"If word of that map gets around town," Sterling said, "we'll have most of the men in the Territory coming after us. McAllen."

"Corporal?"

"From now on bring up the rear. Stay a good bit behind and keep your ears open. You find anyone else following us, stop them."

"Right."

"We can't go much farther today anyway. Light's getting bad."

"We can't stop," Angus said. "Not if my ma isn't stopping."

"If I lose the trail, it won't be any help to her. We're tired and hungry. Men make mistakes, bad mistakes, when they're tired. This spot looks as good as any. We'll make camp for a couple of hours."

Angus stamped his foot and looked as if he were about to argue. Fiona was dark-haired and dark-complexioned, and her black eyes flashed fire when she was angry. Angus was blond and very fair, but his blue eyes had the same intensity and determination.

"Collect firewood," Sterling said, not giving the boy a chance to continue the argument. "Feed Millie and let her drink. That sky looks clear, so I don't think we need worry about putting up the tent tonight. Mouse, collect what food we have and get the fire going and make supper for us all. Donohue, gather some spruce bows to provide us with a mattress."

"I'd suggest ..."

"I don't care what you suggest. Mind you, don't wander too far away. Get yourself lost and I'm not wasting time searching for you. In case anyone else from town has a mind to follow us, we'll take shifts sitting guard. While you're setting up camp, I'm going up ahead to scout around."

And he left before anyone could think of another thing to argue about. Damn nuisance bringing a bunch of civilians into the wilds. Have to argue about everything.

Chapter Twenty-Five

Ray Walker had never been a lucky man. Born in the slums surrounding the great Glasgow shipyards, where luck was in exceedingly short supply, he'd been raised to use his fists almost from the cradle. His father was a good man but none too bright, out of work more often than not, usually because he didn't always remember to do what he'd been told. Ray's mother worked long hours at the fish canning plant and then hurried home to take care of her family. She gave birth to twelve children in twenty years but only three of them survived. Ray and his two wee sisters.

Ray Walker began working on the docks when he was twelve years old, handing over what money he earned to his mother to pay the rent on their stinking tenement flat and buy food for the younger children.

When Ray was fifteen his father died, coughing up blood until there was so much he drowned in it. Ray stayed at home until his youngest sister was safely wed and then left. He sent part of his wages to his mother, visited his sisters and their wee ones on a Sunday, but otherwise could pretty much be counted on to get in a fight on a Saturday night and drink up what remained of his pay packet.

One night, not long after his mother died, finally crushed by life, Ray was with a woman — a cheap slag who prowled the shipyards — in the filthy flat she worked out of. She said something that offended him, he never remembered what, and he beat her until she passed out.

He quit his job the next day, said goodbye to his sisters, and left Glasgow. Not because he was afraid of the police, no one cared about a slag getting herself smacked around, but because he realized he was on a very dangerous path indeed.

He went to London, worked at odd jobs, mostly stayed away from the pubs and the prostitutes, and saved his wages until he could buy passage to the New World. He wanted to go to America, but as it happened, when at last he went to purchase his ticket, the next ship out was bound for Halifax.

Life was still hard, but he never thought it any harder than that of most of the poor people he came across as he made his way across the continent.

He used the last of the money he'd made working on the Vancouver docks to buy supplies and passage to the Klondike.

He got off the boat in Skagway in August of 1897.

And had his first bit of luck in all of his forty years.

He met Fiona MacGillivray.

She'd been like a dream, Fiona. Not because she was beautiful and proper and charming, but because she was as smart and cunning and unscrupulous as ever a man Ray had known.

She reminded him in some ways of his mother. Or perhaps what his mother might have been able to be if she hadn't wed at fourteen and given birth to twelve children by the time she was thirty-five.

He'd never felt anything sexual toward Fiona. He could rub her feet when they ached at the end of a long day, or watch her arranging her hair in front of the cracked mirror in her office, and find no strain in his trousers or shortage of breath.

She was, quite simply, the best thing that had ever happened to him. She was as tough as they came, tougher than most, and a true Scotswoman, holding loyalty to family and clan above all. And he, Ray Walker, was part of her new-world clan. He trusted her completely, but nevertheless he checked the ledger every week and popped into the bank on occasion to ensure the business accounts were as they should be. They ran a hugely successful business, and Ray Walker had no worries about the future. He'd stay in the Klondike as long as there were miners to be mined and salt away most of his share of the profits in anticipation of the day the gold rush ended.

And then there was Irene Davidson. Not beautiful, like Fiona, but also a woman with a determination to make a success of the part she'd been given in life. He might even think of proposing to Irene one day.

Today he wasn't feeling so confident about his future. Fiona wasn't here and he wasn't sure how long he could manage the business without her. He tried to cheer himself up by remembering that if anyone could find her and bring her back it would be Richard Sterling. To Ray Walker, it was as obvious as the pack of men shoving themselves toward the bar that Sterling was in love with Fiona. About the only thing clearer was that she was in love with the Mountie. Too bad neither of them were prepared to admit it. To themselves or to each other. Yet.

The Savoy was packed early on Monday morning. The front room full to the point of bursting at the seams. Men lined up at the bar, three deep, elbow to elbow.

Fiona had once remarked that nothing seemed to abate the flood of drinkers and gamblers pouring through their doors, and once news of the kidnapping of Mrs. MacGillivray and the hunt for a mountain of gold had spread through town, everyone gathered, wanting to be part of the excitement.

There must have been a hundred men lined up at the door at ten o'clock, when Ray opened up. All the talk was of a tropical valley full of gold no more than a few days' hike away. Ray'd been there when Inspector McKnight said he'd give a blue ticket to anyone who whispered word of Sheridan's map. He should have known someone would tell. Lancaster perhaps, the doddering fool, or young Constable Fitzhenry trying to impress a dancehall girl. Before twenty-four hours had passed, half the town knew about it.

Men were bent over tables and the bar counter, sketching out copies of the map Angus had tried to reproduce. They got further and further from reality. Some had paths heading west to Alaska, some due north to the Arctic Sea, some back down the Chilkoot to just outside of Dyea.

Old Barney was regaling the crowd with stories of other great treasure hunts. He told a fresh-faced cheechako that, once his glass was refilled, he'd tell them about the crystal mountain he'd seen years ago, far in the distance. Pure glass it was, as clear and brilliant as a jewel around a lady's neck. The man ordered another whisky, and when his back was turned, Barney gave Ray Walker a cheeky wink.

"Bad business," Joe Hamilton said.

"Mounties have set out after her," Ray said. "They'll be back soon." He wiped the mahogany counter with his rag.

"I'd like to help," Hamilton said. He leaned across the bar and lowered his voice. "I went after them, yesterday. But Sterling told me to get back to town, tell you he's found her trail. I know where they're going."

"Do you now?" The man beside Hamilton turned. He was alone and drank his whisky very slowly. He looked Hamilton up and down, taking in the rotten teeth, the filthy clothes, the hat with half the brim missing, the acrid odour of rough nights and hard-working days. "The corporal was right. Man can't go rushing off into the wilderness, friend, unprepared. How about I provide everything we need in the way of supplies, and you show me the way? Finish your drink. We'd better be going now, before anyone else gets the same idea."

Hamilton grinned. Ray started to say something but at that moment the dancer Betsy came through the doors. Fiona didn't allow the girls onto the premises when they weren't working. Not only was having women in the bar a shady matter of the law, but she thought it reduced the value of the dollar-a-minute dance if men could drink with them any time they liked. Ray crossed the room to tell Betsy to get out. The man offering to travel with Joe Hamilton called to Murray, "Bartender, I'll purchase two bottles to take with me."

But Betsy wasn't here to drink or to meet friends. She spoke to three men sitting at the big centre table. She didn't bother to sit, and the men did not stand. She put her hands on the table and talked in low, serious tones. As Ray approached, she straightened and scurried out. The men at the table stood as one and followed her, leaving unfinished drinks in front of them.

When Ray turned back to the bar, Hamilton and his new friend were gone.

Chapter Twenty-Six

We walked along the dry edges of the creek bed, and both Sheridan and the horse seemed to find the going easier than yesterday. As the day progressed, the trees got increasingly small and scruffy, the spaces between them growing. The tops of the distant mountains were draped in white, and a strong wind was blowing, bringing the scent and chill of snow with it.

Had I made a mistake, once again, in not taking my chances and fleeing while Sheridan slept? We were heading toward nothing. We would not round a corner and see a white church steeple in the distance; we would not happen upon a welcoming inn at the crossroads (there being no roads); we would not see a smudge of yellow smoke marking a town or village on the horizon; we would not encounter a cheerful, ruddy-faced farmer bringing eggs and cheese and vegetables to town for market day.

Nothing lay ahead except the endless forest, distant mountains, and the frozen sea beyond.

The elevation rose, gradually but steadily, as we travelled. Suddenly, the woods cleared and the path broke open on the left. I could hear the welcoming sound of water moving swiftly, and the horse needed no encouragement to follow it. A flock of geese lifted into the air and flew low overhead, honking loudly as they settled into formation. A Kingfisher came from the opposite direction. Its wings didn't move, but it travelled fast above the water, drifting on the wind. The clearing was full of wildflowers in shades of yellow and white, and low bushes were thick with clusters of dark purple mossberries.

I was opening my mouth to mention the berries, when a flash of movement caught the corner of my eye and I looked downstream. A moose stood knee-deep in a patch of gently moving waterweeds. It lifted its head and looked at me, a long strip of grass dripping out of both sides of its mouth. It was the most ungainly, ugly beast, all knees and joints and ribs beneath a massive head, but its eyes were beautiful, huge and liquid brown. Sheridan had put his rifle on the ground and was bending over the water, filling his bottle. I didn't draw his attention to the animal.

It took another mouthful of grass before turning and walking away without a sound. It disappeared into the bush with only a gentle sway of branches to mark its passing, and I wondered that such an apparently lumbering beast could move so silently and gracefully.

"Tomorrow," Sheridan said, "I'll do some fishing. For now, I want to keep moving while the weather's good."

"Do you know if the berries on that bush are safe to eat?"

He eyed them. "Better not try. Anyway, we don't need them. I've enough food to last until we get there."

I doubted that. I'd seen what he had in the saddle bags. After the tent, bedroll, blankets, dishes, frying pan, and coffee pot, almost no room remained for food to sustain two people for more than another day or two.

Sheridan might be able to live on his obsession, but I could not.

I might come to regret not mentioning the moose.

Chapter Twenty-Seven

If he hadn't been so worried about his mother, Angus would have enjoyed his adventure in the wilderness. On their way to Dawson a year ago, as they'd travelled down the Yukon River from Lake Bennett in a boat hastily made of green logs, with a sail which the day before had been a tent, it had taken his breath away to see how completely empty — how vast — this land was. They'd stayed on the river, and all he'd been able to do was watch the countryside moving slowly past. They heard the howling of wolves at night and had seen moose several times, wading in the long grasses. At one spot, a grizzly bear, a gigantic creature of flashing teeth and claws, was fishing in a stream that fed into the river, tossing fish onto the rocks as easily as a woman might pick berries. In Dawson about all anyone seemed to want to do was dig up and cut down the wilderness as fast as possible.

He lay awake for a long time, listening to the night and watching the glow of the fire as the men took turns keeping watch. Mr. Donohue had gotten lost when out searching for wood and blundered around, bellowing. Sterling had refused to let anyone go after him, figuring that he'd have two lost people, so they kept shouting until Donohue followed the voices and eventually found his way back. He'd not been pleased, covered in scratches and insect bites, and he'd lost his cap. But Sterling said nothing, and Donohue tucked into his supper quick enough. Supper had been good, too. Beans and thick slabs of bacon with bannock cooked over the fire and strong sweet tea. Mrs. Mann had packed a seed cake for Angus, and he was pleased to be able to pass it around after dinner while the men smoked their pipes.

Other than worrying about his mother, the only thing spoiling the grand adventure was the mosquitoes. Dratted creatures got into everything. After they'd eaten, Sterling passed the frying pan around and told them to rub cold bacon fat on their faces and hands. Whether it was that, or just that it was late, the insects hadn't bothered him too much once he'd lain down and pulled his bedroll around him. The spruce bows Mr. Donohue had gathered made a surprisingly soft and comfortable bed.

Angus woke to the scent of coffee. He rubbed sleep from his eyes and sat up. Corporal Sterling crouched over the small camp stove.

"Morning, sir," Angus said.

Sterling turned with a smile. "Morning, Angus. Get water, will you. Porridge for breakfast."

"Will we find my ma today, sir?"

"You know she hates being called ma, so don't say it just because she's not around to hear."

"Sorry, sir."

"In answer to your question, I don't know. But the trail's good and clear. Get that water. The sooner we eat, the sooner we'll be on our way."

They had breakfast and packed up without wasting time. As yesterday, Corporal Sterling went ahead, moving slowly, head bent and eyes on the ground. Angus chafed with impatience. He wanted to run up the trail, yelling and calling out for his mother. Where else would Sheridan have taken her but along this track? Nothing but solid wilderness lay around them, other than the river, getting smaller and smaller as they went upriver, and a rough path beside it.

They rounded a bend, and Sterling let out a low whistle. Angus put on a burst of speed, pulling Millie along after him. A wooden cart lay on its side, the single wheel sticking out at an angle.

Sterling put up a hand, and with muttered curses the men crashed into each other behind him. Then they saw the broken cart, and everyone stood, listening to the silence of the forest. Eventually, Sterling said, "I don't think anyone's around. Don't move while I see what there is to see here."

He studied the cart and then examined the ground. From where he stood, Angus could see people had been here, as well as a horse. The remains of a campfire smouldered in a circle of rocks. Sterling crouched down and put his hand over it. Then he got to his feet and, cursing, kicked dirt onto it. "Coulda burned the goddamned forest down."

Everyone spoke at once.

"Can you tell how long ago they were here?"

"Was my ma ... mother ... with him?"

"We're getting close."

"What do you suppose they've done now, without the cart?"

"Think they're much further ahead?"

Sterling held up his hand once again. "I don't think I need worry about destroying the tracks. They're plenty of signs they've been here. Have a look around. If you see anything of interest, let me know."

A couple of empty food cans were on the ground by the fire pit. Horse hooves stamped out a circle at the edge of the clearing and went down the bank to the river. A set of smaller prints, from bare feet, were amongst the booted ones. Sterling let out a long breath. He'd been acting under the assumption that Fiona

MacGillivray had come this way although there'd been no sign of her since the man at the riverside camp had noticed a green dress and pretty feet. He felt a great weight lift off his chest.

"Angus," he called. "Look."

Angus looked. A smile broke across his face. "My mother?"

"Almost certainly."

"Why's she not wearing her shoes?"

"I'd say they were here about twelve to fifteen hours ago. They must have travelled all of Sunday night. Looks like they stopped to eat here, no doubt because the cart broke and Sheridan had to repack his supplies. That much is obvious. There's a patch of ground over there where it looks like someone lay down, but I don't see any trace of a tent or otherwise setting up for sleeping. I'll conclude they didn't make camp here, but kept on going."

"I told you we were wasting time stopping last night!" Angus shouted.

Sterling turned to him. "Would you rather have blundered past here in the dark?"

Angus studied his feet.

"So, if they didn't sleep here, they would've stopped later to make camp." Sterling did the calculations in his head. "Right now we're a good twelve or more hours behind them. But they have to sleep sometime and that'll give us a chance to catch up. Don't worry Angus. Your mother's a resourceful woman. I've no doubt she'll try to find ways to slow him down."

Donohue laughed. "Wouldn't want to have Fiona MacGillivray against me, I'll tell you that."

"My mother," Angus said, giving Donohue a poisonous look, "is only a woman. And she is being held prisoner by that … that man."

"Only isn't the word I'd use," Mouse O'Brien said. "Corporal?"

"Let's go."

Chapter Twenty-Eight

"This must be it," Sheridan announced.

"Be what?"

"The Indian trail that'll take us north."

I peered ahead. There did seem to be a path of some sort on the far bank. The trees were spaced a bit farther apart and the ground was firm, without too many rocks or saplings.

"Must have travelled faster than I figured," he said. "I didn't expect to come across this trail until tomorrow."

Oh dear. He really had no idea of where we were. No doubt any track in the wilderness would serve as a sign to Paul Sheridan that he was following the route for which he searched.

"Only another couple of hours," he said. "Then we'll make camp for the night." The horse and I groaned in unison.

"My feet," I said, "are not going to take me much further." I had pulled off my shoe and sock to examine my left foot. It was not in good shape. I held it up as evidence, waving a tiny bug away.

"You'll be fine," he said. "The going's much easier from now on."

I doubted that very much.

I pulled my shoe back on and took off my hat and made an attempt to refasten my hair. At first glance, my wedding hat appeared to be ridiculously impractical, but it was proving to be a god-send. It kept the sun off my head, and I'd bent the black ostrich feather down to sweep across my face and brush the insects away. I'd ripped out the stitches holding the veil up and wrapped it around my neck for protection. Thank heavens this dress did not have a plunging décolletage.

Paul Sheridan's face and neck, I was pleased to see, were dotted with lumpy red bites.

"Fill up these water bottles, will you, Fiona." He scratched at the back of his hand. "Might be a while before we come to another river."

I looked again at the small track leading into the bush. Sheridan was making some adjustments to the horse's packs. I yanked the clump of grapes off my hat and dropped them into the mud.

Chapter Twenty-Nine

"Corporal Sterling!"

McAllen, who'd been bringing up the rear, came jogging up the trail. He ran past Donohue, O'Brien, and Angus MacGillivray. Sterling stopped and waited for him.

They'd been walking for a couple of hours since finding the abandoned cart. The path along the riverside was rocky, but every once in a while they could see the horse's hoof prints, the tread of a man's boots, and that of a smaller shoe with a dainty heel. Angus was pleased to see his mother had her shoes back on.

The track was clear and easy to follow, as it kept close to the meandering river and the banks were not too steep. Sterling moved swiftly, never looking back to make sure the others were keeping up. Angus's feet were starting to ache, and Mr. Donohue grumbled every time he tripped over a root.

Only Millie seemed to be enjoying the outing. She walked with her head up and her tail swishing from side to side and occasionally gave Angus a look that he could almost believe was a grin.

Up ahead, McAllen reached Sterling. He pointed back down the trail, and Angus turned to look. He could see nothing. Sterling came back.

"What ..." Donohue began.

"Quiet," Sterling snapped.

They could hear a bird in the trees to their left. Overhead, a hawk circled. The river gurgled cheerfully as it rushed over rocks. A grayling leapt out of the water, the sun flashing on its dorsal fin and sleek silver scales. Leaves rustled in the light wind. Then a branch broke, and they heard a man shout, "Anyone there? Help!"

"Oh, for crying out loud," Sterling groaned. "Of all people. I'd much prefer to sneak away, but I suppose we can't let him wander out here forever. Give him a shout, Constable."

"Over here," McAllen yelled.

The others joined in, calling words of encouragement. Angus jumped up and down, trying to give power to his voice. Millie barked.

"I hear you. Keep calling!"

They saw a flash of scarlet and then a man stepped out from behind a poplar. He was old, overweight, and breathing heavily. He'd lost his hat and a bad scratch leaked blood down the side of his face. A twig was stuck in his hair, and the knees of his uniform trousers were thick with mud. It looked as if he might collapse at any moment. Not a pace he could maintain much longer, even though he was not weighted down by supplies.

"Sergeant Lancaster," Sterling said. "What brings you here?" He hid his surprise that the man had been able to move fast enough to catch them up. People could do anything, sometimes, if they wanted it enough.

Lancaster rested his arms against his legs as he caught his breath. "Whew," he said at last. "Good thing you were making so much noise. Must of taken a wrong turn somewhere."

"Good thing McAllen heard you blundering around," Sterling muttered under his breath. "I asked what you're doing here."

"No need to use that tone of voice, Corporal." Lancaster lowered himself with great care onto a dead log. "Figured you'd need help out here."

"Did Inspector McKnight send you?"

"Not exactly sent me, mind. He seemed doubtful about your mission so I ... uh ... figured I'd lend a hand." He gave them all a big smile. Even Angus could tell the sergeant was prevaricating.

"Where's your bedroll? Food?"

"Well, I uh ... lost it. Came across a bear you see, big grizzly mother with cubs. I had to run for my life."

"Sergeant Lancaster, with all due respect I cannot take you into the wilderness without supplies. We've each brought only sufficient for our own needs."

"Not to worry. I'll live off the land."

"No."

"What?"

"I said no. Go back to town, Sergeant. Please, sir."

"Mr. Sterling, I am here and henceforth I will lead this expedition. Not only do I outrank you, but I'll have you know that I have asked Mrs. MacGillivray for the honour of her hand in marriage."

Donohue laughed. He'd taken the opportunity of a break to dig a heel of bread and some cheese out of his pack. "I wonder what she had to say to that," he said around a mouthful.

"She's thinking it over."

"I bet." Donohue offered Angus a piece of cheese, which he declined.

Angus wanted to yell at the fool of a man. Lancaster was a good boxing instructor, and Angus was learning a lot (although the lessons were kept secret from his mother, who would not approve), but otherwise he was useless. Sterling had told him something of Lancaster's story. He'd been a good policeman once, tough but fair. Then he led a group of raw recruits into the open prairie and lost them in a sudden snowstorm. None of the men had died, but they all gave up fingers or toes to frostbite, and Lancaster had never forgiven himself. Since then, he'd never been able to make an effective decision. He stayed on in the NWMP because the officers respected his past, although he wasn't given much in the way of responsibility.

"No," Sterling said. "Go back to town."

Lancaster turned purple. He grabbed a low hanging branch and pulled himself upright with much effort. "Young man," he said to Constable McAllen, "I'm placing Corporal Sterling under arrest for insubordination. You will escort him back to Dawson."

"Are you crazy!" Angus shouted. "How's that going to help my mother?"

"Don't interfere, Angus," Sterling said.

Mouse O'Brien spoke for the first time. "How about you share my things, Sergeant." He threw a glance at Sterling. Angus saw the corporal give a slight nod in return. "I've more than enough food. You can walk with me. Tell you the truth, my old leg is acting up and I might need a hand if the trail gets much rougher."

"Very well." Lancaster sighed heavily to show everyone he was doing O'Brien a big favour.

Without another word, Sterling turned and marched back down the trail, his back stiff and his step firm enough to shake the forest floor. They all fell into step behind him. Lancaster said to Mouse, "Fine wedding, old chap. Your bride was most beautiful."

"I'm missing her, I can tell you. In fact," Mouse shouted so loudly a hawk sitting at the top of a dead spruce took flight. "I'm almost regretting coming on this venture."

Sterling lifted a hand in acknowledgement without turning around. Angus wondered if something was being said that he didn't understand.

They walked for about another hour. Angus was beginning to regret not accepting Mr. Donohue's cheese. Sterling had quickened his pace and disappeared long ago. Lancaster was complaining about his foot while telling Angus to keep his chin up and be brave. The old sergeant's breath came in rasps as he told Mouse he'd travelled all night hoping to catch up with them. He suggested they stop for a rest, and Mouse said, "A few more miles I think."

Eventually they caught up with Sterling. He was standing in the middle of the trail, his face a picture of confusion. Another track broke off from the main one, disappearing into the trees. It looked very new, the ground only lightly disturbed, tree branches freshly broken. The larger trail, continuing along the river, was scuffed and the tracks were erased.

"This might be the old Indian trail marked on Sheridan's' map," Sterling said, rubbing at his chin. "I'm not sure which way we should go."

"It looks like someone deliberately ..." Angus began.

"Angus," Sterling said, "take the dog down to the water and let her have a drink while we decide."

"But."

"Now, Angus."

Grumbling, Angus slipped the packs off Millie's back. She shook herself free and jumped down the bank into the cold water. She swam in circles, her mouth open and tongue moving.

"As I recall," Mouse said, "from the map, the path branches away from the river and heads inland. Might be this one."

"No," Angus shouted, "on the map it ..."

"Hey!" Donohue cried, "Watch that dog."

Angus whipped around. Millie was paddling happily.

"Close one," Donohue said. He scrambled down the bank and put his arm on Angus's. "Better keep a close eye on her, boy. Those rapids can be deceiving."

"Rapids? What rapids?" The green water drifted gently past. Angus could see stones and pebbles resting on the bottom. Small fish darted in and out of the crevices.

"Shush," Donohue whispered. "Be quiet and play along." Angus had no idea what he was getting at.

"Looks like no one's been following the main trail for a few days at any rate," Sterling said. "But someone did turn here, and recently."

"Sure looks like it," O'Brien said. "What do you think, Sergeant Lancaster?"

Lancaster peered myopically up the trail. "Those tracks are fresh all right. We'll go that way."

"I'd hate to make a mistake," Sterling said, sounding more unsure of himself than Angus had ever heard. He wondered what was the matter with the man. Was he so unnerved at the thought of being charged with insubordination he'd lost his common sense? The map showed the trail leaving the river and going north from the east bank. This trail went west. Why, it might even end up taking them right back to Dawson.

"This is the way we're going," Lancaster said, very firmly.

"I don't know," Sterling said.

"Perhaps we should split up," O'Brien offered.

"Good idea," Lancaster said. "Sterling, you continue along the river. As this path looks the mostly likely, I'll go there. McAllen'll accompany me. Where's McAllen anyway?"

Sterling looked around, as though the constable might pop out from behind a tree. "Gee, I don't know. He must have gone on ahead, not realizing we'd stopped."

Angus noticed Sterling was no longer carrying the rifle.

"Never mind, Sergeant," Mouse said. "I'll come with you. We'd better get along. Why, we might catch up with them before nightfall." He plunged into the woods.

"You're a good man, O'Brien," Lancaster said. "Angus, are you coming?"

"Uh," Angus said, "I uh ..."

"The boy's only slowing us down," Mouse shouted. A couple of steps off the main trail and he'd disappeared, but they could hear branches breaking and ground trembling. "My god, I see something."

"Send McAllen after me when you catch up with him," Lancaster shouted over his shoulder as he dashed into the woods.

Angus climbed the river bank and Millie followed, shaking off a gallon of water. They stood and watched the path, saying nothing for a long time.

"Where," Angus asked at last, "does that trail go?"

"No more than 100 yards east and then it circles around to join up with the main trail south of here. Turn right, and follow it all the way back to town."

"How do you know that?"

Sterling chuckled. "Made it myself. We've lost precious time. Angus, get the dog ready and we're off."

They rounded the next bend and the horse and boot and shoe prints returned. Angus turned and looked back. Something had been brushed over the ground to make the trail disappear.

Constable McAllen was sitting on a bolder. He had the Winchester resting on his knees and his pack on the ground. He got to his feet and held out the rife to Sterling.

"Anyone else following us," Sterling said with a growl. "I'll shoot them on sight."

Chapter Thirty

In the great cities to the south, it would have been well after dark. Both the horse and I were asleep on our feet when Sheridan finally decided it was time to make camp for the night. We'd stopped only once, for a quick meal of dry bread and meat cold and grey and as tough as the legs of the horse.

I'd decided the horse, who was bearing our belongings so uncomplainingly, needed a name. He would henceforth be known as Soapy.

The path we were following spread out into a small clearing, where there were traces of a fire circle and the tramped earth was clear of rocks. We were not the first people to make camp here. I hoped the regular inhabitants would return, and I could beg an escort to Dawson or the nearest NWMP post.

Sheridan cleared a space of pebbles and twigs for the tent while I gathered fuel for a fire. I hobbled about in Mr. Sheridan's socks and knew that tomorrow I would scarcely be able to walk. Supper was again a totally unsatisfying mess of fried corned beef and tinned potatoes.

We sat around the fire after our inadequate meal, saying nothing. I never thought the time would come that I'd miss Mrs. Mann's plain, practical German cooking, but this night I did. No need to worry about Angus going hungry under her care. I watched sparks drifting into the trees, rising up into the sky like an offering to ancient gods. I wondered where Angus was and what he was doing.

By my reckoning, it was Monday night, the early hours of Tuesday. No doubt my absence would have been noted. The question that nagged at me was what would anyone do about it? Angus would be sure to remember Sheridan had told him about taking us in search of his Gold Mountain. Angus would alert the police. Would they charge into the wilderness in pursuit?

Quite possibly not.

The Mounties had their hands full keeping law and order in the town and the territory. They wouldn't be able to mount an expedition to rescue one wilful female, even if they wanted to. Inspector McKnight would no doubt be quite happy to see the back of me. Richard Sterling, on the other hand ... I thought of his handsome face, stern most of the time, but with a twinkle in his eye he wasn't always able to control. I heard his deep voice say my name. Fiona, he called me sometimes, when his professional demeanour slipped a fraction. I wasn't sure what the corporal would do. He seemed ... fond of me. Fond enough to go against orders and come after me?

Angus? Dear heavens, I could only hope that hot-headed Angus — I had no idea from where he inherited that trait — would not rush single-mindedly into the wilds.

I had some friends in town. Ray Walker for sure. Mouse O'Brien. Big Alex McDonald and Belinda Mulrooney. But Ray had a business to run, and Mouse should be tucked up in bed with the blushing Martha Witherspoon. Big Alex and Belinda would be able to get a search party together, but they were busy people and that could take days.

I doubted very much Sheridan knew where we were, so how on earth could anyone else find us?

If I didn't come back, Ray would look after Angus, with the help of Mr. and Mrs. Mann, Richard Sterling, and Helen Saunderson. They wouldn't be able to raise him to be the fine gentleman I intended him to become, but they would raise him to be a good man.

The ground was very cold beneath my bottom. I shifted and glanced at Sheridan. He was bent over the fire, puffing on his pipe, staring into space. Flames reflected in his eyes. When I'd been with the Travellers, we'd once come across a preacher standing on a rock at a crossroads outside Oxford, announcing the end of the world to farm families heading to town for market day. Fire burned in his eyes so intensely I'd thought it might devour him from inside. No rational thought, no logic lay behind the words of the itinerant preacher. Farmers laughed at him and boys threw rocks, but he kept on preaching. No reality could interfere with the commitment, the surety of his vision.

We'd come across him again, when he stepped out of the night and asked if he might warm himself for a spell. He sat beside our fire eating nothing but a piece of bread and a single slice of cheese. He stared into the flames, seeing visions and mumbling words no one else could understand.

Like Paul Sheridan, the preacher had been tall and so thin it was as if his body itself was being consumed by the fire inside. Sheridan had that same look now, and it sent a shiver down my spine.

I groaned and got slowly to my aching feet. "Good night, Mr. Sheridan. Don't waste water cleaning the dishes. Rub them with a bit of sand. That will take the worst of the dirt off."

I went into the tent, took off my hat, and lay down. I was still wearing my green satin dress. When I got home, I wouldn't even make rags of the thing.

I heard the horse whinny and the sound of Sheridan relieving himself in the bushes. The flap of the tent opened. He came inside and grunted as he made himself comfortable. I felt his weight beside me, and then his arms slid around me. He buried his face into the back of my neck and began kissing it.

"Release me," I said.

His hands moved upwards, seeking my breasts. He groaned and pushed his hips against me.

"Mr. Sheridan," I said, employing my most imperious tone. I struggled to sit up. He pressed me back down, his lips seeking my mouth, his hands moving.

"If you intend to offer me insult ..." I grabbed his right hand and twisted it. He grunted with pain. I looked directly at him. Outside, the waxing moon was throwing enough light into the tent that I could see the slack face and gaping mouth inches above me. "... Then get it over with. Whereupon I will return to Dawson. If, however, you still want to continue with this expedition and to install me as your ... consort ... be warned that from this moment on you will forever be required to sleep with one eye open. Because I will kill you the first opportunity I have, and it will not matter if that means I will be alone in the wilderness. You said I fight like a man. Be warned, Mr. Sheridan, I carry vengeance like a woman."

He jerked his hand out of my grip. "I meant no offense," he mumbled. His eyes slid off my face and his mouth snapped shut.

"Ensure it remains so," I said. "You may take your bedroll and sleep outside from now on. The sky is clear, hopefully it will not rain. Good night, Mr. Sheridan."

He scurried out of the tent like a rat escaping a sinking ship.

I lay on my back, eyes open until I heard him settle and the snoring begin. Then I stretched out, enjoying the luxury of space.

My virtue is of no consequence to me. I have precious little to lose, at any rate. I would most certainly not follow Mr. Sheridan to the ends of the earth to extract revenge and willingly die in the attempt.

But it did no harm to let him think so.

I woke to the sound of a soft whisper calling my name and fingernails scratching at the canvas walls of the tent.

"Fiona. Are you awake?"

"No. What do you want Mr. Sheridan?"

"The mosquitoes are real bad out here, Fiona. Can I have your hat to protect my face some?"

I tossed my new hat, the cream-coloured one with the saucy turned-up brim, the black ostrich feather, the long veil cascading down the back, out of the tent.

Chapter Thirty-One

Angus woke early. Clouds had moved in, and Sterling suggested they put up the tents in case it rained in the night. He lay on his back with his eyes open, staring up at the grungy white canvas. Fingers of light were stroking the tent walls and seeping through the cracks. Constable McAllen snored heartily. Otherwise, all was quiet.

Angus crept out of the tent. Graham Donohue had been given the last watch. He was stretched out on the ground, jacket under his head, Millie curled up against his belly. Both of them sound asleep.

Some watch, Angus thought. He didn't bother to be quiet as he nurtured the campfire back to life. He put some of the water he'd collected before going to bed into the coffee pot and measured out the beans. He would much rather be having tea for breakfast, but they hadn't brought any tea, and Angus was trying to pretend he liked the coffee. Donohue awoke with a shout, which startled Millie, and she jumped to her feet with a loud bark. The newspaperman sat up, rubbing his face. He saw Angus watching him. "Just resting my eyes."

"Sure."

The newspaperman untied the dog. "Might as well take Millie into the bushes with me."

Angus fed a bit of kerosene into the stove and lit a match to start it up. He didn't want to cook breakfast; he wanted to be running down the trail after his mother. He would never say so, but he was getting increasingly worried. He thought they'd come across her the first day, with or without Paul Sheridan, sitting by a fire at the side of the trail, nibbling on a piece of toast, sipping tea, and demanding to know what had taken them so long. But she'd been gone more than two days, and she and Sheridan were moving at the same pace as their pursuers.

Suppose Sterling lost the trail?

Angus's eyes filled with water. He wiped at his face with the back of his hand and looked around to make sure no one had seen him cry. Sterling was up now, down at the river splashing water on his face. McAllen continued to snore, and Donohue and Millie were out of sight in the bush.

They'd been walking for two days, and the vegetation was changing. The trees were getting smaller and sparser, although the underbrush was still thick. Sterling had said he'd never been there, but he'd been told that the boreal forest ended not far out of Dawson, and the great empty tundra of the true north began, stretching all the way to the ice-covered sea. On the tundra, Sterling said, a man could see for miles in all directions.

"We brought food for five days," Angus said when Sterling joined him by the fire. "We've been out for two now, and that means two back. How long can we," he swallowed, "keep going?"

"Long as we have to. Don't worry about that. In this country, least in summer, no one has to go hungry. I'm getting tired of beans and bacon anyway. I'll try and get us a duck or goose today. Rabbit maybe. Have you ever hunted?"

Angus wanted to say yes, but he shook his head.

"Perhaps you'll get the chance. But right now, I'm afraid it's porridge."

McAllen came out of the tent, wiping sleep from his eyes. "Fish'd be nice. I'll see what I can do."

"Not now!" Angus said, "We have to go. We don't have time for fishing."

"We need to make time to eat properly," Sterling said. "Coffee's not ready yet. Constable, see what you can do."

Angus felt almost guilty enjoying the fresh trout McAllen cooked over the open fire. In only a few minutes, he'd caught enough that they could toss a few fat chunks as well as the guts to an eager Millie. Once they'd eaten, they broke camp, loaded up, and continued walking north. The river had been getting smaller and its banks flatter and broader, becoming a creek and eventually a stream, trickling down the centre of the watercourse.

The horse and the people with it had come down from the high banks, where the trail wound among the tress, to travel on the packed earth of the drying riverbed. The ground had hardened quickly after the latest rain, but it was soft enough to record the passage of any large creature. Small clumps of earth had stuck to feet and hooves before being kicked lose, and damper spots showed the edges of shoes in muddy outlines.

They'd only walked for about an hour when Sterling stopped. He walked toward the riverbank, and Angus could see that a patch of earth on the bank was smoothed down. "Someone sat here," Sterling said. He pointed out the outline of a bottom, the depression of their weight, and handprints where they'd pushed themselves back up.

"Hey!" Angus shouted. "What's that?" An unnatural shade of purple lay on the ground. Sterling knelt as Angus peered over his shoulder.

Sterling put his fingers around the object and lifted it up. It was a clump of grapes. He tapped it with his fingernail. It was hard, not real grapes. The sort of fake object used to decorate a lady's hat.

"My mother bought a new hat for the wedding," Angus said. "It has grapes, just like that."

"So it does," Donohue said. "I thought it a most attractive hat."

Sterling cast around for a few minutes, but didn't find anything else Fiona might have dropped.

Angus watched him, thinking. Had the grapes dropped off her hat, or had his mother left them here deliberately? The creek floor was mostly rocks at this point, gravel and small stones. Hard to see any prints. Sterling waded into the creek, the water scarcely coming up past his ankles. He climbed the bank. Then he turned and waved for the others to follow.

Angus's boots were not waterproof. The shock of the icy water almost took his breath away. But in a couple of steps he was standing on the far side. The bank was disturbed where a horse's hooves had scrambled for purchase.

"Two people," Sterling said. "One climbed here, and the other," he pointed a couple of feet downstream, "over there."

"Can you be sure we're still following Fiona and Sheridan?" Donohue asked. "Not someone else?"

"The trail's mostly unbroken from where we picked it up outside town, but other than that, these are definitely not Indians. Indians wouldn't leave a trail as obvious and clumsy as this one. Could be trappers, prospectors, sure. But coming the same way, in the last couple of days, with a bunch of fake grapes? Safe enough to assume not."

Footprints, human and equine, led into the forest.

"Far as I remember," Angus said, pulling out his map, "there should be a place where the trail branches off from the river. Do you think this is it? Those mountains in the distance could be the triangles here."

"They left the river here, at any rate." Sterling gave Angus a grin. "Your mother gave us a sign. If I hadn't seen that ornament we might have carried on up the creek for a spell before realizing the trail had stopped." He handed the grapes to Angus, who tucked them into his jacket pocket with the map.

Chapter Thirty-Two

The next time I awoke, it was by a frightened horse. Branches broke and Soapy screamed. Something fell to the ground, and I heard metal clanging against rock. Sheridan yelled, sounding genuinely frightened. The rifle was lying against the sides of the tent, where he'd left it in his haste last night. I picked it up and scrambled outside. It was daylight, and the sun was a cheerful yellow ball in the soft blue sky.

Sheridan was backing away, heading into the bushes. The horse reared up in terror, its front hoofs thrashing, trying to break free of the rope tying it to the tree. A loud grunt came from the vicinity of the campfire. I got to my feet, holding the weapon as though I knew how to use it.

A bear was sitting on the ground, the frying pan in front of its face. Eyes as small and black as currants watched me without much interest, and a pink tongue moved in and out of the mouth. It was licking the pan.

It wasn't a very big bear, not that I know what a big bear looks like, and it was black, not brown. I tried to remember what Angus had told me about the wildlife of the Yukon. Grizzlies were the big ones, the dangerous ones. They were brown in colour with a hump on their back. At least I think that's what Angus said. I sometimes don't pay as much attention as I should when my son tries to educate me about things he finds fascinating.

I gripped the rifle and glanced around. No sign of any cubs. I assumed that was a good thing.

"Off you go," I said, waving the rifle in front of me. "There's a good boy."

He tossed the pan aside and lumbered to his feet.

"Shoot, Fiona," Sheridan cried from behind a tree. It was more of a sapling than a tree. The bear would be able to rip it up by its roots if it so desired.

"Shoo." I lifted my skirt with my free hand and waved it in the air. "There's nothing for you here."

The eyes studied my face. Looking for a meal? I tightened my grip on the rifle. I might be able to use it as a club if necessary. I thought I saw a flicker of understanding deep within the impenetrable black eyes. The bear grunted once. It turned and lumbered into the woods. Trees bent and branches snapped, and then it was gone.

"Why didn't you shoot?" Sheridan shouted at me when he'd crept back into camp.

Best not to tell him that I didn't shoot because I didn't know how to operate the rifle. "Why didn't you wash the dishes last night, as I instructed you?" I replied. "Go and settle poor Soapy before he succumbs to heart failure."

At least the bear had cleaned the frying pan. I nursed the fire back to life and dug into the sacks, looking for coffee. The bag containing the oatmeal had been ripped open and the precious grains scattered across the ground. My heart sunk as I uncovered a couple of cans of vegetables and a single package of bacon. Our supply of food was getting perilously low.

Twigs broke behind me as I gathered up what I could of the oatmeal. "You'll have to fish today. We're almost out of supplies."

"If I see any more geese or ducks, I'll shoot them. I'm not wanting to delay by going hunting."

I lifted my eyes to the heavens. An eagle flew overhead, circling on outstretched wings. No doubt checking us out for size and weight. "You'll delay a lot more if we starve to death."

"We're almost there. Come and see, Fiona." He unfolded the map. Almost against my will, I looked.

He punched his finger against the paper. A blue line led north from what was supposedly the Klondike River; a black line broke off from it heading east. "That mountain range." Sheridan pointed to the peaks in the distance. "Would be here." He tapped at a row of triangles on the paper. The triangles could be the Black Cuillins of Skye or the Himalayas for all the detail on this map. "And the valley," Sheridan pointed at the red circle before the triangles, "is here."

He had taken down the tent and was rebalancing the load in the packs prior to readying the horse for the day's travels, and I was attempting to comb some of the knots out of my hair with my fingers when I announced, "I will not be able to walk any further. My feet are a mess. I will ride Soapy."

"The horse has to carry our things," Sheridan protested.

I smiled at him. "You'll have to do that then."

The sun was touching the tops of the trees when we broke camp. Paul Sheridan walked ahead as he had before, but with the largest of the saddlebags slung across his back beside the rifle, the bag containing the knife draped over his front, leading the horse upon which I balanced precariously. The third bag had been tied to the horse, resting against the back of its neck so I had something other than the mane to cling to, and the dull axe was fastened to its side. I had expected the horse would give me difficulty as I tried to mount, but like me it no longer seemed to be able to be surprised and had stood patiently beside a fortuitously placed boulder while I clambered aboard.

I could almost pretend I was a fine lady out for a Sunday excursion in High Park.

The train at the back of my hat caught on a tree branch and I grabbed for it. A length of lace ripped loose. Fortunately, enough was left behind that it would still provide a veil to offer some protection from ravenous insects.

Before folding his map and putting it away, Sheridan had said, "Another day or two if we make good time."

I would attempt do my best to ensure we did not make good time.

Chapter Thirty-Three

The days were beginning to blur into each other. By my account today should be Tuesday. Then again, we might have fallen off the world into a place where time moved in a different rhythm and there really was a tropical valley and a mountain made of gold ahead of us.

The question then would be, could I ever get back to *my* world?

The mountains in the distance did seem to be getting closer.

In the early afternoon, the trail met a small river, and we stopped there for something to eat.

I simply could not sit on that horse another moment and slithered down from Soapy's back, not bothering to hide a groan. That morning, I'd taken the last of the bread and put it in the smaller saddlebag. I fished it out. It was all we would have for lunch. The banks of the creek were lined with bushes fat with blue and purple mossberries. If they were poisonous, too bad. I began gathering the fruit while Soapy stuck his head into the water and drank silently.

I looked over the creek at the bright blue flash of a kingfisher, gliding low above the water. Its wings were stretched out and not moving. As I watched, a hawk dropped from the sky. Both the kingfisher and I screeched in shock. It headed for the trees, the hawk in close pursuit. The two birds dodged and weaved in the air above the creek, swooping and feigning and soaring in a three-dimensional chase of life or death.

The kingfisher turned sharply, almost directly in front of my face, and raced for the treetops. The hawk overshot, pirouetted in the air without slowing, turned, and followed.

And they were gone.

"Wow," Paul Sheridan said. "That was something."

I placed the heel of bread and the berries onto a rock, and we sat down to eat. The fruit was tart and delicious. It left purple stains on my fingers and hands. Sheridan was quiet, and I wondered if he had any doubts at all about the viability of his mission.

The sun was very warm and the air very still. Slowly, I became aware of the silence. A bird chirped, water brushed against the banks of the creek, and the horse munched on grasses and shifted his feet. I couldn't remember the last time I'd been so aware of silence. In Dawson the racket never stopped; the Chilkoot trail groaned with the effort of men stretched beyond endurance; in Skagway, trees were constantly being chopped down and buildings built up; the boat from Vancouver had been packed so full some people didn't even have a cabin.

Even when I'd walked the hills of Skye with my father, we couldn't go far before we'd come across a crofter wanting a chat, his wife cooing over the *bonnie wee lass*, their rambunctious children chasing each other and screaming in delight.

I leaned back and drank in the silence. I felt my chest rise and fall, and for perhaps the first time in my life, I was aware of my own breathing.

"I'd knew you'd come to love it," Sheridan said. His face was soft and round and dreamy. For a very brief moment, I found myself almost liking him.

I stood up and brushed off my torn, tattered, mud-encrusted skirt. "I prefer my dance hall, thank you. As those berries appear not to have done us any harm, I'll collect more for supper."

Before I could move, a flutter of wings and the sound of many bodies hitting the water had us looking once again at the creek. Geese, seven or eight geese, large and fat, had landed on the water, and more were streaming in behind them.

"Time to go." Sheridan started to stand.

"Mr. Sheridan," I said. "Speaking of supper."

"What?"

"For heaven's sake, man. You may not need to eat, but I do. I will dine on goose tonight."

"Oh," he said. "Good idea, Fiona."

His first shot missed, but before the geese were aware they were in danger, Sheridan had killed two.

I refrained from clapping my hands.

Fortunately, the creek was shallow enough that Sheridan was able to wade in and capture his prize.

He tied the two geese to the largest saddlebag, and once again we set off. He made a strange sight, moving up the trail ahead of me, back bowed under the weight of the packs, horse lead in hand. Two dead geese flapped against his legs.

Chapter Thirty-Four

They walked all through the day as the sun moved in an arc over-head. This track didn't appear to be much used. It was narrower than the other path, and the bush crowded in close. In places, they had to walk in single file. Angus's feet were aching and Millie was dragging on her lead, and he was about to ask if they could have a rest, when Corporal Sterling stopped abruptly. He lifted his finger to his mouth and gestured to Angus and the men to be quiet. The wind rustled the tops of the trees. Sterling sniffed the air. Millie barked.

Donohue said, "What's up?" and Sterling shushed him. Angus shifted his weight. Millie gave a low whine.

Moving slowly, Sterling laid the rifle on the ground beside his feet. "The White Queen sends her greetings," he said in a loud voice.

The bush separated and men were standing there. Three men. Indians. Two of them not much older than Angus, and one who looked to be about as old as time. The old man nodded. The young ones did not move.

Sterling reached into his pocket and pulled out his pipe, bag of tobacco, and matches. He extended the tobacco. The old man nod-ded again and dug out his own pipe. Without a word, they squatted to the ground. Sterling lit a match and held the fire out. Only when the old man's pipe was breathing smoke did the Mountie light his.

Donohue threw a look at Angus and got out his own pipe while McAllen crouched beside Sterling.

The two boys studied Angus. One was in overalls, more patches than original fabric, the other wore trousers and a yellow waistcoat. They both wore dusty and torn broad-brimmed hats. They looked enough alike to be brothers, cousins at least. The old man wore a woollen cap and had a blanket wrapped around his stooped shoulders and a moose-skin shirt beneath.

Millie sniffed the young men's feet. Angus remembered the last of Mrs. Mann's seed cake. He looped the dog's lead around a tree and brought the food out. The Indian boys accepted. "Thank you," the taller one said. They smiled at him around mouthfuls of cake.

Sterling and the old man exchanged greetings. The old man did not speak English, but they seemed to make themselves understood with smiles and hand gestures.

"Will you please ask your grandfather," Sterling said to the boys, "if he has seen a white man and woman. They travel with a horse, and were on this trail no more than one day ago."

The taller boy said something, and the man answered.

"My grandfather says I can answer your questions. The white people came through the woods. They made much noise. We are hunting, and Grandfather said the game has been disturbed and so we must go to another place."

"My mother, did you see my mother?" Angus shouted.

"Shush!" Sterling said. The old man moved his hand, and the shorter of the Indian boys said, "My grandfather says your son may speak. She is your mother? She is very beautiful. My grandfather has never seen a white woman. He wondered if she was your queen. I told him your queen is very old."

"When was this?" Donohue asked.

"Yesterday. Late in the day."

The old man spoke and the younger ones answered. Sterling puffed at his pipe. "My grandfather asks if this man has stolen your woman," the taller one said.

"Yes," Sterling replied. He did not explain.

The old man muttered darkly and shook his head.

"Very bad to steal from the Redcoats," the boy explained. He pointed to the Winchester lying on the ground. "You should know the man you follow has a rifle like that one."

The old man rose to his feet with a smooth grace that belied his age. Sterling and McAllen stood also.

Sterling held out his hand. The old man took it. "*Mahsi Cho*," Sterling said, giving his thanks. "Before you go, can you tell me what's up ahead?"

The old man shook his head. He exchanged sharp words with his grandsons.

"One more day will take you to the place where the trees end," the boy said, shifting uncomfortably.

"And beyond that?"

The Indian boys looked at each other. The old man grumbled deep in his chest. No one said anything for a long time. Millie whined.

"It is forbidden," the taller one said at last.

"What's forbidden?"

"There is a small river on the flat land beyond the trees. It is forbidden to travel beyond the river. We do not cross the river."

"Why?"

The boy shrugged. "When our people first came to this land, a hunting party went there. They did not come back, and another party went to find them. They also did not come back. Many years have passed, but no one from our people has crossed that river and returned."

"There's a white man who knows no better, a trapper," the other said. "He lives at the edge of the forbidden zone. If you want to know what lies beyond he might be able to tell you."

The old man muttered.

"When I was very small, a woman from our tribe left us to be with the white trapper. My grandfather says she will never be allowed to return. Her family will never speak to her or to her children. She is gone too close to the forbidden."

"Thank you," Sterling said again.

The old man nodded, and then they were gone, leaving only the movement of the bush behind them and the cry of a raven.

"Wow," Angus said.

"What's that nonsense about a forbidden zone?" Donohue said, tapping ash out of his pipe. "Probably don't want anyone going into the good hunting grounds."

"Don't be so sure," Sterling said. "They looked highly uncomfortable talking about it."

"Primitive superstition."

Sterling said nothing. He simply picked up the Winchester and set off down the trail. Angus grabbed Millie and followed.

"Sir," he said, when he caught up to the Mountie. "How did you know they were there? The Indians I mean. They were so quiet."

"Bear fat and woodsmoke and tobacco. If the wind hadn't been coming this way, I wouldn't have known."

Chapter Thirty-Five

Judging by the light, we stopped to make camp much earlier than we had the day before. Perhaps even Paul Sheridan was running out of steam. Or maybe he just wanted to tuck into those geese.

He was collecting wood for the fire and tent poles, and I was trying to remember how best to get feathers off birds, when a breaking branch caught my attention.

A man stood under a small spruce, watching me.

I got to my feet slowly.

He was a white man, short and thin, with a grey-and-black beard that hung over his chest and long dirty grey hair tied back from his face by a bandana. He was very dark, but it was difficult to tell if the colour came from the sun or was simply dirt. He carried a rifle and had a hunting knife stuck in the belt at his hip.

"Good day," I said. "I do hope we won't get any rain this evening."

He grunted.

Sheridan heard the voices and hurried over. He thrust out his hand. "Hi. Sheridan's the name and this is my fiancée, Fiona."

The man looked at Sheridan's outstretched hand for a long time. Then he extended his own and the two men shook. His hands were caked with dirt, the yellow nails alternately broken and overgrown. Two fingers on his left hand were rounded stumps.

He cleared his throat, and when he spoke, it sounded like an instrument that had not been used for a long time. "Nothin' around here for city folks."

"We're just passing through," Sheridan replied. "Too many people in the Territory these days for my liking."

"Nowhere to pass through to," the man said.

I'm not accustomed to being ignored. "Indeed," I said, "then perhaps you can direct us to the nearest mounted police fort or other government officials."

The man looked as surprised as if Soapy the horse had spoken. Then he laughed, showing two brown teeth in an otherwise black and empty cave. "Your woman ain't gonna last long in the wilds."

"She'll be fine," Sheridan said. "We're prospecting. I've heard word there's a good strain of quartz up north and west some. Might mean gold."

"Don't know 'bout that," the man said, studying me. He did not look too terribly impressed. He obviously thought Sheridan was out of his mind to bring a woman such as me into the wilderness.

We had something in common.

"Do you, uh, live around here?" I inquired.

The man spat a load of chewing tobacco into the ground. I took that to be an affirmative.

"If so," I continued, "I'd appreciate the opportunity to clean up and have a night's rest. We have two fresh geese as you can see, and would be happy to share."

"Be quiet, Fiona," Sterling said in a loud whisper. "The man's a trapper. Probably doesn't like company."

"Don't usually. But I figure you folks need some help. For one night anyway. Sorriest couple of folks I ever did see." He shook his head. Something flew out of his beard. "Where's the rest o' your stuff?" He peered around our makeshift camp, seeing one horse, one rifle, and three saddlebags.

"We're travelling light," Sheridan said.

The man laughed. "Plumb crazy. But folks have been sayin' that 'bout me for years. Figure you've got me beat, Sheridan. Name's Edmund."

Edmund?

"You c'n come home with me, spend the night. Figure your lady might find some things she c'n wear. Proper clothes, like." He looked at my feet. "Maybe even shoes. Then in the morning you c'n be on your way." He turned his head and shot another glob of tobacco onto the ground.

I doubted that Mr. Edmund's accommodation would be any more pleasant than sleeping out, but if he had clothes I could wear, perhaps he also had a wife and family. I would pay very handsomely for an escort to the nearest government office. "What an excellent plan," I said. "Lead on, Mr. Edmund. Not too far, I hope?"

He looked into my face. The corners of his mouth turned up and he sniffed. I felt the small hairs at the back of my neck rise, and a line of ice water moved down my spine.

Sheridan was gathering up the things I'd unpacked. "I promise you, I don't have plans to remain in this area," he said.

"See that you don't," the trapper said, his eyes on mine.

I scrambled to mount Soapy once again. It was not a very dignified performance.

Edmund led the way, not looking back to see if we followed. Scruffy bushes of Labrador tea and dwarf willow, punctuated by the occasional spruce or birch tree, closed in around the almost non-existent trail. If the trapper decided to abandon us, we really would be lost. I bent low over Soapy's neck and felt branches breaking against my back.

We hadn't gone more than a few miles before I caught the scent of woodsmoke in the air. The trees spread out, and I could sit upright again as we climbed a gentle hill. Below, the woods had been hacked down to create a clearing beside a small lake. A single log building sat in the clearing, masses of purple and white wildflowers growing out of the sod roof. A high cache, a shack mounted on tall poles, was behind what I took to be the house, and a patch of earth had been dug to create a vegetable garden, green plants laid out in neat rows. About ten large white dogs were chained in an enclosure next to the woods. As we descended the hill, the dogs, straining against their chains to reach us, set up a hysterical chorus and two children ran out of the cabin, squealing with excitement. One stretched out a hand and touched Soapy's neck. The horse stamped its feet but didn't shy away, and I gave the child what I hoped was a friendly smile. It was a girl, face smudged with dirt but her hair was clean and her clothes didn't smell too bad and her brown eyes shone with curiosity and intelligence. A black bruise darkened her left cheek. The other child, a younger boy, stood back and stuck his thumb into his mouth. I guessed he was about two years old.

By the time we reached the house, a woman had come outside. She waited for us by the door, hands wrapped in a faded pink apron. She wore a brown homespun dress that once would not have been out of place on the streets of Dawson. Now the fabric was thin to the point of transparency in places, and the dress was so many-times-mended, it seemed to be held together by nothing but patches and neat stitches. Her hair was black, hanging down her back in a thick braid. Her eyes were very dark, her face round, her cheekbones flat, and her skin brown. She was an Indian and she was hugely pregnant.

She didn't smile as I rode up to her front step. I slid down from Soapy and held out my hand. The woman did not accept it, and I wiped it on my hip. "Good day," I said cheerfully, "how kind of you to offer us hospitality. It's been a most exhausting journey."

She said nothing, and I wondered if she spoke English.

Edmund handed the woman the two geese with a grunt. She scurried back inside. Most of the buttons at the back of her dress were undone so that her stomach would fit into the garment.

I ducked my head and followed. The outside of the cabin was a jumble of fishnets, snowshoes, wooden crates and barrels, animal hides and traps, but inside it was clean and tidy. There appeared to be only one room, with a pile of blankets against the side wall, a lumpy horsehair sofa against the near wall, a hand-carved pine table in the middle of the room, and a big iron stove at the back. Nailed to the wall beside the stove was a board that served as a counter. Clean dishes, pots, and pans were stacked beside a bucket of soapy water, and the shelves were piled high with cans and packages of food. A tea set, with a blue and gold pattern on a white background, sat on the table. Spode, if my memory served.

Uninvited, I sat on a rough-hewn tree stump that presumably served as a chair. I pulled off my socks and studied my feet. They were raw and weeping — quite disgusting. The rough wool had rubbed against the blisters and re-opened them. My left sock was thick with blood, old and new. The floorboards creaked, and I looked up to see the Indian woman standing in front of me. She held out a bowl containing a lump of yellow paste as foul-smelling as it looked. I tried not to shudder as she pushed the bowl toward me.

"For sore," she said, making rubbing gestures. "Good."

I accepted the offering. "Thank you. My name is Fiona."

Her eyes darted around the room. Sheridan was settling down at the table; Edmund had slipped outside, unbuttoning his trousers as he went. The children watched us, wide-eyed.

"Josie," the woman said in a whisper before hurrying back to her kitchen alcove.

I dipped my finger into the muck and applied the ointment to my feet.

Edmund returned and got a stone pitcher down from the top shelf. He slapped it on the table, Josie brought him two mugs, and he sloshed liquid into the cups. I smelt raw liquor. Clearly, I was not going to be offered any, but that suited me perfectly well.

"None for me, thank you," I said, loudly. "Do you have tea? I'll make it if you like."

I did not care for Edmund and I did not trust him. He looked to me like the sort of man who could smell weakness a mile off. I'd betray no weakness in front of him.

I wanted to be on our way, and soon, but I did want to rest my feet and have a cup of tea and some goose for dinner. Good heavens, was that a bag of rice on the top shelf?

"Tea," Josie said. "I make tea."

"Thank you."

Josie served a piece of — could it possibly be — lemon with the tea. I stared in amazement at the thin yellow slice. "Where on earth did you get that?" I cautiously poked it with my finger, fearing it would disappear into a puff of smoke. I lifted my finger to my lips and tasted. Lemon, for sure.

"A traveller," Josie said with a shrug, turning back to the stove.

The tea was hot and wonderful. She served it in one of the delicate blue-and-gold china cups, and when I'd finished I snuck a surreptitious peek at the bottom. As I'd suspected: Spode.

Such a tea set being here was no odder, I supposed, than Fiona MacGillivray drinking from it in a trapper's cabin in the Yukon wilderness.

Edmund didn't talk much, but Sheridan chatted away about his plans to become a gold prospector. He kept touching his hand to his chest, the pocket where he kept the map, and I knew he didn't trust Edmund either.

Josie took the geese outside and returned in minutes with two naked birds. The little girl sat at my feet, staring up at me with awe, and the boy clung to his mother's skirts while she cooked.

For dinner we feasted on goose and rice and berries. Best of all, we also were served carrots and chard. The carrots weren't fresh, probably stored from last year, but the chard was green, crisp, and absolutely delicious.

Being raised in a proper British household, I attempted to make conversation over the meal, but everyone stuffed food into their mouths so fast there was room for nothing else, and I soon gave up.

Dinner over, Edmund leaned to one side, farted with gusto, and stood up. "Goin' ta feed the dogs," he said.

"I'll help," Sheridan said.

Edmund grunted. The children followed them outside.

Josie had refreshed the water bucket and was wiping the dishes. I stood beside her. She pushed her sleeves up prior to plunging them into water, and I could see a line of deep purple bruises running up her left arm. Her hands were red and chapped, her nails broken and cuticles torn.

"I need your help," I said, my voice pitched low. "I don't want to be with this man."

She kept her eyes on her task, hands moving.

"I have money, friends, influence in Dawson. In town. I have a son."

"In the town you have these things. Here you have nothing."

"Will you help me?"

She didn't reply.

"If you don't know the way to the nearest government post, an Indian village will suffice. You must know the way to the nearest village."

Nothing.

"You can come with me. Take me there. I'll look after you. You won't have to come back here. You can ride the horse."

"I won't leave my children."

"Help me," I repeated.

"Mrs. Fiona. I cannot help you. I cannot help myself." She jumped as Edmund's voice rounded the corner of the cabin and she scurried into the corner like a rat.

Chapter Thirty-Six

They came across the second camp not long after leaving the three Indians.

Branches had been chopped from a small poplar, a fire pit laid, kindling collected, and a square of ground cleared of rocks and pebbles. Buds on a willow had been snapped right off, almost certainly by a feeding horse. Sterling poked at the remains of a campfire: cold and wet.

"They spent the night here," he said. He leaned over a rock and lifted something into the air with a big smile on his face. Angus and Donohue studied it.

Hair. Three strands of long black hair.

"Mother," Angus whispered. He held out both of his hands and Sterling placed the strands into them.

"It's possible the hair's from someone else, but we'll assume your mother was here."

One set of footprints were considerably different than the others. "Bear," Sterling said. "Not a very big one."

"Might it have been here after they left?"

"Looks like oatmeal over here, Corporal," McAllen said. "Scattered around in the dirt. And some threads from a sack. Bear musta gotten into the bag. Sheridan doesn't know enough to cache the food and cooking utensils. Bear wandered in looking for breakfast."

"Gave the horse a good fright," Sterling said. "He just about pulled that tree down trying to get away."

"Is my mother all right?" Angus said.

"Almost certainly. I see no signs of a fight, no bloody ground, nothing's been dragged away. If it was a black bear they would have been able to scare it off."

Sterling did not mention finding spots of blood on the ground between the tent and the fire. There wasn't much blood, only enough, he hoped, to have come from a small cut or a nick. Fiona's shoes were not suitable for a walk in the wilds, so it was possible she'd hurt her feet. He said nothing to Angus.

Sheridan was not at all concerned about hiding his tracks. Perhaps he didn't think anyone would follow, or care if they did. Seemed a strange attitude for a man with a treasure map in his pocket to have, but then again, Sterling thought, simply having a treasure map in one's pocket was strange enough.

At the edge of the clearing he found a length of lace hanging from a broken tree branch. It had a couple of spatters of mud, but otherwise was clean and pure and white. Angus put it carefully away in his pocket next to the strands of hair, the bunch of fake grapes, and the map.

Sterling consulted his pocket watch. "It's shortly after seven now. I'm going to assume Sheridan's stopping for a full night's sleep. They've put up a tent and made a proper fire. Say they slept until six or seven. The excitement with the bear would have slowed them down a bit, and they'd have to put things back to rights. Say another hour. If so, they might have broken camp around eight or nine. We're less than twelve hours behind them. We're gaining. We'll put in another couple of hours and stop for supper and some sleep. But I want to be on the trail not long after sunup."

Chapter Thirty-Seven

Edmund and Sheridan settled themselves at the table and set about downing the contents of the stone jar. Perhaps only I noticed that Sheridan didn't drink any more than was required to be polite. The children crept into the pile of blankets and lay down, huddled together. Josie pulled a fish net onto her lap and began to sew. Her eyes were round and watchful and, I thought, frightened.

Before anyone could offer us bedding, I told Sheridan it was time to put up the tent. He looked almost grateful at the suggestion and pushed away from the table, patting his belly and burping loudly. He was not uneducated and not ill-mannered, so I assumed he was putting on this show for the benefit of his new friend Edmund.

No one came outside with us, and Sheridan erected the tent in considerable haste. "May I come inside tonight, Fiona?" he asked in a most respectful voice. "I promise I won't lay a hand on you until we're properly wed."

"Very well," I said with a deep sigh, as though I were making a great concession. I had, in fact, decided this night I'd be safer with Paul in the tent than without.

I woke to the sound of the dogs barking. Sheridan was sitting up, pulling on his boots. "I suggest we leave immediately after breakfast," he said.

I agreed.

We had nothing to contribute to the morning meal, but it appeared that Edmund kept his family well fed, if nothing else, so I didn't feel guilty on that account.

Josie was stirring a pot over the stove when I knocked politely on the open door. Edmund was nowhere to be seen. The girl came over and touched my dress. "Pretty," she said with a shy smile.

Pretty was most certainly not the word I would use. The hem was thick with dust, mud splattered all up the back, one sleeve was torn from when I'd fought with Sheridan back in Dawson, the neckline was ripped, and the right shoulder had a gash where the branch of a tree had grabbed at me. It must stink to high-heaven of horse and smoke and unwashed Fiona. The first night on the trail, I'd removed my pearl necklace and earrings and tucked them away in one of the packs. I went outside and found them and presented them to the girl. I held the gifts out, and her black eyes opened wide. She stretched her hand to take them, but her mother hissed at her with a glance at the open door.

"They're not genuine pearls," I said, understanding. "No value. Like a toy."

She nodded at the girl and the child grabbed them and dashed across the room. She buried herself in the blankets to examine her prize.

Breakfast was lumpy porridge and powdered milk. I added a several spoonfuls of sugar to give myself a boost of energy. Edmund was his typical scowling self. If he noticed his daughter proudly wearing new jewellery, he didn't mention it.

Sheridan excused himself, saying he had to pack up our things, and Edmund and the children followed him. I heard the trapper explain that if he found us in his territory after today he'd shoot us.

Pleasant host.

Josie cleaned away the bowls and then, to my considerable surprise, brought out a large fruit to serve as dessert. I hadn't seen anything like it before. It was about the size and shape of two cricket balls lying together and had a thick, lumpy green skin.

Rather than take a knife down from the shelf by the stove, she picked up a good-sized hunting knife from Edmund's place at the table, pulled it from its sheath, and sliced into the fruit, revealing bright green flesh surrounding a single large brown pit. She dug out the pit, scooped out the flesh, and placed a generous slice onto a plate, which she passed to me.

"Try," she said. "Very good."

I expected it to be crisp and clean, like an apple, instead it was as soft and creamy as butter. Absolutely delicious.

"Where did you get this?" I asked, picking up the discarded rind and studying it. I could not imagine anything this wonderful growing in the near-Arctic. I thought about the lemon I'd enjoyed with yesterday's tea.

She shrugged. "Strange people pass by in the night. They don't come to the door, but they leave food and small things for the children."

She got up from the table, pressing her hands into the small of her back, and went to a shelf over the beds. She sorted through it, pulled out a sweater, and held it out to me. I almost declined, but didn't. She was offering me a gift, and it would be unkind to refuse it. I had quickly discovered she had no clothes or shoes that would come near to fitting me, but this sweater was very large and well knitted.

If the nights started getting cold, I'd need it.

"Ready Fiona," Sheridan yelled from outside.

"Thank you," I said.

Josie returned to the table and picked up the knife she'd used to slice open the strange green fruit. With a quick glance toward the door, she shoved it back into its sheath, and then handed it to me. "Take. Hide."

I grabbed it and wrapped it in the sweater. "Tell me where your people live. I'll go there. I'll send them to you."

She shook her head and rubbed her giant belly. "They will not come," she said. "Go now. Do not return to this place."

Chapter Thirty-Eight

There had been no sign of any other pursuers since they'd managed to ditch Sergeant Lancaster, but Sterling still insisted they maintain a night watch. He wasn't worried about Lancaster. Mouse O'Brien would steer him down the trail, and they'd soon find themselves back in town. Lancaster would pretend to be annoyed, and then head off to the mess to relate how he'd gone in pursuit of the fair Mrs. MacGillivray and, after giving orders to Sterling, had reluctantly decided his duty was at the fort with his men.

Richard Sterling sat by the fire, smoking his pipe and listening to the soft breathing and snores around him. Not too far away, a wolf howled and the undergrowth rustled. Firelight flashed on a pair of small yellow eyes. He was sorry to have lost Mouse. The man's size alone could be counted on to pretty much put the fight out of anyone so inclined. He wasn't much for the wilderness, none of them were, but he had a good head on his shoulders.

Despite his earlier attempts to sound positive in front of the others, they were not making good enough time. Sheridan was moving faster than Sterling had expected, and if Fiona was riding the horse she wouldn't be slowing him down. He'd have to hope Sheridan would take a wrong turn and double back or at least stay put for a while so they could catch up.

Hope. Was that all he had? Even if he did catch up to them, it might be too late. The wilderness was not a safe place for people who didn't know how to use it. He thought about Fiona's soft voice, the way she said his name — always very proper, with rank and surname. About the way she kept her beautiful face stern and impassive as she went about her business, but sometimes she'd look at him out of the corner of those amazing black eyes and the ghost of a smile would touch the edges of her mouth, and he might even think she had winked.

He loved her. He'd never dared to express the thought before, but now it came into his head fully formed. He loved her. And he couldn't bear to lose her before he'd had the chance to tell her so.

Foolish thoughts. Half the men in Dawson wanted Fiona MacGillivray. Sergeant Lancaster had asked her to marry him and she laughed and barely tolerated his attentions. What did he, Richard Sterling, a preacher's son, a farm boy from Saskatchewan, a corporal in the Mounted Police, have to offer a woman such as her?

He would save her life, if he could. That would be enough.

He tapped out his pipe on a rock, stirred the embers of the fire, and woke Donohue to take the next watch. Sun-up these days was around four o'clock; he wouldn't get much sleep tonight.

Chapter Thirty-Nine

And so we set off once again. I fastened all the buttons on the sweater and wrapped it tightly around me, although it was too warm. Not only was my dress shredding in some most inappropriate places, but I was able to tuck the knife Josie had given me into one of the sweater's voluminous pockets. As I led Soapy over to a rock I could use to clamber aboard, I'd heard the trapper give Sheridan one last piece of advice.

"Turn west, there's nothin' to the east o' here."

"Nothing? Can there be more nothing than what's around here?"

The trapper didn't answer, and when I'd hoisted myself onto Soapy and looked up, he was staring at Sheridan. He spat a lump of chewing tobacco onto the ground. The little girl stroked the horse's soft velvet nose. She was wearing pearls around her neck and in her ears.

"River not far from here," Edmund said at last, pointing toward the rising sun. "Small river, movin' slow most o' the time."

"What's on the other side?"

The trapper shook his head. "Don't know. Never been across."

"Why?"

"I've set out to, but somehow always seem to change my mind. Blast it, man, go where you want, just so long as you stay away from my traps. And don't come back here with your fancy woman."

He spat out a lump of wet brown tobacco and stalked into the house.

When we crested the hill, I turned and looked back. Smoke was rising from the roof and the dogs were barking. Josie stood in the dusty yard watching. I lifted my hand but she did not wave back.

I could read the passage of time on Paul Sheridan's face. His dark stubble was getting longer, his clothes torn and stained by sweat, grease, and dust. His face and hands were covered in scratches and infected insect bites. The bags under his eyes were heavier and darker every day, but the fire in them didn't let up.

I looked no better. My hair was a tangle of knots, sticky with the residue of pine sap, and I'd given up all attempts to keep it under some sort of control. It hung down my back and across my face, and my hat, which should perch attractively on top of a carefully arranged bundle of hair (and be secured by a hat pin, I might add), was pulled down low on my head in an attempt to keep it on. My dress was torn in a hundred places and the skin of my legs and arms as well. The trail was now so narrow, Soapy could barely fit through in places. The lower branches of pine trees die and snap off as the trees grow and make a formidable barrier. My face was scratched by numerous broken branches. I had to remain alert, constantly, otherwise I might get a pointed stick in the eye.

Sheridan walked ahead, laden down with our packs. As he was breaking the trail he was having a rougher time than I, but he never seemed to mind. He chatted about his plans for his new kingdom. First thing, he'd send to the Outside for workers and supplies. Then he'd build me a grand house with a big front porch so I could sit out and catch the cool breezes. The house would, of course, have hot water, piped in from the hot springs.

He asked if I wanted gold faucets for my bath, or would that be too pretentious. I didn't answer. I wasn't interested in playing his games. I was thinking about the contents of our packs, and getting quite worried about the amount of food left. Then it occurred to me for the first time that something was lacking in the things Sheridan had brought for his venture.

He had no mining equipment.

Not even a pan for sifting river gravel.

"Mr. Sheridan!" I cried. "We must return to Dawson immediately."

He spun around. "What? Why? Are you ill?" Soapy took advantage of the break to lower his head and search for something tasty.

"You neglected to bring mining utensils."

"Won't need them."

"Why on earth not? I thought the purpose of this expedition is to mine for gold."

He walked back to stand beside the horse. He put his hand on Soapy's neck and looked up at me. "Don't you trust me yet, Fiona?"

I didn't bother to answer.

"The gold'll be easy to collect. Nuggets so large I'll have trouble lifting them out of the stream. No need for a pan. I've got the axe, that'll loosen the mountainside enough to reach in and pull out handfuls of gold."

I shivered in the warm sunshine and the thick sweater. Until that moment, I'd thought Mr. Sheridan had an excess of gold fever but was confident he'd soon come to his senses and turn back. My only worry had been that we might, by then, be hopelessly lost. Now I truly understood the depths of the man's madness.

He wasn't the only one: Dawson overflowed with men who believed they were about to make it rich, to become one of the legendary Kings of the Klondike. No matter how many times they were told no good claims were left and all that waited for them at the Creeks was relentless labour on behalf of someone else, they refused to give up the dream.

Mr. Sheridan had taken the obsession to an absurd degree.

"There's a clearing up ahead," he said. "I think we need a rest." He slapped the horse's rump. No doubt he would have liked to give me a hearty pat as well. He hadn't tried to touch me since that night in the tent. I felt the weight of the knife beneath my new sweater.

If I had to kill Mr. Paul Sheridan, I would.

We reached the clearing, and as he was swinging the rifle around to rest it on the ground, a bird broke from cover. It looked very much like the grouse back in Scotland, but was quite a bit smaller. It was brown with a small head and a line of red above its eyes. It stopped. Blinked at us. Lifted its wings to take to the air. Sheridan finally got command of his senses and shot the little creature.

We drank a mouthful of water and chewed on dry biscuits and wrinkled carrots the trapper's wife had provided. As I ate the miserly lunch, I thought happily of the meal of roast ptarmigan to come.

The vegetation was getting sparser; what trees there were, stubby and stunted. We climbed a low hill late in the day, poor Soapy barely able to put one tired foot in front of the other. And the other, and the other.

Sheridan reached the top of the hill and stopped dead. Glad of the break, Soapy stopped as well. From my higher vantage, I could see what lay ahead. My heart leapt into my mouth.

It was an open plain, almost completely bare of trees. Dwarf willows turned the rolling hills the colour of ripe plumbs. The hills stretched toward a row of mountains, sharp-toothed and topped with snow reflecting shades of pink and purple in the long light of the western sun. The wind blew toward us, carrying fresh snow and the heady scent of wildflowers and berries.

"Do you see it, Fiona?" Sheridan said, his voice low and full of awe.

One mountain stood alone, closer than the distant range, rising up from the plains like a pointed hat tossed onto a table. A blanket of snow was draped over its top and upper flanks. Sheridan pulled out his map. He pointed to the red circle near the uppermost corner. "Here," he said. He stretched out his hand in front of him. "Here," he repeated. I looked down at the map. It did show a line of triangles marching behind the round red dot. Was he right after all?

I shook my head. Heaven's sakes. That map could be of any place. Some child scribbled on a blank piece of paper and his father decided to have fun and perhaps make a bit of money selling the treasure map. No shortage of mountain ranges in the North. Simply a coincidence we'd come upon one with a single tall peak.

Without another word, Sheridan pulled on the horse's lead and descended the slope of the hill at a fast clip. The ground was soft, thick with moss. A golden eagle circled overhead, and off to my left, the long tail of a fox disappeared into a clump of shrub.

Sheridan broke into a run in his eagerness to push forward. Soapy trotted behind and I clung to the horse's mane. At the bottom of the hill, we came to a river. It was a creek really, moving lazily across the vast tundra. The banks were shallow and the water so fresh and clear, I could see gravel sparkling on the bottom. Small fish darted between the stones, silver bodies glistening in the sun.

"The promised land," Sheridan said, holding his arms out wide. "Why should I not be king, king of all that lies before me?"

I rolled my eyes and muttered, "I'd rather go home and be queen of my own bed, thank you very much."

Sheridan put his foot into the water.

He pulled it back.

"Perhaps we won't go on today," he said.

So surprised was I, I forgot to say, "Good idea," and instead said, "What? It's scarcely six o'clock."

He dipped his foot in again. "We don't know when we might find another water source. Best make camp here." He hesitated, one foot in the water, one still on the shore.

"Let's at least get across the stream. That clump of spruce will give us some shelter and you need wood to make a fire and erect the tent."

Sheridan seemed to be battling with himself. His body jerked and his legs shook. Was the man having a seizure? I was capable of cold-bloodedly stabbing him in the back if such should be required, but I wasn't able to stand by and let him die of a fit.

Legs kicking, I slid off Soapy's back. I approached Sheridan and touched him on the arm. "Are you all right?"

He jerked. "Overly tired, my dear." His smile was sickly and his face white as death. "We'll rest here." He pulled his foot out of the water. "Don't know what came over me. Feel fine now." Colour flooded back into his face. "Let's go on."

He put his foot into the water again and the scene repeated itself. His body shook and the blood again drained away from his face. I took his arm and pulled. He stumbled against me.

"As you say. Best we make camp here. You sit for a minute." I looked around. Not so much as a boulder large enough to provide a chair. Sheridan collapsed to the ground like a rag doll.

He might look exhausted and seriously ill, but he still had the presence of mind to cradle the bag containing his knife to his chest.

Soapy watched us with interest. I untied the saddlebag from the horse's neck and dropped it on the ground. I'd give the beast a drink and then lead him up to a lovely green patch of moss a few yards away. After three days of walking, the horse was looking somewhat thin.

I took hold of the rope tied to Soapy's neck and walked toward the water. He followed me willingly enough and put his right front foot into the stream. Without warning he reared back and screamed a scream the like of which I hope never to hear again. The rope burned as it tore out of my hand, and Soapy flailed at the air with his front legs. I fell backwards, crashing down on the rocks and pebbles of the riverbank. My head swum and pain flooded my right wrist where I'd unthinkingly tried to break my fall.

When I looked up, Soapy was nothing more than a speck disappearing over the crest of the hill, heading back the way we had come.

I let out a long piercing scream. Rage at the horse. Rage at Paul Sheridan. Rage at my own stupidity for letting myself be dragged this far.

"Fiona," Sheridan said. "Couldn't you have taken more care? Now you're going to have to walk the rest of the way. Good thing you got the bag off him first."

Using my left arm, I hurled a rock at him. It missed by a very wide margin.

I clambered to my feet and rubbed my aching bottom. How quickly the trappings of civilization desert us.

"As you're up," Sheridan said. "Take the axe, will you, and cut some branches for the tent."

I flexed my wrist. It was painful but not too bad and there wasn't a problem with movement. I took off my disgustingly filthy socks before wrenching the axe out of its pack. Sheridan was watching me, a stupid smile on his face. I hefted the axe. It wasn't heavy and the blade was dull and rusty. I looked at my captor. He continued to smile.

I sighed and, holding the axe high, stepped cautiously into the water. I almost expected it to be boiling hot, but the water felt cool and refreshing on my aching feet. Tiny fish darted forward to nibble at my toes. Stones dug into the soles of my feet, but I crossed the creek in a half-dozen careful steps. The far bank was not as rocky and I could move between patches of emerald green moss, soft and cool. I wiggled my toes. Josie, the trapper's wife, had given me some of the yellow paste to take with me and it did seem to be doing a good job healing the sores.

When I looked back, Sheridan was taking the tent and bedrolls out of the pack. He saw me watching and waved.

Now, I really was in a pickle. I'd lost the horse. I wouldn't be able to outrun Sheridan, not in bare feet or leather-heeled socks or evening slippers. Ahead was the flat plain, the tall snow-topped mountain.

And a great deal of nothing.

Chapter Forty

They walked in silence most of the day. Angus missed Mouse O'Brien's hearty laugh and cheerful conversation. Donohue cursed every time he tripped over a root, and even Millie was beginning to droop.

At one point, they heard water up ahead and came to a small, cheerful stream, moving fast over rocks. The mud by the water was heavily churned, the grasses torn up, and a patch of horse manure, fresh, lay on the ground. Ravens rose with loud cries as the men approached. Sterling went over to see what the birds had been dining on: scatterings of bread crumbs.

"They stopped for something to eat," he said. "And to water the horse. I don't think they stayed long. We'll rest here for a short while. Angus, do you have any more of that seed cake?"

"Sorry, sir. Gave the last of it to the Indians."

"Oh, well. At least it was well spent."

They shared bread, now stale and hard, and cheese and filled their water bottles. The water was so cold, that as Angus put his hand in, his fingers began to numb almost immediately.

Then they hoisted their packs once again and continued on their way.

"Where do you think we are, Corporal?" McAllen asked after hours of walking. McAllen carried the rifle and had shot two rabbits to throw into the dinner pot. He'd shown Angus

how to use the weapon, but so far Angus had missed everything
he aimed at.

"Damned if I know," Sterling growled. "Sorry, Angus. We're
well north of Dawson, somewhat to the east. I'm hoping we'll
come to the tundra before too much longer. There's not many
trees, so I've been told, and a man can see all the way to the
horizon. If that's so, and that's where they're headed, we might be
able to catch sight of them. We're going steadily north-north-east
now."

"Like the map shows," Angus said.

"Right."

"That's good, I suppose," Donohue said, sounding quite
unsure of himself. "Sheridan's sticking to the map and not
wandering blindly all over creation."

"I suspect," Sterling said, "he's simply following whatever
trail he comes across that's going in the general direction."

They found another campsite. This one was barely disturbed.
Sterling studied the ground. "I'd say they stopped and started to
make camp. There are twigs gathered, but the fire was never lit.
Well, well, look at that." He pointed with his toe to a big brown
blob.

"We haven't seen any other signs of chewing tobacco," he
said. "If Sheridan used it, he'd surely have brought it out before
now."

"You think someone else was here?" McAllen asked.

"I do." Sterling tested the air. "What do you smell?"

Everyone sniffed.

"Smoke," Angus said.

"Woodsmoke," McAllen added.

"Smoke indeed."

"More Indians?" Angus asked. "Maybe they've seen my
mother too."

"A handful of prospectors and trappers live out here, as well as Indians. They don't usually care for visitors from Outside, and certainly not anyone from the government or police. Nevertheless, we'll pay them a call." He looked up, over the tops of the trees, but could see no trace of smoke. "The prints go in that direction, not back to the trail we've been following, so let's see what we can find."

The scent of woodsmoke got stronger, and in the distance, dogs set up a chorus of frantic barking. They crested the hill to see a homestead below.

As they approached, Sterling bellowed, "Hello, the house!" Millie barked out her own greeting.

By the time they reached the clearing, a man had come outside. He was a white man, dirty and scruffy, with unkempt hair and a long, tangled beard. His right cheek bulged with a lump of chewing tobacco, and he cradled a rifle in the crook of his arm, watching them approach through narrowed, unfriendly eyes.

"Greetings," Sterling said. He stopped about ten feet away and waited for the man to speak.

He studied them each in turn, his eyes lingering on Angus's face for a long time. At last he said, "Howdy. What brings the Mounties to these parts?" He did not lower the rifle.

"I'm Corporal Sterling from Fort Herchmer. This is Constable McAllen, Mr. Donohue, and Mr. MacGillivray."

"Edmund Whiteside. I don't like folks on my land, uninvited."

"Mr. Whiteside, I'm looking for a white man and a woman. They have a horse with them. Have you seen them?"

"Might of."

"When would that have been?" Sterling asked. Donohue and Angus and McAllen stood beside him, saying nothing. Even Angus was learning to keep his mouth shut and let Sterling take the lead.

He heard light footsteps on the wooden floors of the cabin. A child's dark head poked out of the door. Another one, younger, smaller, joined her. The older child wore a dress far too big for her over-dirty trousers with rolled up hems. She had pearl earrings attached to her ears and a long strand of pearls draped around her neck.

Angus sucked in a breath. "Those are my ma's pearls." He stepped forward and the child darted inside. The man growled and lifted the rifle.

"Mr. Whiteside. I don't want any trouble. The woman I'm seeking's obviously been here. I also recognize the necklace."

Whiteside peered at Angus. "Your ma, boy?"

"Yes, sir."

"You've the look o' her, though the colour's wrong. Your wife, Corporal?"

"A subject of her Majesty in need of assistance."

Whiteside grunted and lowered the weapon. He tossed his head in the direction of the open cabin door. Sterling took that to be an invitation. "Come on in," the trapper said, "and we'll talk about it. Don't suppose you have any grog on you?"

"No."

"Too bad."

Angus unloaded Millie's packs and tied her to a stump while the men followed Whiteside. The hysterical barking of dogs came from the kennels at the edge of the property. Realizing that none of her kind were coming to greet her, Millie circled three times and then tucked her tail beneath her rump and settled down for a nap.

The cabin was small and dark, crammed with goods and heavy with the scent of tobacco and grease. A pregnant woman stood beside the iron stove. Her skin was brown, her cheekbones high and flat, and her eyes as dark as a Yukon winter night. Her hands were wrapped in her apron, caressing her belly, and a thick black braid hung over her shoulder. Her right eye was shades of black and purple, almost swollen shut, and a matching bruise marked the side of her mouth.

"Ma'am," Sterling said, removing his hat.

At a grunt from the trapper, the woman got a stone jar down from the shelf and brought it and mugs to the big table in the centre of the room. The girl crept into a pile of blankets against the far wall, leading the boy by the hand. The boy buried his head into the bed, but the girl watched them with an unblinking stare.

Whiteside splashed liquid into mugs. He lifted his own and drank deeply.

Sterling almost choked on the fiery hot liquor. It burned its way down his throat all the way to his stomach. McAllen took a tiny sip. Donohue swallowed his in one gulp and leaned back with a satisfied grunt. Millie settled, Angus came in. Whiteside began to pour some liquor into an extra mug. "No," Sterling said, sharply.

The corners of Whiteside's mouth lifted up. He downed his drink and wiped his mouth with the back of his hand.

"When were they here?" Sterling asked.

"Who?"

"Don't play games with me," Sterling said. "I'll have you taken into town if you don't co-operate." He glanced at the woman, who'd retreated to her place by the stove. Her hands rested on her enormous belly and her face was expressionless. An empty threat, and everyone knew it. Take the man away and the woman and children would starve come winter.

Was this the woman the Indians had told him about? Who'd left her tribe to live with a white man and would never be allowed back?

He'd wondered about that. Plenty of Indian women set up with white men, very few with benefit of clergy, and lived with them until the men decided they'd had enough of the wilderness and abandoned their half-white families. Most of the women went back to their tribe easily enough. What had the old man said? This particular woman had gone too close to the forbidden?

"Just messin' with ya," Whiteside said. "Yeah, they was here. A pretty woman and a city man. Won't last another month in the wilds. First sign of snow, they'll be rushing back to town fast enough."

"I can only hope so," Sterling said. "They were here last night, I assume."

"Yup."

"And they left when?"

"This morning. Couple hours after sun-up."

"That's great," Angus said, jumping to his feet. "We're almost on them."

"Hold on a minute," Sterling said. "Where'd they go?"

"Now that I can't rightly say. I told him I find him on my trapline, I'll kill him. What'd you think about that, Redcoat?"

"I think that if you killed him, the NWMP would see you hang for it."

"You could try at any rate." He poured himself another drink. This time he did not offer the jug around. "But before you do that, you c'n arrest the woman."

"Why?"

"Stole a knife." The man looked at the Indian woman. She turned her head away. "One o' my best skinning knives. And here after my family and me showed 'em such nice hospitality."

"She needs the knife to defend herself," Angus shouted.

"Forget about it. Don't matter none to me if'n she sticks it between his ribs."

"Once again," Sterling said, feeling impatience rise in his chest like heartburn. "I ask you where they went."

"He said he were lookin' to go prospectin' to the northwest. I told him to make sure he did."

"Did they go northwest?"

"Nope, they's heading east." The man shifted in his chair, suddenly uncomfortable. "No one goes there."

"Why not?"

He chewed at a scrap of loose skin on his right thumb. It came away in a spurt of blood. He sucked at it, eyes on the table.

"I asked why not? What's to the east?"

Outside, a black cloud moved across the sun, plunging the cabin into deep gloom. A gust of wind rattled the shutters on the windows and a cold breeze blew between the cracks in the log walls. Millie howled, and the trapper's dogs answered.

Donohue muttered under his breath, McAllen's eyes darted around the room, and Angus glanced toward the door. Only Sterling continued to stare at the trapper.

"Don't recon I know," he said at last. "Never been there. There's somethin' strange there. Somethin' not right. Indians 'round here say that land's cursed. Don't go much into worryin' 'bout Indian superstition, but that land over the creek? No, I don't go there."

"Does no one go there?" Donohue asked.

"Sometimes the dogs hear folks passing through, heading west. Always at night, come to think of it. They don't stop, they don't talk. Sometimes, they leave things for the woman an' the kids." His eyes darted toward her. "Presents. Fruit or nuts."

"You make them sound like fairies," Donohue said, "Elves. Storybook creatures."

Whiteside stood up. "I got work to do. Winter's comin' and it's gonna be a hard one."

Sterling rose also, and the others clambered to follow. "Show me the path they took, and we'll be out of your way."

They went outside. Whitehead pointed toward the small hill. "They went back the way they came."

Angus untied Millie. McAllen and Donohue started off. Sterling hesitated. "Your wife," he said at last, "is close to her time. You might want to get her to Dawson. There's doctors there now."

Whitehead spat a lump of tobacco, barely missing the toe of Sterling's boot. "Indian women don't need doctors. She'll manage."

Sterling walked away. Angus fell into step beside him.

What happened in a man's home between him and his wife was no one else's business. That's what everyone said.

Still didn't make it right.

Chapter Forty-One

We camped on the side of the creek. It was not a good location — I had to cross the water several times to fetch wood for the fire, and there was no shelter for our tent. I considered refusing to do the work, but Sheridan was behaving in such a strangely apathetic manner, it seemed if I didn't do it, no one would.

I gathered twigs and brush to start the fire and was fortunate enough to come across some good-sized dead branches in a clump of spruce. It took me several trips to lug it all across the creek, and I was not in good humour when I pushed Sheridan aside and rearranged the kindling into a pile that might actually burn.

I lifted the ptarmigan. It was a very small bird and wouldn't provide much of a meal for two people.

I thought of my own knife nestled in my sweater pocket.

I did not bring it out.

"If we are going to eat, give me your knife so I can skin this thing."

"I'll do it," he said. He held out his hand and I passed the bird over. Once it was roasting over the fire, Sheridan pulled himself to his feet and began collecting rocks to hold down the edges of the tent.

I opened the last can of potatoes to accompany the meat, and we ate our meal hunched close to the fire, now dying into embers. As I munched on the badly-cooked ptarmigan, I watched long shadows crossing the rolling hills in the east. I thought of Scotland and the bare beauty of the Highlands I missed so much. My father accompanied the earl and his guests many times on hunting trips and cared for his shotguns. He never allowed me to touch one of them, much less learn how to use it. If the hunting had been good, and sometimes even if it hadn't, the kind earl would send my father home with a couple of good grouse for our pot. I smiled, realizing why I'd suddenly come over all affectionate for Scotland. This ptarmigan, as badly cooked as it was, reminded me a great deal of those fine Scottish grouse.

I finished my meagre dinner lost in thought.

A strong wind came up as we were preparing for bed, bringing with it the scent of snow off the mountains and wild-flowers from the plains, and our tent was storm-tossed all the night long. Once again, I insisted Mr. Sheridan retire outside. "Not proper," I said with a sniff.

He spent the night buffeted by the wind.

The miserable fire went out while we slept, and the cold woke me. I rummaged through the food bags — which did not take long — and located about one half a cup of oatmeal.

"Mr. Sheridan. We cannot continue. We simply don't have adequate food."

He had rolled out of his blanket when he heard me exit the tent. At my words he lifted his eyes to the horizon, and I was once again reminded of that preacher, sermonizing reverently to farm families who replied with laugher, jeers, and thrown rocks. "Another day, I suspect, Fiona. And we'll be there."

"Perhaps not. Now that we've found the way, I suggest we return to town and outfit ourselves properly. Plus collect Angus. Why we can be back in a week! Well-equipped and ready to face the unknown like true adventurers." I almost gave a proper British rah, rah, but decided that might be laying it on a bit thick.

He gave me a long look. "Really, Fiona. Do you think me that much of a fool?"

I sighed and crossed the creek one more time to collect firewood. My head was stuffed full of wool. There have been times in my life when I've gone without adequate food, and I'd seen what hunger could do to others. It's hard to think straight when your body's shutting itself down to conserve energy.

I'd hoped Paul Sheridan would tire of this foolishness and I'd be able to talk him into going back to town. Clearly that wasn't going to happen.

I'd have to take my chances.

I should be able to find my way back to that dreadful trapper's house. Without Sheridan to contend with (or sympathize with) he might be willing to take me ... someplace in exchange for a handsome reward. Even dressed in torn rags and a cast off sweater with my hat yanked down over my head and my hair like a rat's nest, I clearly looked like a woman of means.

Didn't I?

I fingered the knife concealed deep in my pocket.

I looked back. Sheridan had picked up the rifle and was standing very still, the weapon held up to his face, his finger on the trigger, facing the edge of the creek where a line of scruffy bushes dipped toward the water.

I studied my surroundings. The creek meandered across the plain, running more or less parallel to the line of mountains on the eastern horizon.

Enough of this. It was long past time to be on my way home. I wasn't taking another step in the direction of that mountain. Mr. Sheridan seemed unwilling to cross the creek. I had absolutely no idea why that might be the case, but I'd take advantage of it. He wouldn't shoot me.

Would he?

Even if he did shoot, unlikely he'd hit me. I was a good distance away.

I'd tucked my socks into the folds of my dress while wading across the water; I had nothing to return to camp for.

Setting my back straight, I lifted my head and began to walk along the edge of the stream. According to Sheridan's ridiculous map, we were going north and east. This creek was heading south. I would simply follow it, steering west with the sun. With luck I could slip back across the creek once I'd lost the odious Mr. Sheridan. Perhaps I could even find Soapy. The horse was no fonder of the wilderness than I and would be glad of my companionship.

I'd taken three determined steps when the rifle went off. So started was I that I leapt into the air. My naked right foot landed on a rock and my left slid into a small depression. I lost my footing completely and fell, hard. My hands dug into sharp stones and my right wrist, the one I'd hurt yesterday, twisted under my weight. Pain shot up my arm, lancing into my shoulder, pain so sharp and unexpected I screamed.

"Fiona!" Through the haze of pain and confusion, I heard Sheridan shout my name. "Oh, save us, Fiona! My beloved."

Water splashed as he stumbled across the creek. I'd rolled onto my back, after checking the knife was still in place, when Sheridan dropped to his haunches beside me. "My darling, I'm so sorry. Where are you hurt?" His hands began to explore my body.

I swatted them away. "Everywhere. Help me up, you fool."

"But, but," he said. His eyes were wide with fear as they studied me. He reached out as reverently as if he were touching a holy relic, took my forearms, and turned my palms up. They were dotted with tiny stones and flecks of blood.

"Oh, Fiona. I thought ... I can't bear to imagine what I thought. If I lost you ... I don't know how I could go on."

He thought he'd shot me.

And he'd forded the creek, which for some reason seemed to terrify him, to get to me.

Another chance lost.

I wasn't shot, but my hands hurt like the blazes, my wrist screamed in protest at any movement, and my knees were torn and bleeding.

After Sheridan settled me on a patch of moss, apologizing profusely for frightening me, and went back across the creek to collect our things. He seemed to have no further trouble with the water.

As I watched him go, I felt a touch of almost-affection for the man. He was trapped in the grip of sheer madness and nothing, such as my unwillingness to be his consort, would dissuade him from following his goal. Once we — I should say, he — got to this mountain and found that it was nothing out of the ordinary, would he recover his senses? Or descend completely into insanity?

I brought my wandering sentiment under control sharply. As much as Mr. Paul Sheridan might care for me, I must never forget that he did not have my best interests at heart. I was alone in the wilderness with a madman.

A large ragged hole had been torn in my dress at about the level of my knees. Propriety be damned. I tore off a strip from knee to hem, dipped the cloth into the water, and used it to clean blood from my hands and legs.

Sheridan's eyes almost popped out of his head at the sight of all that exposed flesh. I glared at him and he blushed to the roots of his hair. He began piling twigs for our morning fire. I settled my back against a not-too rough tree and watched him work. For breakfast he served me coffee and the last of the oatmeal.

After we'd eaten, Sheridan repacked our possessions — a pathetically small bundle — and politely asked if I'd mind carrying some of the lighter things. He put the coffee pot and the frying pan into a sack. They made a tiny lump at the bottom of what had once been our food packs. I considered telling him we might as well leave them behind, as we had no more coffee and nothing to fry. He gave me a sheepish smile that would have been attractive had he had a full set of teeth, and I reached out and took the offering.

His own knife, he kept to himself.

Chapter Forty-Two

They walked most of the night, stopping only for something to eat and a few hours sleep when it was darkest. Angus chafed at taking even that short break, but Sterling reminded him, once more, they would do his mother no favours if they missed signs in the darkness. Fiona and Sheridan had left the trapper's cabin not more than eight or nine hours earlier. If they stopped to sleep a full night, the pursuers should catch up to them today.

Angus was in charge of supper tonight. They were having rabbit, roasted over open flame, and the smell was making his mouth water. Of like mind, Millie was attempting to edge closer to the meat. He wished he'd been able to bag a rabbit or ptarmigan, something to contribute to dinner. McAllen had been patient and helpful, showing the boy how to steady and aim the Winchester, how to squeeze the trigger, to anticipate the recoil, how to reload. Despite not killing anything, he felt like a man, proud of his newly learned skill.

"Do you think we've been particularly lucky," Angus said, struggling to open a can of beans, "that the trail's been easy to follow and people have seen my mother?"

Sterling puffed on his pipe. Firelight danced on the sharp bones of his face and illuminated the depths of his eyes. He'd placed his broad-brimmed hat on top of his pack, and dark hair curled around the back of his neck. The stubble on his face was coming in black and thick. Angus had checked his own face this morning — to his great disappointment there were still no signs of whiskers.

"They say," Sterling said slowly, "in the far north, where the sun never sets at all in the summer and never rises in the dead of winter, a man can travel hundreds of miles without coming across another human being. Whole ships, great sailing ships, and all their crew have disappeared into that empty land, leaving not a trace behind to tell of their fate. Here, there's usually someone around, in summer anyway. Indians, trappers, prospectors, not to mention whisky traders and missionaries. Sheridan hasn't been trying to hide his tracks. If he had, then we might well not be able to follow them so easily."

Angus was about to announce the rabbits were ready when Millie's ears shot up and she leapt to her feet with a bark. Sterling grabbed the Winchester and stood up, pipe clenched between his teeth. Donohue and McAllen froze in place. Angus stopped breathing. Within the dark forest, leaves rustled and a branch broke.

"North-West Mounted Police," Sterling shouted. "Lower your weapon and come forward."

They heard a sharp puff of air. A horse whinnied and the trees parted. A thin brown horse walked into the clearing. It was wearing a bridle, and a rope trailed between its front legs. Sterling lowered the rifle. McAllen stepped toward the animal and spoke to it in low soothing tones. The horse pawed the ground and allowed the constable to stretch out one hand and stroke the soft nose.

"McAllen," Sterling ordered, "tie it up. Angus, pull out a handful of oatmeal and give it to him while McAllen gets it secured."

The horse sucked up the offering and allowed McAllen to grab the rope and loop it around a tree.

"Where do you suppose he's come from?" Donohue said. Millie returned to guarding the dinner.

"No wild horses in this part of the world," McAllen said, studying the animal. "And this one isn't wild in any event."

"Fiona?" Donohue said. "She was riding a horse, Whiteside told us. Is this it?"

"I'll assume that's the case until I know otherwise," Sterling said.

"How do you suppose ..." Angus said.

"No point in supposing anything," Sterling interrupted. "We don't know what it's doing on its own. At a guess, probably got loose and wandered away from your mother's campsite and then decided it didn't want to be out here on its own after all. The horse is clearly unharmed." It ripped up vegetation and munched happily, ignoring the watching men.

Angus stroked the long neck. "Wish he could talk."

"McAllen, load some of our gear onto the horse when we're ready to go. Give us a bit of a break. It smells as if those rabbits are starting to burn. Mr. MacGillivray, better see to your duties."

Angus wanted to leap on the horse's back and gallop off down the trail. Surely they were close now. He curbed his impatience and began serving supper.

He fell asleep listening to the horse's breathing, the stamp of hooves on the hard ground, and the tearing of leaves and grasses. He awoke when Sterling poked his blankets with his foot. "Time to go." The sun was low in the east. Angus didn't have to look at his watch to know it was only about four o'clock.

The horse seemed happy enough to have a couple of packs slung over its back, and they set off without bothering with breakfast.

After all, it had only been three hours since supper.

A strong wind had come up during the night, bringing with it high, fast-moving clouds, and the temperature had dropped noticeably while they slept.

Two hours walking brought them to the edge of the forest. Before them stretched the tundra, empty and beautiful. They stood at the top of the hill for a long time. Even Angus felt the urge to pause and stare.

"Wish I'd thought to bring glasses," Sterling muttered.

"Do you think that's it?" Donohue slowly lifted his hand and pointed at the single peak rising out of the plain. "Gold Mountain?"

"It might be where Sheridan's heading," Sterling snapped, "but it sure isn't any gold mountain."

"Does that mountain have a name?" Angus asked. "The one standing all on its own. It must be quite a landmark."

Sterling rubbed at his chin. "Don't think it's on any map. Least not any map I've ever seen. McAllen?"

The constable shook his head. "Never even heard anyone talk about it, and there are Mounties and traders with Taylor and Drury who've been up this way."

They soon came to a small creek. Once again there were signs of a fire and camp. The creek was only a few feet wide, and on the other shore they could see more evidence that someone had been there very recently.

Sterling slapped Angus on the back. "Not much longer now, son. We'll find your mother."

"Poor Mother," Angus said. "She swore she'd never set foot in the wilderness again, and now look where she is. I really do want to get her home."

"I'm supposed to be going to Forty Mile next week," McAllen said. "Hope we're back in time."

"We will be," Sterling said. He stared across the land and saw Fiona in his mind's eye. He swallowed the lump of emotion that threatened to choke him. "We'll get your mother back to the Savoy, Angus, where she belongs."

"Gold Mountain." Donohue's voice was dreamy. "Perhaps it really is true. There are hot springs around, everyone knows that. Why not one so big it can heat a valley? And gold. A mountain of pure gold."

"No point in standing here talking," Sterling said. "Let's go."

McAllen went first. He crossed quickly, checking for deep spots or places where a man might lose his footing. But the water was very shallow, and he gestured for the remainder of the party to follow.

Graham Donohue put one foot into the water. Then he took it out again. Angus watched as he put it back. And then took it out. Donohue shook himself, all over, and retreated a couple of feet. "I'm awfully tired. Let's have a rest before we carry on."

"Are you crazy?" Sterling said. "We stopped for coffee less than an hour ago."

"I have to catch my breath. You go ahead."

Sterling was leading the horse. He got several feet across the creek when the rope jerked tight. He looked back. The horse was standing at the water's edge, its feet locked, eyes wide with terror. "What on earth?" Sterling waded back to the animal. He gathered up loose rope so his hand was under the horse's neck. "Come on, fellow." The horse refused to budge. It took a step back, pulling Sterling along with it.

"What's the matter?" McAllen called.

Sterling studied the clear water beneath his feet. Tiny silver fish darted around the pebbles. Nothing that should frighten a horse, but no matter how hard he pulled on the rope, the animal refused to take a step forward.

"Get over to the other side, Angus," Sterling said.

Angus stepped into the water. Millie put her front paws in and stopped dead. Angus pulled on the lead. Millie pulled back. She whined and the short hairs on the back of her neck stood on end. "Come on, Millie," Angus said. "I'm not going to carry you."

The dog growled at him, her teeth bared. Angus blinked in surprise. "Mr. Sterling, she doesn't want to come either."

Sterling looked around. McAllen was on the other bank, his young face curious as to what was taking everyone so long. Donohue had sat down, removed his right boot and sock and was rubbing his naked foot with a look of mind disinterest.

"Never seen anything like this before," Sterling said. "It's as if they're mutinying. Donohue, will you get the heck up. We're not waiting for you. This is obviously the way. Mrs. MacGillivray was here last night and I suspect they're not more than a few hours ahead of us, if that."

Donohue shook his head. "Sorry. Don't know what came over me." He put his footwear back on and stood.

"Don't you show me your teeth," Angus said to Millie, pitching his voice deep and low and giving a growl of his own. He pulled hard on the dog's lead. "Now, come on." She snarled and resisted. "Don't you want to help Mother? You helped her before. She needs you again."

The big white dog looked at him for a long time. Angus stared into her eyes, wondering what thoughts were going on behind them. Then she gave a single loud bark and ran across the creek with such speed it seemed as if her feet didn't touch the surface of the water. It was all Angus could do to keep his own feet from being pulled out from under him.

Graham Donohue stood with one foot in the water. His face was lined with strain as if he were involved in a game of tug-of-war and his side was losing. Then all the tension drained out of his face and he stepped back.

"Not today," he said. "You men carry on. I'll catch you up later."

"Are you nuts?" Sterling said. He was still in the creek, still gripping the horse's lead. Icy water was beginning to find its way through the stitching in his boots. Unlike Millie, the horse wasn't budging. "Stay here, then," he said, swallowing a string of curses. With short, angry movements he untied the bags from the horse's back. All Donohue was carrying were his own things. Sterling threw the rope to the newspaperman. "Mrs. MacGillivray may need to ride. Be sure you're here when we get back or I'll see that you get a blue ticket. Hear me, Donohue?"

Donohue waved his hand in the air. "Just need a short rest, then I'll follow. This seems like a nice spot." He lay back and closed his eyes. The end of the rope was loose in his hand and the horse stood beside him.

Sterling and McAllen exchanged glances. "Strangest damn thing I ever did see. Begging your pardon, Angus."

Chapter Forty-Three

The closer we got to the solitary mountain, the quicker Sheridan moved. At times he would practically gallop on ahead and then have to turn around and wait impatiently for me to catch up. Now that we'd lost the horse, Sheridan carried all of our supplies: the rifle, depleted food sacks, tent, blankets, dishes, and the rest of the cooking equipment. I carried only the coffee pot and frying pan. To my delight, my feet were doing better. I continued to apply the yellow paste every chance I got, and although the stuff smelled like the inside of Joe Hamilton's rotting mouth, it was working.

It had turned cold overnight, and I was glad of the sweater the Indian woman had given me. I was reminded of how soon winter arrived in the North and how dreadfully cold it could get. How long had we been walking? I'd lost track of time completely. I tried to count the campsites we'd set up, but other than the night at the trapper's cabin, they all seemed to blur into one. It might have been a week. It might have been a month. Was it still July? August nights could turn to frost, and it would snow at the higher elevations. I wouldn't last long out here in a pair of men's socks, a tattered dress, and one old sweater.

Then I thought of the food. We had no coffee left, no oatmeal, just a couple of cans of vegetables, some corned beef, and a handful of powdered milk. Difficult to tell how much oatmeal we'd lost when the bear ransacked the packs. When I'd first

looked into the food sack after my abduction, I'd figured we
didn't have enough food for a week. Sheridan had shot a small
amount of game to supplement our rations, but not much.

Therefore, I surmised, we hadn't been out here for a week yet.

I heard a sound on the wind. I stopped walking and looked
behind me, ears pricked.

Angus?

I sighed, and felt tears well up behind my eyes. Angus.

I hadn't been a very good mother to Angus, but he repaid
me with total devotion. He was a better son than I deserved. Not
that I had much choice, as I'd been alone in the world and had
to earn our living. But ...

"Fiona, hurry up," Sheridan called. "Not much further."

I turned and trudged after him. The mountain did seem to
be getting closer. It filled my vision. The sky was cobalt blue,
the top of the mountain pure white, snow sparkling in the sun.
The ground was mostly soil with lichen-covered rocks scattered
in patches. The plain across which we walked wasn't completely
flat. Brown hills, covered with blankets of red, purple, and yellow
flowers, spread out gently on either side of a small depression,
which seemed to be headed straight for the mountain. Almost as
if it were a road.

I had no choice but to walk on. I had nothing to eat, and
only Mr. Sheridan and his rifle stood between me and starva-
tion. When we reached this mountain and he discovered it was
only a mountain, as cold and barren as any other mountain in
the Territory, I would make one last attempt to persuade him
to return to civilization. If he refused, then I would simply
have to walk away and hope I could reach help before I starved
to death.

The sun cast long shadows in front of us as we began to
climb, and the sky to the east was heavy with approaching clouds.

We'd walked all day, but I felt strangely invigorated. Most of the pain in my feet had gone, as had the ache in my legs, and my wrist had stopped throbbing. We'd rested briefly, long ago, to take a drink from a lazy little stream and eat the last of the stale dry biscuits. Yet I wasn't particularly hungry. Perhaps now that this dreadful journey was about to end, one way or the other, my body and mind simply wanted to get on with it.

The path climbed gently but steadily, the carpet of green moss soft beneath my feet. Two hawks made wide, lazy circles overhead. A ptarmigan broke from a scrap of undergrowth as Sheridan passed, wings fluttering in panic. He didn't break stride or swing the rifle into shooting position.

"Mr. Sheridan," I called.

He turned and waited for me to catch up.

"I suggest," I said, "that you might wish to find us something for our supper."

"Huh?"

"We need to eat. I expect you to hunt for my dinner."

"Oh, yeah, right." He laughed. It almost looked good on him. "I'm so darn excited, Fiona, I completely forgot about eating. Do you need to rest, my dear?"

"That might be a good idea," I said. We'd reached the foot of the mountain. Naked black rock rose straight up, as though it were a wall. Most of the vegetation had fallen behind us as the elevation got higher, and only a few tough lichens and tiny alpine flowers covered the rocks. It was noticeably colder. I shivered and wrapped my sweater around me.

Sheridan swung one of the packs off his back and pulled out a blanket. He placed it around my shoulders. His fingers lingered and I felt their soft pressure. For a moment, I almost forgot myself and started to lean back into them. "Take care you do not forget your position, Mr. Sheridan," I said sharply, pulling my shoulders tightly together. The fingers moved away and he mumbled an apology.

A conveniently positioned boulder rested at the side of the trail. I sat down and arranged my tattered, cut-off, shredded, mud-encrusted skirts around my legs. I didn't bother to reprimand Sheridan for staring.

He didn't sit, just paced so anxiously I couldn't possibly relax. After a few minutes of this, I got to my feet. "Very well. Let us continue. If we must."

He galloped off in unseemly haste.

I watched him go and ran my fingers across my knife.

I was letting my guard down. Sheridan had been exceedingly kind and most solicitous on our journey. Apart from that one incident, he'd acted like a perfect gentleman.

I mustn't allow myself to forget that he tackled me in a dark alley, fought with me, knocked me unconscious, dragged me off against my will, and threatened to stick a knife in my belly if I didn't co-operate.

Once again, I heard that sound on the wind. "Mother."

Dear Angus. I hoped he wasn't too worried.

"One moment, Mr. Sheridan," I called. "I see a small stream. Let me fill the bottle."

He tossed it over his shoulder without turning. He stared, back stiff and straight, at the wall of rock ahead.

I gathered up the bottle and bent to a small trickle of water tumbling through a pile of boulders on its journey down the mountainside. The bottle was not yet half empty, but I feared that as we climbed, water would become hard to find. I knelt on the bank, the feel of spongy, velvet-soft moss soothing on my knees. The water was not much more than an inch deep, but clear and pure, the bottom a bed of gravel and small rocks. Overhead the clouds briefly parted and a long beam of sunlight illuminated the scene. I stopped in the act of placing the bottle into the water. One of the stones was positively gleaming, the light from the sun bouncing off in a thousand directions. I turned my head and took a quick glance up the trail. Sheridan hadn't moved.

I slipped the frying pan out of the bag. Dipping it into the water, I scooped up rocks, gravel, mud, and water. I tilted the pan and allowed the pure clear water to flow out, the way Angus had told me men searched for gold. When the water was gone, black sand dotted with golden specks and two big golden lumps remained.

I let out a long sigh.

"Don't dawdle, Fiona," Sheridan said.

"Coming," I replied. I slipped the two nuggets into my sweater pocket and poured the grey rocks and gold dust back into the creek. I forgot to fill the bottle.

* * *

It was almost noon when Constable McAllen sprained his ankle. He was bringing up the rear, carrying the rifle, watching out for something to put into the dinner pot. An enormous golden eagle circled lazily overhead, coasting on a thermal, and the young Mountie tilted his head back to watch the graceful movement. He stepped into a hole, his foot twisted beneath him, and he fell to the ground with a cry of surprise and pain.

"Not broken. Thank heavens," Richard Sterling said, leaning back after examining McAllen's leg. "Think you can get up?"

Angus took one arm, Sterling the other, Millie barked encouragement, and they lifted McAllen to his feet. He took one step and bit back a moan of pain. "I'll be all right," he said, when he could speak again. "Just needs loosening up a mite."

"I doubt that," Sterling said.

"Get me a branch, Angus," McAllen said. "Something I can use as a walking stick."

Long, low hills spread out around them, and the black and white mountain lay straight ahead. Not a tree was in sight, and no bushes with a branch any wider than Angus's little finger, nor much longer.

"I'm leaving men scattered all over the bloody countryside," Sterling mumbled. "I'm sorry, Constable, but if you can't walk, you can't come with us."

"Angus, give me a hand." Angus hurried to get under the young officer. McAllen wrapped his arm around the boy's shoulder and leaned on him. McAllen wasn't a large man, but Angus almost staggered under the weight. "This'll do until we can find a branch I can use," the constable said, in a failed attempt to sound cheerful and optimistic.

"And we'll never catch up to Fiona," Sterling said. Angus tried to give McAllen an apologetic look. He'd been thinking exactly the same thing.

"There's nothing for it, but you're going to have to wait here, Constable," Sterling said.

"I won't hold you up. I'm feeling better all ready." McAllen unwrapped his arm from Angus and hopped forward on his good foot. "See?" Angus hovered beside him, ready to catch the Mountie should he collapse.

"Walk to that rock over there," Sterling said, pointing about five feet in front of them.

"Sure." McAllen alternately hopped and took baby-sized steps. When he reached the rock, he collapsed with a groan. His face was red and streaked with sweat.

"I'll leave you the stove and some coffee and food. There isn't much around here to use to prop up the tent, but you need shelter. Angus, collect a few good sized rocks and we can create a small cave off the side of the hill." Angus rushed to do as he was asked.

Finally, McAllen stopped insisting he would soon be able to walk. "Sorry, Corporal."

"Not your fault. I can't leave you the rifle. We know Sheridan has one. We'll be back shortly."

Angus tried to give the downcast constable an encouraging smile as they moved off. It was only him now. Him and Corporal Sterling. And Millie.

They walked for several hours before Sterling stopped.

"What?" Angus said. Millie whined.

"Look ahead. What do you see?"

Angus looked. Solid black rock of the mountain wall rose sharply up from the brown plain. A path, wending slowly upwards, appeared to be carved out of the mountainside. The top was wrapped in snow and mist. Thick black storm clouds were moving in fast from the east.

Angus said, "We're almost there."

"Look at the path on the right. Is something moving?"

Angus sucked in a breath. "Mother," he whispered. Then he shouted, "Mother."

"I suspect so," Sterling said. "Can you see how many people there are?"

Angus narrowed his eyes and stared. Something was moving for sure, almost certainly people. "Two maybe." When he looked at Sterling the corporal had a touch of a smile at the edges of his mouth. He shifted the weight of the rifle. "Unload Millie. We'll leave everything here. Now we need speed." Sterling tossed his pack at the side of the trail. Angus and Millie's things joined it. Only the rifle remained. Sterling talked as they walked. "I need you to listen to me, Angus, and listen good. We have no idea what state Sheridan's in or what he's capable of doing. We know he has a weapon, and we have to assume he's prepared to use it. He didn't bring your mother all this way to allow her to turn around and come back with us. You'll do what I tell you, when I tell you, and nothing else. Do you understand, Angus?"

"Sure," the boy said. He was hurrying now. The people ahead had disappeared, probably as the path twisted or ducked behind a wall of rock, but his heart was singing. Mother.

He felt a weight on his shoulder, pressing him down, slowing his pace. He lifted a hand to knock Sterling away. The Mountie grabbed his arm and held it tight. "If for one minute I have reason to believe you won't do as you're told, I'll leave you behind."

"You can't. I won't let you."

"Angus, this is not a lark. Look at me."

Angus looked. Sterling's eyes were dark and his face set into tight lines. "This is a police operation. Are you going to obey orders? Or not?"

Angus lowered his head. "Yes, sir."

"Good lad." Sterling shifted the rifle once again and strode on ahead, his long legs eating up the ground.

Angus wanted to be a Mountie. He'd known that meant sometimes he'd have to do things he didn't particularly want to do. Maybe even things he objected to. He'd assumed, without thinking much about it, that he'd follow orders for the good of the force and to uphold the law.

He never thought his mother would be his first case. He gave Millie's lead a tug and they set off at a trot after Corporal Sterling.

Chapter Forty-Four

I said nothing to Sheridan about finding gold. Could the man's foolish fantasy be reality? Was this indeed a gold mountain? Back in the Savoy, we enjoyed a hearty laugh at the expense of men who came to the Yukon expecting to pick nuggets off the ground like windfall apples, yet today I'd done that very thing. I touched my pocket. I'd pushed the nuggets in deep, past the knife. They weren't particularly big nuggets; I'd seen larger ones laid down to finance a night of drinking or a serious hand of poker, or as a gift to a dance hall girl.

But considering it had taken all of about one minute's effort, I'd done rather well.

I eyed Sheridan. He was ahead of me, moving fast. The path was increasingly steep, carved between enormous boulders and walls of rock. Perhaps it had been a watercourse long ago, picking its way down the side of the mountain. Surprisingly, the path wasn't too rocky but smooth hard-packed earth in most places. As we climbed, it got steadily colder, and I shivered in my sweater and tattered evening dress. Fingers of icy mist swirled around the path, getting thicker as we walked. Ahead and above us, the mountains disappeared into the clouds.

I ran my index finger across the sheathed blade of the knife. Sheridan's back was protected by the packs he carried, but his front was exposed. Easy enough to slip around him so

I was on the higher ground and thus taller than he, murmur sweet nothings into his ear, stroke his cheek with my left hand, playfully lift his head up.

Expose the throat.

A single silent swipe with my right hand, and that would be the end of Mr. Paul Sheridan.

And then what? I stopped and turned around. We were very high and the limitless tundra lay at my feet. The carpet of flowers and grasses and rock, far below, stretching as far as I could see, reminded me of the Highlands when the heather bloomed. It was so quiet up here, not even the sweet murmur of leaves rustling in the wind. Sheridan had turned a corner and passed out of sight. I heard a scratch on rock and looked up to see two sheep watching me. They stood on a ledge that was scarcely more than a crack in the solid surface. They were white with brown horns swooping upward, curling at the edges. Large brown eyes blinked at me, and their mouths moved as they ate unseen grasses.

I imagined a city at the bottom of the mountain. Dance halls and bars and waffle bakeries and tent shops. Doctors and dentists and pickpockets. Mining officials and priests. Gentlemen and drunkards and layabouts. Prostitutes and percentage girls and laundry women. The tundra churned into mud, wildlife fleeing. Everything beautiful and powerful subdued or broken in service of the all-encompassing lust for gold.

Who would rule here? The North-West Mounted Police, as in Dawson, or the likes of Soapy Smith, as in Skagway?

Or me?

I wouldn't be a queen and Gold Mountain would not be my kingdom. This was Canada, after all. A dominion in the British Empire. Not unclaimed territory. But I could stake a claim. I could make a great deal of money. I would be rich beyond all my dreams.

First, Mr. Paul Sheridan would have to go.

Without warning, the sheep leapt from one crevice to another and were gone. I heard a sound, someone calling. Perhaps it was the wind, whistling through rock. Something moved at the edges of my vision. I pulled my eyes away from the horizon and focused on the path below, twisting and turning down the mountain. I'd thought I'd seen something, but all was still and nothing moved.

"Will you hurry up, woman."

I turned to see Sheridan standing on the path several feet above me. His hands were on his hips and he was breathing hard. He looked positively angry.

"I'm getting tired," I said, putting on a pout. "I want supper. I don't suppose you've managed to shoot anything." I waved my hand to indicate our surroundings. "I can't imagine where we're going to make camp. There's not enough wood to start a fire and not a flat piece of ground on which to lie within miles."

"Stop your moaning," he replied. "You'll have all the comfort you need soon enough. Now get moving."

I lowered my head submissively and took a step. He turned and continued on his way. I slid the knife out of its sheath, to check if it would come clear easily, and then put it back.

Soon enough.

Chapter Forty-Five

I don't know from where I got the strength. I'd scarcely had a decent meal for a week, and I hadn't eaten for hours. The water bottle was empty, and we hadn't come across water in a long time. Perhaps Sheridan's enthusiasm, as he bounded ahead almost as easily and surely as the mountain sheep, was giving me some energy. Or perhaps my own thoughts drove me forward.

With sufficient funds, not only could I return to Scotland and extract my revenge on Alistair Forester, the man who murdered my parents, but I'd no longer have to worry about the law and my past, uh, profession. No British policeman would arrest an excessively wealthy lady for stealing silver or jewellery. The nobility did it all the time. At the end of a country house party, more than one householder had waved away the last of the guests only to discover valuable items had been unwittingly gifted to their visitors. If a maid pocketed a cheap trinket, she'd be sacked, a footman would face a stretch in Wormwood Scrubs, a hanger-on such as I would be socially ruined if not jailed. Lord or Lady Fitzjames-Worthington-Montague would be assumed to have taken the item by mistake, and it would be impolite to ask for it back.

With my newfound wealth, I'd purchase a country estate of my own, send Angus to Eton and then to Oxford or Cambridge. Eventually buy him a title. Set him up as a proper gentleman.

So happy was I with these thoughts, I almost bumped into the back of my captor. It was well after suppertime and long shadows crossed our path. Tendrils of cold mist curled around our heads and feet. The mountain closed in around us and sheer black rock rose up on either side, as straight as if it had been cut with a giant's knife. The path narrowed to not much more than a foot wide, as if a doorway of sorts had been carved out of the stone. I squeezed forward to stand behind Sheridan and peered over his shoulder.

I gasped.

We stood high above a valley. Mountains, black and sleek, rose up on all sides. Below us, hawks and eagles circled. A wide blue river flowed lazily across the landscape, and plumes of white steam drifted into the air from several places on the valley floor. Everything was green and verdant, the ground hidden by vegetation: tall trees with large flat leaves and dense undergrowth. The sun was lowering itself behind the peak opposite where we stood, and the hills were bathed in a clear golden glow. The air at my back was Yukon-summer cold, bearing the threat of snow and icy winds. Ahead of us it blew soft and warm, perfumed with what might have been citrus.

The trail dropped sharply away and descended in a straight line, eventually to disappear into a clump of trees heavy with vines.

Gold Mountain.

Sheridan stepped backward. His mouth hung open and he looked into my eyes. He said nothing as he dropped slowly to his knees. A single tear travelled down his left cheek.

He lifted his face to mine.

His throat was wide and white, rimmed with a torn and dirty collar. His Adam's apple bobbed. "I found it," he said in a whisper. "We've made it, Fiona, we've made it."

I gripped the handle of my knife and slowly pulled it out of its sheath. I envisioned piles of gold stacked at my feet, diamonds on my fingers and emeralds in my ears and loops of pearls around my neck. Gowns of silk and satin and lace. More beautiful than ever, I'd bask in the adoration of all who encountered me. Angus would be prime minister some day. Sir Angus of the Yukon. Lord MacGillivray of Skye. He'd marry an insipid, buck-toothed great-granddaughter of the Queen, and I would take tea at Buckingham Palace and be the grandmother of a future king of England.

"Thank you, Mr. Sheridan" I said, "For bringing me here."

I pulled the knife free.

"You are needed no longer."

A dog barked.

For a fraction of time, I assumed it was a wolf. Then I remembered Angus telling me wolves do not bark, they howl. Only dogs bark.

Another bark, followed by an excited shout, from the path we'd recently ascended. A gust of wind came out of nowhere, carrying the single word "Mother." The word lingered in the air like mist.

I looked at my hand, knuckles white on the handle of the knife.

What on earth was I doing? Was I seriously contemplating slicing a man's throat? I didn't even want to take tea with the Queen, nor to have a dreary daughter-in-law and buck-toothed grandchildren. Paul Sheridan knelt at my feet, submissive as a lamb to the slaughter. He had not heard me speak. I shoved the knife away and gave my head a proper shake.

"Someone's coming," Sheridan said. He pushed himself to his feet. The small pack he'd worn across his chest for the entire trip, the one containing his knife, dropped to the ground. I kicked it aside.

We went to the edge of the trail and peered down in the direction from which we'd come. Through the swirls of white mist we could see movement far below. A man and a dog, ascending. No, two men. My heart moved into my throat. A man and a boy and a big white dog. The man was dressed in a red tunic and black boots and wore a broad-brimmed hat. The boy had a shock of too-long blond hair. Their heads were down and their backs bent as they concentrated on climbing.

Angus. It was Angus. And Richard Sterling.

He'd come for me.

"My escort," I said. "It's time for us to part, Mr. Sheridan. I'll not be continuing, but I truly wish you well."

The man's eyes were as round and white as Soapy the horse's when he'd refused to cross the creek.

Sheridan swung the Winchester off his back. "You belong to me. I'm not letting you go."

"No!" I yelled. "Don't shoot. Angus, run."

Sheridan lifted the rifle to his face, laid his cheek against the barrel. I saw his finger inch toward the trigger.

I launched myself at him and threw my entire body against his left side, throwing him off balance. He staggered and the weapon fired. From below came cries of alarm and increased barking. Sheridan braced his legs and brought the rifle back up. I grabbed the barrel and we wrestled for it.

"You're mine," he hissed, the sound like a snake moving through grass, "mine." His eyes were very cloudy.

He managed to wrest the weapon out of my hands. Shifting it, he struck the side of my head, hard, with the butt. I staggered backwards; stars moved across my eyes and my head swam. I dropped my forearms to the ground and broke the fall before my skull could strike rock. I pulled myself to a sitting position and sat on the hard ground, blinking. Paul Sheridan moved in and out of focus. There were two of him, and then three, and finally just one. But that one was bracing the rifle barrel against a rock and settling back into shooting position.

I clambered to my feet, pulling the trapper's knife free with one smooth movement. I again threw myself at Paul Sheridan. All the while I was screaming, trying to gather strength for myself as well as warn Richard and Angus. And, hopefully, frighten Sheridan.

He swung around and lifted the rifle in defence. I raised the knife high and brought it down, slicing it across his arm, wrist to elbow. The blade was very sharp, and it cut deeply. Bright red blood spurted. Sheridan said not a word, but threw the rifle to the ground and faced me. His mouth was set, his eyes so round, the surface so white, I wouldn't have recognized them. He was breathing very deeply and hissed as air passed in and out of his mouth. He moved fast, sending a fist toward my jaw. I pulled back in time and thrust the knife forward, but he leaned aside and my blade sliced cold mountain air. We circled each other, eyes fixed, hearts pounding, hands up.

All I had to do was to keep him away from me and from that rifle, give Richard time to get to us. And Angus. Oh, heavens, don't let Angus be the first to arrive. I could hear shouting from below and the dog barking. Richard would be moving carefully, not sure if the shooter was reloading or if he had another weapon. Angus would be scrambling up the hillside pell-mell, heedless of danger to himself.

I dared to glance toward the trail. That was a mistake. Sheridan saw my attention shift and he came in low, his left arm up and out, prepared to take another cut if he could get his right fist though my defences.

I ducked down and slipped under his arm. I was aiming for the centre of his belly, but he slid to one side at the last second and the knife cut only his jacket. His fist crashed into my face and I fell. I landed hard, once again, but kept my grip on the knife and held the blade pointing up and out. Sheridan swung his foot at my face, and I brought my weapon up, slicing into his calf, just above his boot.

He stepped backwards. Blood was pouring down both his arm and leg now. He stared at me through those crazed eyes. His chest heaved and his breathing was ragged, but he'd not said a word.

"I'm not going with you," I said. "You will have to kill me, and you do not want to do that."

The white cloud faded from his eyes. He blinked. "Fiona," he said, in a voice full of sadness and of pain. "Fiona. I will always love you."

He headed for me, and I braced myself for another attack. Instead he dodged and ran around me. I swivelled on my rear end, and the last I saw of Mr. Paul Sheridan, he was standing in the stone doorway, surrounded by a blaze of golden light from the setting sun. He took one step, and then another, and disappeared.

The barking was getting closer. "I'm here," I yelled. "He's gone. It's safe."

I staggered to my feet, thrust the knife behind a boulder, gathered up the rifle, and dashed a few yards down the path, whereupon I fell to the ground and arranged myself so I was draped across the trail in a dainty swoon.

Chapter Forty-Six

They were nearing the top of the mountain. The trail was steep and the going difficult. Angus would have run on ahead had Sterling let him, but he cautioned the boy that they didn't need another twisted ankle — or worse. Thick damp mist spun around them, and visibility wasn't much more than a few feet. Rock, sheer steep black rock, rose up on either side.

"Mother," Angus cried, and Sterling looked up. The mist had cleared, for a moment, and they could make out a figure standing above them. It was tall and thin and ghostly, dressed in rags, topped by hair as tangled as brambles and the remnants of a hat. Richard Sterling's heart knew who it was.

Angus dropped Millie's lead and put on a sprint, and Sterling barely had time to reach out and grab the boy by the arm. "Caution," he warned. "We don't know what's up there."

Angus fought against the restraint, but he wasn't strong enough to free himself. "It's mother. My mother. She's alive. Let me go."

"No. Wait. I'll go first."

As if to underscore his point, a shot rang out. The noise bounced off the rocks around them, echoing across to the plains far below. Sterling heard rock shatter as he dove behind a boulder, dragging the boy with him. Millie launched into a chorus of barks.

"Stay down." Sterling swung his own rifle around and raised it. "I'm going up and you are to stay here, Mr. MacGillivray, until I call the all clear. Make no mistake, that is an order."

Millie bounded on ahead. Sterling paid her no mind. He moved cautiously, only moving from the cover of one rock to another when he could see a safe path. Sheridan had the high ground, never a good thing in any battle, whether entire armies were clashing or it was one lone man against another. Sterling kept the back of his mind focused on Angus. How long would the boy be able to remain in place?

If his mother called out, not long at all.

It was quiet now, up above. He could hear nothing over the dog's barking. The mist drifted across the path like curtains, constantly opening and closing. An advantage, he knew, as the shooter above would have to wait, nervous and anxious, to get a good shot. Fiona had disappeared, stepped back from the edge. No doubt she lay cowed in the shelter of a boulder, shocked at the sudden display of man's violence.

Acid spurted into his gut. He tightened his grip on the rifle and broke cover, gaining another two or three feet. Then he rested, back against the mountain wall, weapon in front of him, finger resting on the trigger, barrel pointing up, listening.

Millie had disappeared. Unafraid, she'd rushed on, still barking.

A woman's voice broke the silence. "I'm here. He's gone. It's safe."

Sterling lost all the vestiges of caution. He broke cover and ran at full speed up the twisting mountain trail.

He rounded a corner and there she was. Fiona lay on the ground while Millie jumped on her and licked at her face. Her long black hair was a rat's nest trapped in the wreckage of her church hat; under a homemade sweater, her green dress was so thin and torn it wouldn't serve to make rags; her arms and legs and face were covered in streaks of dried blood, ugly scratches, and purple bruises.

She was the most beautiful thing he had ever seen.

He wanted to do nothing but drop to his knees and take her into his arms and hold her forever. But Sheridan was still up there somewhere, despite Fiona saying he was gone. There was no place the man could have gone.

Richard Sterling bent down and grabbed the rifle that lay on the ground.

Angus's footsteps pounded against the bare rock, and the boy almost shoved Sterling aside in his haste to get to his mother. Fiona burst into tears and wrapped her arms about her son.

Keeping his eyes on the path ahead, Sterling said, "Mrs. MacGillivray. I trust I find you well."

Chapter Forty-Seven

Millie reached me first and spread warm sticky drool all across my face. She was followed by Richard Sterling, who took one look at me, saw I was alive, and scooped up the rifle. Then came Angus. He fell to his knees beside me, crying, "Mother." I touched the top of his blond head and I didn't have to pretend to cry.

"Mrs. MacGillivray," Richard said. "I trust I find you well."

"Somewhat the worse for wear," I replied, "and in desperate need of a bath. But I will live."

"Sheridan?"

"He's gone."

Richard started up the trail.

"No!" I shouted. "No need to go there. He, uh, fell over the cliff. Yes, he fell over the cliff. Lost his footing. It was a long way down. A terrible accident."

The sun had descended behind the mountain; the swirling mist was cold and damp. I couldn't see Richard's expression. No doubt he was checking out the marks of the fight on my face. I pulled Angus close and buried my head into his chest.

"Do you have anything you need me to fetch?" Richard asked.

"No. We came on this impossible journey with few possessions as it was, and nothing's left."

"We have to get my mother to help," Angus said. He stroked my hair, and I felt time shift. My child was mothering me. Millie nuzzled my hand, hoping for a scratch.

Richard hesitated. He looked up the path. "What's up there?"

"Nothing. A dead end. A wall of sheer rock on one side and a sharp drop-off on the other."

"We'd better get you down before dark. Can you walk, Mrs. MacGillivray?"

"With Angus's help, I'm sure I can."

Thus, we descended the mountain as long shadows wrapped themselves around us. I leaned on Angus while Richard carried both rifles. Millie was allowed off her lead because no one had a free hand to take her, but she didn't wander far from our legs.

"We have a horse waiting for you, Mother," Angus said.

"A horse? How lovely."

"I suspect you know him," Richard said. "Small, thin, brown thing."

"Soapy?"

"Soapy?" They chorused.

We were making surprisingly good time. It was almost as if the mountain wanted to be rid of us. My head most definitely did not feel right, but I leaned on Angus's arm and said nothing about it. I wanted to get out of the shadow of this strange mountain as fast as possible. It was dark when we reached the plains, but the storm clouds had passed, and the moon was full and it cast enough light for us to walk by. I stopped for a moment and looked back. The mountain was a black shape bathed in white moonlight.

Had there really been a green valley with trees with broad flat leaves wrapped in vines as fat as my arm? Had the air truly smelled of oranges and lemons? Had the hills glowed with specks of gold?

Totally ridiculous. A figment of my rattled head, stressed nerves, and empty stomach.

In the fight with Paul Sheridan, the two stones I carried in my pocket had not been dislodged. I fingered them. No doubt in the light of day they would turn out to be nothing but hunks of worthless rock.

We came across a couple of packs abandoned at the side of the trail, and Richard announced we would rest here for a few hours.

I was suddenly ravenous and devoured a tin of cold corned beef with three dry, stale biscuits before Angus could get a fire started. Richard handed me a blanket with a shy smile, and I wrapped it around me. I closed my eyes and knew nothing more until sunlight was warm on my face.

Angus's long, lean body was curled around me, and time was set right. He was my child once again. I touched his tousled head. Richard Sterling sat by the embers of the fire, his pipe clenched between his teeth. He turned, although I hadn't made a sound. "Feeling better?"

"Yes. Thank you." I coughed and studied my fingers. "I mean, thank you. For coming after me."

He concentrated intently on patting down the tobacco in his pipe. "My duty, Ma'am."

"Of course." Nothing more than his duty.

Angus started and sat up abruptly. His hair was dishevelled and his eyes bleary from sleep. "Ma. I mean, Mother. You're here. I was afraid I was dreaming."

"I'm here," I said. "And I also am not sure what was a dream and what was not."

"Most of our equipment's a few hours back," Richard said. "If you don't mind having a biscuit for breakfast, when we get to the stove I can make up some coffee and oatmeal."

"That would be delightful."

I watched Angus feed strips of dried fish to Millie. "I must say, Corporal Sterling. I'm surprised you brought my son on this journey." I smiled. "Although I'm glad you did."

"Can you imagine trying to leave him behind," Richard replied. "We didn't come alone."

That was a somewhat cryptic statement, but rather than explain, he hoisted his pack and set off down the trail.

After a few hours of walking, Richard began calling out. I smelled smoke, and wonder of wonders, coffee. Someone answered, and we rounded a corner to come across a canvas shelter held down by rocks, a cheerful fire blazing, and young Constable McAllen holding a tin cup toward me in offering.

I laughed. "This is a most pleasant surprise." Angus escorted me to a rock by the fire, and McAllen served coffee while Richard poured water for Millie. McAllen was limping badly and I asked what had happened.

"Just a sprain, Ma'am. Almost better now."

Richard handed him Sheridan's rifle. "This should do as a crutch. It's not loaded."

We relaxed for a long time. Breakfast was hot oatmeal and fresh flatbread McAllen had prepared earlier. The men enjoyed their pipes, and Angus sat very close to me. I put my arm around him and he didn't pull away.

"Is Mr. Sheridan dead?" he asked after a long silence.

"Yes, dear. He attempted to fire a shot at you and Corporal Sterling, warning you to keep away, but he lost his balance and fell over the cliff. It was a long way down, and I could see his broken, lifeless body below. Probably for the better. The poor man wasn't entirely sane."

"It's kind of you to talk about him that way, Mrs. MacGillivray," Richard said. "After all, he did kidnap you and put you through much hardship."

"Yes, but he wasn't quite right in the head. This Gold Mountain, I mean the idea of a gold mountain, disturbed the balance of his mind." As it had disturbed mine. I decided never to think of that again.

"Strange place," Richard mumbled.

"Where's Soapy, by the way? You promised me a ride."

"You mean the horse?" Angus replied. "He's on the other side of the creek. Wouldn't cross, so we left him with Mr. Donohue."

"Graham Donohue? Good heavens, you mean he came after me as well?"

"Yeah," McAllen said. "When we got to that creek he came over all strange. Said he was tired and couldn't go any further. Odd that."

Odd indeed.

"Can you walk that far, Mother? Then we'll get you on the horse and you can ride back to Dawson in style."

Fortunately, the path to the creek was flat and mossy. I doubted I could walk through the forest in what remained of Sheridan's socks. They had been amazingly good socks, but there was a tear in the leather of the right heel that was threatening to expand, and the ball of the left foot was almost worn through. The precious yellow paste I'd been applying to my blisters had been left at the top of the mountain with the rest of Sheridan's meagre belongings.

"Mr. McAllen and I will support each other." I gave the young officer a radiant smile. He blushed to the roots of his hair. I looked back toward the way we had come. It was just a mountain now, standing alone where it rose out of the plains, snowy top sparkling in the light of the sun, but I needed to be as far away from it as possible.

"Let us be on our way then. I'm simply dying to get this dress off and have a bath."

If it were possible, I'd say McAllen coloured even deeper. Richard Sterling sucked in too much smoke.

We heard them long before we saw them. For a moment, I thought I'd fallen into such a deep sleep they'd carried me all the way back to town. Someone was playing a banjo and a woman was singing in a voice that cracked on every high note. A man laughed and several dogs barked.

On the other side of the creek, the one that had given Soapy and Paul Sheridan so much trouble, a mini-town had sprung up. There were several tents, a couple of big fires, and groups of people standing about chatting. I smelled roasting meat and fragrant tobacco. Clothes and blankets laid out to dry were tossed over rocks and three donkeys and a horse searched for grasses at the water's edge.

"What the...?" Richard said, stopping himself from emitting a profanity at the last moment.

I realized my mouth was hanging open and snapped it shut. "Corporal Sterling did all these people accompany you?"

"No," Angus answered. "We left Mr. Donohue here with your horse."

A man dipped a long spoon into a pot hanging over a fire. Several other men stood with him, holding empty bowls in their hands, and he began to dish out soup. They squatted to the ground and dug in. Another group was sitting on blankets spread out around their own fire. A man strummed a banjo, a woman sang off key, and a man drank deeply from a bottle that looked to contain whisky. The woman was Betsy, one of my dancers, the banjo player part of the Savoy orchestra, and I recognized the man as a regular customer at my bar.

A tent was set up upstream, by itself. A man came out, doing up his trouser buttons. Another man entered, after slapping something into the waiting palm of Joey LeBlanc, Dawson's most notorious Madame.

Graham Donohue was crouched over a large, flat rock. Several men were with him, and they all held cards in their hands. Someone reached out and scooped up a pile of coins, bills, and a single gold nugget. Graham threw his cards onto the ground in disgust and got to his feet. Then he saw us standing on the other side of the bank.

He raised one hand in greeting, as if he were waving to me from the far side of Front Street rather than watching me return from the dead. Or at least from the sort of thrilling adventure you'd think a newspaperman would be interested in. He said something and heads began to turn. A couple of people waved. The banjo player stopped playing and Betsy, thankfully, cut herself off mid-note. The donkeys and horse lifted their heads and the three dogs tied to a stake in the ground barked a greeting to Millie.

Even the dogs didn't seem too excited at our return.

"Strangest darn thing I ever did see," Richard muttered.

Graham was waiting at the riverbank as we crossed. Noticeably, he did not step foot in the water to approach us. Everyone else gathered behind him. Even Joey LeBlanc and the ugly red-headed whore named Kate, whose skirt was bunched up at the back to reveal a filthy petticoat, joined the crowd.

We crossed the creek in a few steps. The icy water felt delicious on my aching feet.

"Glad you made it back, Fiona," Graham asked. "Did you find it?"

"Find what?"

"Gold Mountain."

"Don't be ridiculous. No such thing."

"Where's Sheridan?"

"Dead."

"Hello, Mrs. MacGillivray," Betsy said. "We're just resting here a mite before coming after you. Thought you might need some help."

Heads nodded and everyone murmured in agreement. Joey LeBlanc grunted.

I had trained in the salons of Belgravia and country houses of Surrey on how to greet one's arch-enemy. I gave Joey a smile. "How terribly kind of you to be concerned, Mrs. LeBlanc. As you can see, I'm well and looking forward most anxiously to returning home."

She turned away and growled something at Kate. The two women stalked back to their tent. No one followed them.

Richard spoke to the crowd. "There's nothing to see. Nothing but wilderness out there, far as the northern sea. I suggest you people pack up and get yourselves back to town. I'm requisitioning one of those donkeys for Constable McAllen, who's injured. Any complaints? I thought not. Angus, get the horse and help your mother."

The crowd drifted away. "Might try again in the spring," I heard the banjo player say. "Ain't a good time to try for Gold Mountain now. Winter's comin'."

Betsy agreed.

"Nothing there," someone said. "Coulda told you that. 'Course I never believed in it, just wanted to see how far you fools would go."

Everyone else, it appeared, also didn't believe in it.

Joe Hamilton approached me shyly, twisting his filthy, tattered hat in one hand. "I'm pleased to see you're fine, Mrs. MacGillivray. I came with Frank over there. We caught up to Betsy and some of the others on the trail. I wanted to help you, but they all decided they were too tired to cross the creek. Seemed strange to me, but then the donkey wouldn't come either, and I didn't want to carry on by myself. I figured young Angus wouldn't let any harm come to you."

I smiled, turning my head slightly against the onslaught of foul breath from his mouthful of blackened teeth. "You were correct about that. Uh, Mr. Hamilton, did you yourself ford the creek?"

"I told Frank and Betsy we had to hurry, that you needed our help, but they came over all tired. I've been carrying wood back and forth for the fires all day. I could have set myself up in business if I wanted to. No one else seems to want to bother."

"Come and see me at the Savoy, Mr. Hamilton, when we get back to town. I might have an offer for you." He didn't ask what sort of offer, just touched his hat and walked away.

Joe Hamilton was well-spoken and clearly educated. He drifted around the docks, making a few cents here and there running errands, though he didn't earn enough money to buy soap to wash either his clothes or himself or purchase a new hat. But he'd always been unfailingly polite to me, and I never heard anyone say a bad word about him. I'd ask Ray to find him a job. Something that didn't involve breathing on the customers.

Angus and Richard sorted out their few belongings and re-loaded Millie. Once that was done, my son helped me to mount my old friend Soapy. The horse stamped his feet but didn't shy away. Richard got McAllen, protesting that he was perfectly fine to walk, while gritting his teeth against the pain, onto an emaciated donkey. Richard carried his rifle; the other had been reloaded and now rested alongside the donkey's flanks. Graham Donohue shifted his own pack. And thus we set off, at the head of a strange ragged procession, back to Dawson. Home.

While the breaking of camp was in process I took the two rocks I'd found in the mountain stream out of my pocket, tak-ing care to keep them concealed from onlookers. It was early

evening and the light was good. I balanced them in my hand.
They were heavy and dull yellow in colour. I pressed my fingernail into the surface of one. It was very soft, and my nail made a
small indentation.

Pure gold.

I put them away, full of thought.

I never saw or heard of Mr. Paul Sheridan again. Perhaps he
died of the knife wounds I inflicted; perhaps he hadn't been able
to survive alone even in that lush wilderness. Perhaps it was so
wonderful he never wanted to leave.

Perhaps he found Gold Mountain to be as difficult to escape
as it was to enter.

Epilogue

Corporal Richard Sterling knocked at the back door of Mrs. Mann's boarding house at seven o'clock on Monday morning. It had been a week since he'd returned from the pursuit of Paul Sheridan and Fiona MacGillivray, and the rhythm of life in the mud-soaked streets of Dawson City had fallen back into its usual frantic pace.

The previous evening, he'd been called into the office of Inspector Cortlandt Starnes, temporary commander of the NWMP in the Yukon. Sterling had stood at attention while Starnes congratulated him on returning one of Dawson's most prominent citizens safely to town. And on *not returning* Soapy Smith's henchman, which was never stated but nevertheless understood.

Starnes then gave Sterling one more order.

Mr. Mann opened the door, pulling his suspenders over his shoulders. "Mrs. MacGillivray asleep," he said. The door began to shut again.

"I'm not here to see her, but Angus. Is he up?"

"Breakfast," Mr. Mann said.

The door opened and Sterling was admitted. Mrs. Mann stood at the stove, stirring the porridge pot. The smell of toast and coffee filled the kitchen. Angus sat at the table, caught in the act of spreading orange marmalade on his toast. He broke into a big smile. "Morning, sir."

"Good morning, Angus, Ma'am. This is Mr. Templeton." Sterling introduced his companion, a short chubby man with neatly trimmed hair and moustache and intelligent brown eyes. He wore a pair of thick spectacles perched on a beak of a nose that would do a hawk proud. He was well-dressed in high boots with a long wool double-breasted jacket over a clean white shirt and tie. He took off his cap when he entered the house and nodded politely to Mrs. Mann.

"I'd like to take Angus away from his duties at the shop once again," Sterling said. "I trust this will be the last time."

Angus jumped to his feet, toast in hand. "Where are we going?"

Templeton laughed. "I see what you mean, Corporal. Eager indeed. Finish your breakfast, son."

Angus stuffed the food into his mouth. "Finished," he mumbled.

"Coffee?" Mrs. Mann asked the new arrivals.

"No, thank you, Ma'am. We breakfasted at the Fort."

Mr. Mann stroked his chin. "If sis is police business then okays."

Millie was waiting outside, a single canvas pack, lightly filled, slung over her back. Angus added the tin containing his lunch to her load and gave her an affectionate scratch behind the ears. Mr. Templeton carried a bulging pack of his own.

Sterling explained their mission as they walked through the morning streets. "Mr. Templeton's a surveyor. The creek we followed heading north isn't on any maps, and the government wants the location marked. We won't be travelling up it this time, just want to make a note of the exact location. Won't take us more than a couple of hours to get there and back, and I figured you deserve to be in on the recording of the new river."

"Can I name it?" Angus said.

Templeton laughed. "Perhaps you can. MacGillivray River is a mouthful though."

"Angus Creek?"

"Sterling Stream has a nice ring."

They all laughed. It was a good day for a walk. It was going to be a scorcher of a day, but the trees and the river would keep the temperature down. Sterling was looking forward to a pleasant outing for a change. A chance to get a break from town and spend some time in the wilderness without a care in the world. They followed the same route they had last week, past the city's outskirts and along the north bank of the Klondike River. Even in the few days since they'd last come this way, the town had grown. Men were hard at work chopping down trees and turning them into building logs. More men, a dark steady river all its own, marched down the other bank, heading south to the gold fields.

"We could name the river after my mother," Angus said. "Fiona River. It was because of her we discovered it."

Sterling thought the peaceful little creek flowing into the Klondike was nothing at all like the tempestuous Fiona MacGillivray. If a river were to be named after her, it should be a great waterway, pouring into nothing less than the ocean. He didn't say so.

The question of what to name the new river became a moot point.

They couldn't find it.

To Templeton's increasing impatience, they walked up and down the Klondike. It had rained several times over the past week, and all traces of their footsteps, the horse and cart they'd been following, and all the people, donkeys, wagons that trooped after them, were gone. They followed the Klondike River much farther than Angus and Sterling believed they'd been, until eventually they met up with a river that *was* on the government maps. They swore they hadn't come this far.

They came back, eyes on the ground, checking every step, eventually hearing the sounds of civilization in the west. Sterling took off his hat and scratched at his head.

"If you're playing some sort of a joke on me, Corporal, I am not amused," Templeton snapped. He shifted his pack. It contained his surveying equipment, and he was hot and tired and bad-tempered.

"No joke. It's just not there."

"The creek might have dried up," Angus said. "Although that's not likely with all this rain. But even then the riverbed should be visible. It was about five feet across, right, sir?"

"The banks were a foot high and there was five feet or so of a watercourse. Open water. No trees or bushes."

They searched for the rest of the day as Templeton got increasingly angry and Sterling increasingly frustrated. Angus had the idea of letting Millie lead the way to possibly retrace their steps. But the dog simply sniffed after rabbits and enjoyed the day's excursion.

The sun was low in the sky when they got back to town, tired and hungry and perturbed. Templeton stalked off muttering something about wasting government time.

Sterling and Angus watched him go. Stoves and cooking fires glowed on the hills of both sides of the river, and light streamed from steamboats and make-shift rafts being used as houses. Kerosene and oil lamps were lit in the dancehalls up and down Front Street. Music, men's voices, and women's laughter poured out of the doors.

They could see Fiona MacGillivray inside the Savoy, drifting across the saloon. She wore a scarlet dress and her thick black hair was piled up under a scrap of a hat more ostrich feather than cloth. She jerked her head toward one of the bartenders, and he hurried to serve a well-dressed man at the end of the bar.

"What do you think happened to it, Corporal Sterling?" Angus asked. "To that creek?"

"I've seen waterways dry up if beavers build a dam upriver, or something blocking the way moves, and the water can turn in another direction. But for the creek bed to grow into fully-treed forest in a week?" He shook his head. "I don't know. Perhaps it's better we don't know. I'm going inside to check everyone's behaving themselves. You better get off home."

"Night, sir."

"Good night, Angus."

Corporal Richard Sterling of the North-West Mounted Police stood on the boardwalk for a moment, watching the tall, lanky boy make his way down the crowded street. When he turned back to the Savoy, Fiona MacGillivray was standing by the window, looking out. She lifted her hand and beckoned him in with a warm smile.

The doors opened and a body flew out, propelled by Joe Hamilton, newly hired bouncer. The man landed face first in Front Street and struggled to his feet with a groan and numerous curses, dripping mud and horse dung.

"Well, if it isn't Ronald Kirkluce," Sterling said. "I thought you'd been run out of town long ago. You'd better come with me."

The astute reader is advised not to attempt to follow the trail of Fiona and Sheridan and parties in search of them. They have, perhaps, stepped off the map into the unknown lands.

Acknowledgements

Sincere thanks to my great critique group: D.J. McIntosh, Jane Burfield, Donna Carrick, Madeleine Harris-Callway, Cheryl Freedman, fabulous writers all. And to Jessica Simon, who provided a ton of useful information about the flora and fauna and scenery of the Yukon. I apologize to Jessica for all my errors, deliberate and accidental. Thanks also to Jerry Sussenguth, who helped with the German accent.

I have attempted wherever possible to keep the historical details of the Klondike Gold Rush, and the town of Dawson, Yukon Territory, accurate. Occasionally, however, it is necessary to stretch the truth in the interests of a good story. A few historical personages make cameos in the book: Jefferson Randolph (Soapy) Smith, Big Alex McDonald, Belinda Mulrooney, Inspector Cortlandt Starnes, but all dramatic characters and incidents are the product of my imagination.

The reader who is interested in learning more about the Klondike Gold Rush is advised to begin with the definitive book on the subject, *Klondike: The Last Great Gold Rush 1896–1899*, by Pierre Berton. Also by Berton, *The Klondike Quest: A Photographic Essay 1897–1899*.

OTHER READING:

Gamblers and Dreamers: Women, Men and Community in the Klondike. Charlene Porsild.

Gold Diggers: Striking It Rich in the Klondike. Charlotte Gray.

Good Time Girls of the Alaska-Yukon Gold Rush. Lael Morgan.

The Klondike Gold Rush: Photographs from 1896–1899. Graham Wilson.

The Last Great Gold Rush: A Klondike Reader. Edited by Graham Wilson.

The Real Klondike Kate. T. Ann Brennan.

Women of the Klondike. Francis Blackhouse.

The Klondike Stampede. Tappan Adney.

FOR INFORMATION ABOUT THE NWMP:

The NWMP and Law Enforcement 1873–1905. R.C. Macleod.

Sam Steele: Lion of the Frontier. R. Stewart.

Showing the Flag: The Mounted Police and Canadian Sovereignty in the North, 1894–1925. W.R. Morrison.

They Got Their Man: On Patrol with the North-West Mounted. P.H. Godsell.

SOAPY SMITH AND SKAGWAY:

King Con: The Story of Soapy Smith. Jane G. Haigh.

The Streets Were Paved with Gold: A Pictorial History of the Klondike Gold Rush, 1896–1899. Stan Cohen.

THE LIFE OF SCOTTISH TRAVELLERS:

Exploits and Anecdotes of the Scottish Gypsies. William Chambers.

Pilgrims of the Mist: The Stories of Scotland's Travelling People. Sheila Stewart.

www.time-travellers.org.uk.

LIVING IN THE YUKON WILDERNESS:

This Was the North. Anton Money with Ben East.

Vicki Delany is one of Canada's most prolific and varied crime writers. She writes everything from standalone novels of gothic suspense to the Constable Molly Smith books, a traditional village/police procedural series set in the British Columbia Interior, to the light-hearted Klondike Mystery series, the first two of which are *Gold Digger* and *Gold Fever*. Vicki lives in Prince Edward County, Ontario. Visit *www.vickidelany.com*.

More Klondike Mysteries by Vicki Delany

Gold Digger
978-1894917803
$18.95

It's the spring of 1898, and Dawson, Yukon Territory, is the most exciting town in North America. The great Klondike Gold Rush is in full swing and Fiona MacGillivray has crawled over the Chilkoot Pass, determined to make her fortune as the owner of the Savoy dance hall. Provided, that is, that her twelve-year-old son, growing up much too fast for her liking; the former Glasgow street fighter who's now her business partner; a stern, handsome NWMP constable; an aging, love-struck, ex-boxing champion; a wild assortment of headstrong dancers, croupiers, gamblers, madams without hearts of gold, bar hangers-on, cheechakos and sourdoughs; and Fiona's own nimble-fingered past don't get to her first. And then there's the dead body on centre stage.

Gold Fever
978-1926607023
$18.95

A newcomer to town has secrets Fiona doesn't want revealed.... It's the spring of 1898, and thousands of people, from all corners of the globe, are flooding into the Yukon Territory in the pursuit of gold, the town of Dawson welcomes them all. The beautiful Fiona is happy to make as much money as possible in as short a time as possible. When her twelve-year-old son, Angus, saves the life of a Native woman intent on suicide, he inadvertently sets off a chain of events that offers his mother's arch-enemy Joey LeBlanc, the madam with a heart of coal, the opportunity to destroy the Savoy Dance Hall once and for all. Unaware of impending danger, Fiona has other concerns: among the new arrivals are a would-be writer with far more tenacity than talent, and her nervous companion. There's something familiar about the newcomer's cut-glass accent, and Fiona MacGillivray is determined to keep her as far away from Angus as possible. Then a killer strikes, and the Mounties are determined to get their man ... or woman.

Available at your favourite bookseller.

www.dundurn.com

What did you think of this book?
Visit *www.dundurn.com* for reviews, videos, updates, and more!